I0679149

The GLOW

Glenn Lazar Roberts

2025, TWB Press
https://www.twbpress.com

The Glow

Edited by Terry Wright

Cover Art by Terry Wright

ISBN: 978-1-959768-96-8

CHAPTER 1

"Back there...what the *fuck* did you do to me?" The face thrust in the open car window: gargoyle gray, yellow streaks on creased eyes, purple bruises closing them shut. Before the driver could speak, the face yanked back and the cop stumbled into the darkness.

With a muffled clump, a car door opened and shut.

Sam rolled up his antique car's window and placed his hands in his pockets and fingered two dimes and a nickel in each. *Balance.* He glanced in his rear-view mirror. *I warned you. When you gave me the ticket, I begged you—but you were like all the others.*

An orange fireball lit the night.

After the heatwave passed, Sam turned the key and breathed deep as his car trembled back to life. The police cruiser burning in his mirror like a pillar of flame, he gently guided his Oldsmobile onto the asphalt, and by the light of the stars slowly accelerated until his car regained its speed.

Dawn came, and the road clicked steadily beneath his tires. With each mile of stunted brush, each road-cut face of limestone cliff that flicked by the window like clips in a camera lens, Sam Trencher willed the layers of tension that overlay his life to ease.

He hand-cranked the front car windows open. Amid the rush of hot dry air, he noted he had turned the window knobs counter-clockwise. A small voice urged him to reverse the process, not to stem the breeze that blew in, swirling paper and trash on the floor, but to restore the balance. *Counter-clockwise requires clockwise.* He rolled the windows up and turned on the clunky cooling as high as it would go. *No hurry. No need to let oneself go.* The clicks of the road returned, and another stretch of limestone cliff peeled away.

He glanced at a paper on the dash, one of several maps that littered his car. With his thumb, he traced the interplay of red and black squiggles, raising an occasional eye for traffic. He wasn't worried. There had been no car for miles, and the hills were rolling softly, so it was unlikely he would drive off the straight two-lane highway.

A bump shook the car, and static erupted from the dashboard as the radio crackled on. He removed the scratched CD before it could play and turned the radio off. Too distracting.

Another minute and he had found the cutoff. He turned, then tossed the map aside. Though surprised so much time had passed that he could no longer rely on memory, he was confident. His car seemed to know where to go. The cutoff became another two-lane road, not as well-repaired as the main thoroughfare, but the road was straight and arrowed into the distance. He floored the pedal and sank into the frayed seat to listen to the soothing hum of the motor.

The painted-wheel sun drifted down, and still he drove. The harsh yellow of afternoon gradually deepened to vermilion and red, the rays flashing blue off the paint of the car's vibrating hood. The prism of a drifting cloud triggered a riot of color. This was his time. Not the night, which would soon be upon him, but twilight. Because in twilight there was hope. There was time to stem the tide, to reverse the errors he had made during daylight and restore the norm. How simple it all sounded: norm; balance. Mere words. A better image, he reflected, was a tightrope—with him an acrobat suspended. Or the proverbial eggshells beneath one's feet, with him the careful walker.

The wheels rolled on, those beneath his car matching the one above, and at length the first stars peeked through the dusk. Scanning the sky, he glimpsed the Pleiades. *Corvus the Crow* the ancients had called it, bringer of evil tidings. How did he know that? He blinked to clear his mind. How did he know anything? After all, nothing had happened to *him* if things became skewed. Since he had first felt these feelings, he had always managed to remain in balance.

An ancient doubt surfaced. Could it all be illusion? He sighed. If only he could believe that, how comforting it would be. He knew, however, in the heart of his being, the truth—he was a criminal and this was his punishment. Oh, he had never stolen, or swindled, or slandered his neighbor, or beaten his wife. He had never tried to hurt others, cast spells, or even laid the evil eye—but inside there was no doubt. By some twist of fate, he had been condemned to be suspended, perched atop a rope, in limbo, striving always to keep the eggshells below intact. Failure would be the end—*his* end. He found an extra penny in his left pocket and he retrieved a penny from a stash of coins on the floor and put it in his right pocket and breathed easier.

Balance.

And he knew what he knew—*she* would still be there.

In the distance, neon numbers appeared on an uplifted sign, and minutes later, his tires squealed into the paving of a brightly lit gas station, the last glow of the sun dwindling behind. A broken sign with sagging electric bulbs waved in the wind. From somewhere a bell dinged.

He waited.

Half a minute passed and no one came. He tapped

the dash with one finger, disturbing the dust that managed to accumulate despite the breeze of the open road. He backed up and rolled over the hose, ringing the bell again.

"Come on. I'm dead tired. I could use some service."

A bald head thrust out of the office, and soon a thin man in a grease-monkey outfit meandered through the twilight in his direction. Trencher cranked both windows down, wondered how long it would take for the old man to recognize him after the passage of so many years.

The thin man passed his gaze over the Oldsmobile. "Nice car." He shifted his jaw and stared at the driver. "Piece of crap. You want I should tank her up?"

Trencher nodded and pointed to the gas-cap.

The attendant went to work with the alacrity of a sloth, but finally the tank was filled, and the attendant stretched out a gnarled hand and took Trencher's carefully offered pair of twenty-dollar bills.

"Nice to see ya again, Len."

The old man leaned close, brows drawn. He made change, peered in the back seat, glanced at the single soiled suitcase. "You ain't from around here."

"You sure?"

He shook his head. "Yep. I'd remember this piece of crap car."

"Your name's Len, ain't it?"

"That's what the sign says. Ain't you hot shit that you can read?"

"Alright, have it your way."

"My way or the highway, Mr. High and Mighty."

"Thanks."

"For what? Get this heap a crap outta here and get lost."

Dividing up the four dollars he had received from

Len as change, Trencher slipped two of the dollars into his wallet in his left back pocket—and the other two dollars into the wallet, its mirror image, in his right back pocket.

He drove.

After a moment, he realized the window on the passenger side was still down. Hastily, he raised the window halfway, then lowered the window on the left the same distance. Stretching his arms in both directions, he steered with his knees while raising both windows at the same time, accelerating to the speed limit.

"Same old Len," he muttered.

The road was another straight shot that led to the center of town. He fumbled for his brights, and a moment later, illumined the valley that had contained his entire world until six years ago.

From behind, flashes of red and blue appeared—a chill gripped his spine. *Please God, not again.* He lowered his brights and clicked his belt, slowed, and the police car sped round and past, racing on some urgent errand. He let out his breath—*not this time.* Other memories surfaced. Could *he* still be here too? Somehow, he knew the answer to that as well. But the implications were cloudy. He had no feelings in that direction.

He regained the speed limit.

A spanking new sign emerged out of the darkness: Welcome to Okwalla, population 33,999. *Well, that's new.* Now plus one. *Once the lemons line up, do they give you an award? Or is a small town's population more like an odometer, making it worth a little less with each new person who arrives? But I'm not new,* he reminded himself. Only returning after a series of busted, pointless jobs, including the last, which had been the most disappointing of all, a fitting capstone to a failed life.

A gleaming *Vacancy* sign took shape, and he slowed in front of the *Haven Motel*. Also new. And out of place given the lack of traffic. He circled. It was worth a try. No point in reappearing in people's lives scruffy and exhausted. He glanced at his soiled clothes. Who was he kidding? He meant there was no point in reappearing in *her* life.

Entering, he expected familiar faces and was again surprised. A swarthy man with a foreign accent and toothy grin greeted him. His badge read: *Mr. Patel.*

"Sign here, please, sir."

"No problemo," Trencher said.

"I'm sorry, sir. I don't speak Spanish."

"Apparently."

"Sir?"

"Nothing. Here you go." Trencher laid down a large bill.

"Cash, sir?" He seemed perplexed. Mr. Patel looked at him askance. "Do you have ID?"

"Yeah, take your pick. Smith or Jones."

The humorless brows furrowed more deeply. "Sir, do you have ID?"

"Yes, I have ID," Trencher said tiredly. He handed over his driver's license, careful to avoid touching the clerk's hand.

Mr. Patel examined it. He read aloud, "Samuel Trencher." He handed it back. "Fine, sir. There is an extra five percent charge for cash transactions, sir. Checkout is eleven a.m., or there is a five percent charge. Please let me know if you need anything—"

"And if I do?"

They both said together: "Five percent charge."

"I get your drift."

"Sir?"

"Nothing. Thanks." *For nothing*. Trencher exited

the office.

Inside his motel room, Trencher threw himself into a deep armchair. He flicked on the TV, became instantly confused and ill-at-ease. He flicked it off.

He showered, dried, and hung up all the towels in a precise row, every corner matching. He inspected the bed and folded the sheets so that left and right were exact mirror images. Inspecting the cover for lint, he picked and discarded several nits. Finally, he crawled to the precise center of the bed, lay upon his back, and felt deliciously cool. In seconds he was lost to the world...

***

With a start, he returned from the Abyss. For a moment he breathed deep—then it came to him where he was, who he was, what he was about. *Damn. I'm still here.* With a frown, he stripped away the clammy, sweat-drenched covers, which had not moved an inch during the night, and immediately Mr. Five Percent floated before his eyes. An electric fan was bolted to the side table, and he aimed it at the bed and turned it on high to dry the sweat from the sheets. He shrugged.

Glancing at his watch, he sucked another breath.

Four minutes to Five Percent.

In three, he had packed his suitcase and was rushing for the front desk.

The toothy manager had been replaced by a woman who looked like Mr. Patel's sister. Trencher tossed her the plastic keycard. "How's Delhi these days?"

She looked puzzled. Laughed sweetly. "Que?"

He closed his mouth, hesitated, then turned away.

Desolation.

Entering his piece of crap, Trencher's mood improved. He decided to cruise down Okwalla's Main

Street. Maybe the memories would trigger more images; maybe better explain the ones he received. Having rushed out of the Haven Motel, he still needed a place to shave. He steered carefully around a thin figure with long gray hair snapped in a ponytail, riding a shaky bicycle. Wrinkled eyes glanced briefly his way as he drove past. Feelings appeared then disappeared as the bike vanished.

Trencher's stomach growled, and his eyes lit on a busy breakfast diner. Several locals were entering.

"The Bronco Grill," he said aloud to himself. With a half-smile, he cruised in front. He felt a tug. The Grill had no parking lot, and all the angled spaces were taken, and as he passed by, he thought he glimpsed a parking attendant scribbling on a floppy pad. Pulling up a side street, Sam pursed his lips. Here, too, every curbside space was taken. A patch of shadow appeared, the brightness of the sun making the shade beneath the huge, full-leaved tree darker by contrast. Hurrying to claim it, he backed in, congratulating himself on a rare perfect parallel execution. He walked to breakfast with a smile.

In front of the Grill, a thin young man in a wheelchair with full-arm tattoos and dirty hair held out a wide tin cup. At arm's length, Trencher gingerly handed him a dollar and felt even better. The young man inspected the bill and stuffed it in a cup half filled with coins and bills. Other patrons approached, and Trencher stood aside and held the glass door open for a couple.

"Thank you, young man," an elderly woman said with a crinkled smile.

Sam nodded. "Opening doors is my specialty."

The couple entered, chuckling.

Trencher followed and let the door go. Before the door swung shut, a man in his late twenties in a fringed jacket and felt-lined Western hat pushed back to reveal a pate of curled sandy hair stepped into its path—the man groaned, holding his elbow.

"Sorry," Trencher mumbled. He thrust his hands in his back pockets and stared at his feet.

The man glanced snidely at a smaller male companion, let fall an if-looks-could-kill glare at Trencher's back, and slammed the door. The pair strolled down the street.

Trencher staked out a booth. Brightened. From the rear of the diner came a willowy brunette decked out in a waitress uniform with short skirt and open cleavage, smiling as she deposited blue plates at a booth packed with customers. Images of cheerleaders during half-time came to mind, and Trencher's mood improved. No mystery where these impressions came from. From behind appeared a sharp-faced boy in a similar server's uniform. The boy approached and whipped out an order form while the brunette disappeared into the kitchen. Pen poised, the boy waited, scowling.

Trencher sighed. *Am I truly to be spared nothing?*

He placed his usual over-easy eggs and coffee.

When his eggs arrived, he ate in silence. As he finished, something seemed to nudge him, and he became aware of two thoughts. The first was that the brunette had reappeared on the far side of the diner and stood staring in his direction, strange red swirls appearing about her hair. Casually, he looked back without allowing his gaze to fall too directly so as not to offend her in case he had misread something—wouldn't be the first time. He glanced at his clothing and frowned. Though cutting a better figure than the night before, he still needed a shave, and his clothes looked slept in.

She looked away.

He peered into his coffee. Where were the signs when he needed them? Could coffee work as well as tea leaves? Looking up, his eyes searched again for the waitress. The brunette was serving an older balding man and a young curvy woman who kept her nose in a cell phone, and although Trencher continued to stare, the red swirls were gone and the waitress did not repeat her glance.

He sipped. Okwalla seemed overrun with strangers. In fact, he had been absent so long that he was tempted to think of himself as one. He pictured in his mind a long queue standing before the Welcome To Okwalla sign and he at the end, numbered ticket in hand, awaiting the dubious privilege of residing in what he had once regarded as the armpit of the universe.

The second thought was of a wheel. For some reason this image came through clearly, and he could not shake it. He recalled the wheels that had rolled through his mind the previous evening and, for a moment, was encouraged by the old hope that perhaps his latest foray into adulthood had not flopped after all. They were signs. He looked at the sullen teenage waiter, and the wheel appeared on the waiter's forehead. He shook his head. A goth tattoo? No, he was certain it was absent when he had first entered, just as the brunette's red swirls had been absent. He leaned back, could not help staring. He waited, stared, sipped his coffee, and gradually the wheel on the boy's forehead took on spiraling stripes that curled around its perimeter—suddenly Trencher understood.

Jumping up, he threw a ten on the table and rushed out of the diner.

He ran to his car.

A tow-truck was parked alongside, and the driver rolled out a pair of chains under the gaze of a silent policeman who calmly eyed a gray-painted, leaf-shaded fire hydrant through broad sunglasses.

It was him.

Trencher approached. "Ca-can I help you?" He struggled to catch his breath, hoping they would believe his lack of breath was due to his hurrying from the diner instead of lack of nerve, when, in truth, it was a little of both.

"Nope," the driver replied as he continued laying out his chains. Turning to stare at Trencher, the cop stood silently with arms folded. Trencher decided he had struck out and would soon have to walk to the police station to retrieve his car, and he opened his mouth to ask permission to retrieve his checkbook and suitcase, when the cop unexpectedly waved the tow man back to his truck. Without a word, the man reversed course and began to retrieve his chains.

Crossing to the police car, the officer returned with pen and pad, scribbled on the top sheet, and ripped it off. He handed the ticket to Trencher. "Welcome back, Sammy."

The chill he had felt the previous night when the police car had passed him returned in full force. "Glad to see you, too, Officer Brant."

The cop slid the pad into a shirt pocket. He paused. One hand wandered to his chin, and he rocked on his heels, regarding Sam quietly, passing his gaze over his rumpled clothes.

"Word of advice..."

Here it comes. "Yeah?"

Brant removed his sunglasses to reveal two intense pale blue eyes staring from a rough-hewn complexion, clean-shaven but for a gray-streaked mustache. He put his hands on his hips, elbows out, and pointed at Trencher with one prong of his sunglasses. "Keep your ass *clean*, Trencher. And I mean *squeaky* clean." Replacing his sunglasses, Brant began to walk away, then paused. "And by the way," he turned, "maybe you shouldn't smoke any *see*-gars while you're here."

Trencher felt himself redden. "I didn't do anything wrong, Brant. I'm not responsible for what happened to my uncle."

"That's a matter of opinion." The blue eyes glared.

"Besides, I was just a kid."

The cop pushed his hat back. "Well, in my experience, *kid*, people don't change. And I'll tell ya what." He stepped close, and the prong tapped Trencher's chest.

Trencher tensed but did not step back.

"I put you in the Army the first time, Sammy. Don't make me put you *somewhere else* the next time around." Brant waited for his comment to sink in. A second police car turned the corner and stopped, and Brant walked away, flopped into his cruiser, and rolled down Main Street.

"For nothing," Trencher muttered. He let out his breath and, with an effort, tried to relax beneath the steady stare of a policewoman with short dark hair who stood watching him from across the street while leaning on the second police car. Then she too reentered and drove off.

He looked away. *I guess she brought the shovel.*

Sam slouched to his car. Remembering his wrinkled clothing and stubble, he decided to see whether the YMCA he had visited once in the old days was still there. He eased the Oldsmobile into the growing traffic and turned, congratulating himself on his skill in avoiding collisions. The way to the Y was to the right and straight down Main Street as he recalled, which would take him again across the front of the Bronco Grill. He smiled. Maybe he could catch another glimpse of the best thing he had seen all day, swirls or no swirls. He had a feeling he would be taking more breakfasts at his former teenage haunt.

He steered into a turn. Across the street he saw a dentist's office, a law office sign that read: *Alexander* in pale stenciled letters, and this time clearly saw a parking cop in blue blazer slap a pink ticket on someone's windshield. Sam looked back to the Grill. For a moment he thought he saw the brunette and craned to look.

A loud metallic clang resounded.

He jammed his brakes—behind, a car swerved, missed him by inches. A tin cup sailed over Trencher's car, change and dollar bills dancing on his roof, and from below his car's hood he heard a groan.

The sidewalk in front of the Grill filled with wide-eyed pedestrians—some rushed into the street to help a young man with tattoos who lay beside a tumbled wheelchair.

Trencher stepped out. What thoughts he might have had of making himself scarce vanished in the growing crowd. His depression gave way to horror, which, he suspected, would surpass all the discomforts he had so far experienced and last far beyond any capacity he might have to endure it. His eyes searched the surrounding streets. Okwalla had no bridges high enough to jump off, but he did see a few decent light-poles that might support a nice rope.

He trudged to the victim, his unshaven jaw open, conscious of the fact that even this street bum with his tattoos made a better appearance than he. *What more? What else could be visited on me to make my life a living hell?*

Red-blue lights flashed. *Yes*, he nodded. *Of course. Thank you, God. Thirty fricking minutes and I'm headed for San Quentin.*

Officer Brant slid from his car. He drew himself to full height, straightened his holster, and did what he did best—strutted. Approaching Sam, he thrust his face into Trencher's. For a long moment Officer Brant stood staring in Trencher's eyes while neither moved, then, with a sudden jerk, Brant turned to the victim, whom sympathetic witnesses had helped into his wheelchair where he sat smiling as they brushed dirt off his muscled, short-sleeved arms. Brant whipped off his sunglasses and pointed them at the young man as he had at Trencher minutes earlier.

"Goddamit, Ralph. How many times I gotta tell ya to stop pullin that goddam stunt of yours? You ain't gettin *no* goddam insurance settlement."

The youth in the wheelchair lost his smile. Slowly he turned his wheelchair around, apparently none the worse for the incident. Bystanders helped push his chair back onto the sidewalk, more picked up his loose change and put it in his cup.

The door to the Grill opened. The brunette appeared, wide-eyed.

Brant snapped his gaze to her. "Get your brother out of the street and tell him to stay in front of the Grill where he belongs. I'm not picking his sorry ass up off the asphalt every time he thinks he's spotted another sucker." He turned his glance on the pedestrians. "Now that's enough. Go home. The shit didn't hit no fan."

They drifted away, though not without a few glares at the stranger who had attempted to run over one of their own.

Turning to Trencher, Officer Brant let his stare fall again, longer than before. For a full minute Trencher endured the inspection, until at last Brant thrust his shades back on and turned on his heel. He strode to his car. Spinning his tires, the car jerked then cruised measuredly up a side street, Brant keeping eye contact with Trencher through his car window as he vanished around the corner.

Trencher hardly noticed. The sidewalk was again empty, except for Ralph, who ignored him and leaned back to nap, and the number of cars eased up as the breakfast hour ended. Trencher puffed out his cheeks, blowing out the tension. There would be no bridge or light pole. Yet.

Two minutes later, Trencher killed his engine in the parking lot of the Y and gently pulled a tote-bag out of his suitcase. Walking carefully to avoid stepping on cracks in the sidewalk and aged tiles of the YMCA's floor, he managed to negotiate the hallways to find the locker room. He took a swim. Changed his shirt. Shaved. The Y was run down and decrepit, but at least he was clean and felt better.

A trip to the library followed. As he entered, the impact of Ralph's attempted swindle and Brant's anger hit. Sam trembled. Without moving, he violently shook, hoping the few patrons wandering quietly about would not notice. Sighting a blond wooden chair placed between two matching windows, he stumbled to the center of the chair where he closed his eyes until the trembling stopped. When he opened his eyes again, late afternoon had come. Surprised, but relieved that he was once again calm, he returned to his car.

He cranked the engine.

He soon found the scene of the crime. A new school had been built where his uncle's house had once stood. He shrugged. Maybe he should have answered his mail for the past six years, but he had had no money to pay the overdue house taxes anyway.

Pausing at a convenience store sporting a Minit Mart sign in need of paint, he walked inside and bought a newspaper from a middle-aged clerk. Avoiding asking about Delhi, he flipped to the want-ads, where he found an ad to share a renthouse on Southmore Street whose cost was in his price range, a mere half-mile from where he and his uncle had lived. Something prodded him, drew him to the address. Again, he wondered at the mysterious process that sometimes rewarded him when he acted on intuition, sometimes backfired in the worst way. Returning to his car, he squinted and tried to look inward—the feeling was strong.

Avoiding Main Street, and every major intersection he could, he drove to Southmore and found the renthouse. It was an old two-story bungalow of yellow clapboards. Trencher nodded. This time he understood. Framed with shiplap, the house needed paint and new shutters, and Trencher felt a small twinge of pleasure as he noted it lacked a man's touch. The day shift was over, and with dusk approaching, he decided it was okay to try the door. Leaving the want-ad on his seat, he rang the bell.

Half a minute and the door creaked open. The Bronco's waitress uniform had been replaced by cutoffs and T-shirt, but there was no mistaking the delicate turn of brunette hair and the fulsome curves that broke every angle.

Soft eyelashes widened. "It-it *was* you."

"Hi, Lori." Trencher sucked a breath, then let it out. "You're going to die."

CHAPTER 2

Lori stood in her living room with mouth open. After a moment she closed it and smiled, shaking her head. "Same old Sam. Nice to see you, too."

She motioned him in, and he parked himself on an expensive leather sofa behind a new glass-topped coffee table. He looked around, noticed that the quality of the furnishings belied the age of the house, and the salary of a waitress.

Crossing the room, Lori shouted down a hallway in a loud voice. "Brother dear! Companyyyy!" She turned back to Sam. "Back in a second."

She disappeared.

Sam sat and let his hand wander over a shawl on the sofa beside him. For a moment, he entertained the possibility that Lori was married, that a tall, confident, tanned giant with bulging muscles and wallet to match was about to enter. He consulted his mysterious touchstone, and for the first time as he fondled the shawl, was certain that a man was indeed in her life, a romantic attachment, though not here, not living with her.

Metal creaked and a wheelchair rolled into the room. Now, here in Lori's presence, Sam recognized him, and again wondered at the undependability of his gift—or affliction—at times tuning him in to facts he could not possibly know, other times preventing him from remembering what he ought: the younger brother of the first and only girl he had ever kissed.

"Ralph. Now I remember you." He forced a smile.

For a moment the youth stared, frowning in silence, his muscled hands cracking knuckles.

A voice came from the hallway. "Tell him you're sorry, Ralph. I *mean* it."

Ralph caught his breath. Looking up, he farted his lips. "I'm sorry, Sam. I didn't recognize you earlier. Otherwise, I wouldn't have done what I did."

Sam shrugged. "No harm, no foul."

Lori returned, having changed into a formal pantsuit. Sam was taken aback. She looked even less like the skinny girl that had changed his life so long ago, triggering the changes that would turn him into a man. Or something.

She sat beside him. He slid to the far side of the sofa, out of arm's reach. "He's tried that same trick two times this summer. He wheels his chair into the street, waits for a stranger, then tips his chair over. He even has a metal bar that he bangs on the car door." She looked at her brother. "It's way dangerous. One day you're going to get killed doing that."

Ralph looked crestfallen. "Who cares?" he mumbled.

"I care. And I don't appreciate your acting like a child about it."

"For *crissakes*, Lori, not another lecture."

"You need one."

He looked skyward. "Kill me now."

"I know it's hard."

He lapsed into silence, inspecting his shirt. "You've no idea."

Lori looked back to Sam. "You're still doing that *thing*." Her tone was matter of fact.

Sam blew out his cheeks. For a moment he was uncomfortable, aware that Ralph's presence seemed increasingly like that of a chaperone. "Yeah." He shook his head. "Some things I know. And some I just can't figure out. It's always been that way. But it's worse now."

She frowned. "I heard you joined the Army."

He nodded. "After my uncle died, I disappeared. I wasn't given a choice. I was run out of town by *you-know-who*."

Lori looked puzzled. "Officer..."

"Yeah. Him."

She brightened. "I remember our last night together. How we talked." She stopped smiling. "But you were supposed to come back the next day. You never came back. No phone call. No nothing." She looked sad. "Six years is a long time, Sam."

There it was. It was coming. He tried to ward it off.

He took a breath. "The Army didn't work out. I was a draftee among volunteers. They didn't take kindly to how I avoided everyone, and how I was constantly rearranging my stuff. When I began rearranging other people's stuff and always avoiding contact...that was the end. They put me in a room with carpet on the walls and asked me to talk to a guy with glasses and a beard. I was soon back on the street. Some pay saved up, but no benefits."

Lori shook her head. She smiled sympathetically.

"After that I tried driving a taxi. I worked hard at it and at first I actually made some money."

"Good for you." She contracted her shoulders, stretching her back.

"Then I started making change before the customers paid me. I simply knew how much change was due ahead of time. So I handed it over." He looked down. "Not the smartest move because then they wouldn't pay anything at all." He shrugged. "I went broke."

She laughed. "I can see you doing that."

"So, I was back on the street."

"But you didn't come back—"

"To Okwalla?" He smiled. "No. I couldn't come back. I just couldn't. Not after Uncle Roy died."

She nodded briefly.

"The whole town thinks I killed him, that I was smoking crack and burned down our house."

"He did take a drink now and then," Lori said. "Not to speak ill of the dead."

"He still does. On the other side. At least that's what he tells me when he appears."

Lori gave Sam that blank look that he was so used to from their former acquaintance whenever he mentioned his special talent.

"I didn't kill him, Lori. You know that. Not even by accident. And the drugs weren't his...or mine. But strange things were happening. Things I couldn't explain. Anyway, the cabbie thing didn't work out. Neither did a gig as a security guard. I escorted a thief off the store premises when he had my walkie-talkie stuffed under his shirt. I was too busy reading signs and I forgot that I had put it aside. I got fired...and got billed for the walkie-talkie."

She shook her head, disbelievingly.

"I was busy trying to figure out the images I was receiving from other places, other times, other people." Sam paused, looked up. A bouquet of roses had appeared floating in air behind Lori. The flowers did an arc into waiting hands. He sighed again. Looked back at her. "When is the wedding?"

Lori jerked as if struck.

"Am I right? For a moment I thought you were about to go into the plant nursery business."

Her eyes were wide. "Two weeks."

"That's it. That's how it starts."

"How *what* starts?"

"Your...you know what."

"My *death*?"

He nodded, disconsolate.

Lori turned to Ralph. "Uh, brother dear, can I ask you to give us some privacy please. I think Sam and I have some things to discuss."

Ralph paused from inspecting his shirt. He grunted, picked up a TV Guide, and slowly wheeled himself out, one arm rippling a red dagger tattoo.

Sam turned back to Lori, earnest. "That's what I saw. Kept seeing. Cars. The night. You. You don't die at once...you linger in a place surrounded by bright colors and twinkling lights."

"I don't want to hear this."

Sam caught his breath. Paused. "I could be wrong," he resumed. "That's the other thing I wanted to say. After I lost a whole series of jobs, I tried the only thing I had left. The thing that kept me from being stable all those years. I became a psychic."

Lori smiled and shook her head once more. "Like I said. Same old Sam."

"I read cards at first. Tarot. Went to psychic meetings and predicted coin tosses. I could predict 16 or 17 out of 20 tosses of a coin. Over and over. I don't know what you know about psychics, but that's very unusual."

"Couldn't you turn that into a job? Make some money?"

"Oh, I tried. I really did. But communication from the spirit world is not straight-forward. It's not simple. It's images, symbols, strange coincidences, songs at odd times. Ghosts can't really speak to you unless you're in *their* world."

Lori repositioned herself on the couch. "I'm glad you believe in yourself, Sam. Especially after so many disappointments. But I don't believe in magic. I'm a

Christian."

Sam shrugged. "Neither do I. But this isn't magic. It's natural. And it's...just plain weird." He took another deep breath. "And I'm not very good at it. I see the signs. But I can't read them. That's why everything went wrong again." He smiled unconvincingly. Shook his head. "You see, I may be a psychic, but I'm a failed one. I see the signs, but I can't understand them even when they're plain as day. I can't tell what the spirits are trying to say. Except sometimes. And sometimes too late."

"So, you could be wrong about me." She leaned to one side. "Though it was sweet of you to come all the way back to Okwalla just to tell me."

He shook his head. "To warn you."

"Now look, Sam." She grew serious. "Okay, so we used to be girlfriend and boyfriend. But that was a long time ago, and I'm engaged now and getting married in just a few days. It isn't fair for you to show up like this, and just out of jealousy try to break things up."

"Lori, Lori. I wish it were that simple. I'm not here to try to break things up, but in the hope that I'm wrong, that I've misinterpreted what I've seen. I'm not here for me. I'm here for you."

A pitying look settled on her. "Sorry, Sam, but I don't believe in this predisti... predistigita... predisti... astrology." She smiled wanly. "After I marry, Ralph will take a roommate, and I'll be moving out of here and into my new husband's house with my new furniture that he gave me when we got engaged. He's very successful. And, me...well, I can only serve so many blue-plate specials before I go...crazy." She stumbled over the last word.

"Yeah. *Crazy*."

"I didn't mean it *that* way."

"I'm not offended." Sam shrugged. "Prophets are

always scorned in their own hometowns." He shrugged deeper. "And I'm not even a prophet. Just a bum who sees things that aren't there." He looked up. "But a bum who used to love you. And still doesn't want to see anything bad happen to the best thing that came into his life."

"That's sweet, Sam. But six years is a long time. We're no longer seventeen."

A sigh. "I know. I won't try to apologize. I'm not here to cause you trouble. And I didn't come to ask you for another chance. I had to learn something about myself, about the world. I needed time to grow up."

"Me too. And that's what I did."

Sam's eye wandered to her pantsuit that could not hide the maturity beneath. He didn't need to be reminded of that, he told himself. Behind Lori, he glimpsed flowers again, more than before. Still floating in the air, no longer traveling in an arc. *What's it mean?* All he could think of was a plant nursery. From below the flowers rose a trickle of what looked like smoke. *What the hell? If only this came with an instruction book*. Behind it was the usual tightrope that caused him such worry. *How am I supposed to make sense of all this? I'm just a person like any other. How could I be expected to know what I'm supposed to do next?*

A distant voice penetrated his meanderings. "Sam...*Sam*!"

"Huh?"

"You're spacing out. Just like you used to."

"Was I?"

"Yeah. You know you've done that ever since we went to..."

He dropped his gaze. In all the years since that long-ago event, they had barely mentioned the *place*, and never fully discussed what had happened there, that nexus of events that had changed his life so much.

Now still wasn't the time.

He stood. "It's time to go. I have to get settled and think about things."

"You're staying in Okwalla, aren't you?"

"Yeah. My uncle's house is gone, but I'll find someplace." He looked around. "This was your parents' house. Didn't know they had passed."

"They didn't. My mother and father divorced. My mother moved to Italy with a car repairman, and my father is in Reno. He went to jail for shooting cars and won't come back to this state. Ralph got the house."

Sam shrugged. "See what I mean? I can't even make it as a psychic."

She too sighed. Paused a moment. "Do *you* see, Sam? This is my big break."

He slowly nodded. "No need to explain." He brightened. "Breakfast tomorrow at Bronco's?"

"Just like old times?"

"Not just, but almost. I know you're not my gal anymore. But you're still a friend..." He glanced at her questioningly.

Lori stood. Sidling close, she reached for Sam's hand. He tensed and shrank back. Thrusting his hands deep in his pockets he contacted change and counted two dimes and a nickel and a penny in each front pocket. The coins balanced and he relaxed.

Shaking her head, Lori pushed forward and puckered to plant a brief kiss on his cheek. Leaping to his feet, Sam jumped away from the couch and stood watching her.

She sighed. "Some things don't ever change."

Sam had caught his breath. He let it out and smiled. "Do *you* believe that people do?"

"I don't know. That one, I'll have to wait and see."

He hesitated. Pursed his lips. Lowering his gaze, he turned and opened the door.

She glanced at his left foot. “I see you’re still walking good. I’m glad.”

He smiled again.

Lori closed the door behind him.

Depression.

His hands dove again into his pockets and slid over the exactly balanced coins as if counting the beads on a rosary. Under control. But confused. Stepping away from the house, he came out under the wide, star-lit sky. He turned, and out of the darkness red petals showered Lori’s roof like noiseless rain. He scratched his head. “Could it be?”

CHAPTER 3

Charlie jammed the pedal backward to stop the bicycle and took a bite from his morning snack. He showed it to the other members of the posse.

"Apple core," he proposed.

"Baltimore," they answered.

"Who's your friend?" They scanned Main Street for a likely prospect.

"Big fat hen," Iggy yelled.

Taking aim where Iggy pointed, twelve-year-old Charlie launched the nearly whole apple, and with the accuracy of a seasoned pitcher, struck his target on the temple. The girl in pigtails, older than them but distracted with an armful of books and sporting just enough excess weight to make her an easy object of their prank, put a hand to her head. She dropped her books and burst into tears. Charlie looked to the others for confirmation of his skill and pedaled away, letting loose a war-whoop.

Down the street and around a corner, he stopped.

Sam skidded his bike beside him, scattering gravel. "Wow, you got her good. Did you see the look on her face?"

Charlie grinned, absorbing Sam's admiration like a sponge. "What a klutz." He cupped his hands and called back toward Main Street. "Fatty Josey. Fatty Josey. Summer school for a big, fat fool."

Sam stopped smiling and looked behind him. "Maybe you shouldn't yell so loud. It wasn't right to do that, ya know."

Charlie leveled a haughty glance upon him. "Says who?"

Another moment, and more gravel scraped. Iggy halted his bike beside them. "Yeah. That was great." He sneezed, and his glasses dropped to the ground. Straining to retrieve them, he carefully brushed them off and replaced them on his nose. He too looked back. "But don't you know who that was?" He remained upright with one foot on the pedal, poised to resume flight.

"Of course, I do. Fatty Josey. Do you think Apaches care about that?" He sniffed. "I am part Apache, you know." He let loose another of his famous war-whoops. The others broke into the wonder-struck stares that always followed any mention of Charlie's special connection to Indians.

"Gee," Sam said dreamily. "I wish I was."

"Yeah," Iggy added. "I'm gonna ask my Mom. Maybe she married an Indian and didn't know it."

The last of the posse showed up. "You took long enough." Charlie looked down at the slowest member of the club. "You're last." He looked at Iggy and Sam. "But what else can you expect from a *girl*?"

"Yeah," Iggy said. "A *girl*."

The last to arrive was skinny and wore her tangled black hair in a ponytail. "I made it." She panted.

"Who cares?" Charlie snorted.

"Yeah," echoed Iggy. "Who cares?"

A blank look settled on Lori's face. "But you know who that was?" Breathing hard, she looked behind her. "I'm not sure that was a good idea."

"Wimp," Iggy said.

"No." Charlie corrected him. "Wuss."

"Huh?" Sam frowned. "What's that mean?"

"It's Apache for *worse*. And it's only for girls."

All three boys grinned at the choice insult. “Wuss,” they all yelled together at Lori.

Lori stood her ground, still catching her breath.

“Aw,” Charlie said, “don’t worry about Fatty Josey’s big brother. He’s clumsy.” Charlie looked to Iggy for support. “He’s a klutz.”

“Yeah. A klutz.”

“Besides,” Charlie added, “Iggy told me to do it. So it’s the same as if he threw it himself.”

Iggy looked hurt.

Charlie glanced at him and softened. “But we really threw it together.”

Iggy brightened. “Yeah...together.”

Sam looked worried. “Maybe he’s a klutz, but he’s also older than us. And bigger.” Glancing back toward Main Street, Sam got off his bike. With a limp, he walked his bicycle behind some trees as if to make himself invisible. Charlie also stopped smiling, and a moment later scooted behind Sam. Soon they had all taken refuge behind tree-trunks.

“Aw, he ain’t gonna do nothin. Our bikes are faster than him anyway.” Charlie looked sideways at Lori. “Except yours.”

“What’s wrong with mine?” she asked innocently, looking at her spokes.

The others sniggered.

“Just look at it,” Sam said.

“Look at what?”

“*Look at what?*” Charlie mocked her. “Why, look at your bike.”

“What of it?”

They exchanged pitying glances. Finally, Sam deigned to enlighten her. “It’s a *girl’s* bike,” he gently informed her.

Her mouth formed an O of surprise.

“See? You’ll never make it. Girls’ bikes don’t go

fast."

"Yeah. Not like ours. Ours are kamikazes."

"Kamikaze *destructos*," they echoed.

She glanced once at their bikes and frowned. "Mine will, too."

"Not where we're going," Iggy said.

Charlie glared at Iggy, and he lapsed into silence.

"Where is that?" she asked.

"None of your business. But it's gonna be rough. Only boys can do this." Charlie puffed out his chest.

"Do what? Where are you guys going? *Please* tell me."

They looked at each other in silence. "You can't go and that's all we can say. You just can't."

She got off her bike and pushed down the kickstand. She stood with arms folded. "Well, I'm not leaving 'til you tell me."

"It's a secret. And it's not for girls."

Lori tapped her toe. She thought, and after a moment, Sam glanced at Charlie, who twisted a handgrip.

Suddenly she stared bright-eyed. "I know. You're going to the Round House."

The others exchanged crestfallen glances. "Naw." They looked sideways at her. "Why do you think that?"

"Because you snuck away on the Fourth of July when everybody is at the town picnic, and you all brought your bikes, and I know you didn't tell your parents because Sam's Uncle Roy called my house this morning and he wanted to know where Sam was, and you know you're not supposed to go there, and I'm telling. That's why."

Charlie, Iggy, and Sam let out simultaneous groans.

"And if you don't let me go with you, I'm telling Mom, and I'm going to tell her to tell Sam's uncle, and everybody else's Mom, too. And I already told my little brother, Ralphie." She turned an endearing smile on Sam. "Besides, Sam told me last week and invited me to come."

Iggy and Charlie turned on Sam. "Great. *Thanks*, Sam." "Yeah, Sam. *Thanks*."

"And, besides..." Lori sidled up to Sam, batting her eyelashes at him. "Sam's my boyfriend and I'm not letting him go anywhere without me."

Sam reddened. "If you try to kiss me, I'll hit you." To his relief, she refrained from this ultimate insult to his dignity, though a small voice wished that Iggy and Charlie were somewhere else so that he could receive her kiss without endangering his reputation.

Letting her arms down, she smiled. "Oh, come on, guys. Marge went to camp and won't be back 'til next week. I have no one else to play with. I wanna go."

"Okay, okay." Charlie kicked a rock. "But don't fall behind. This is men's work." He glanced around and gathered the others into a huddle. "Here's the plan. We cross the ridge behind town and go through the valley. That way no one will see us. Then we go up the creek along the dirt path 'til we get to the cliff. We park our bikes below. And then..." he raised his head and peered about to make certain no grown-up was spying on them, "we go inside the Round House."

The others shivered.

"*Inside*, Charlie?" Iggy asked. "But...no one has ever been inside."

"My grandpa has."

"Really? Wha-what's inside?"

"Never mind. But my grandpa was there years ago when his grandpa took him. He was an Apache, you know."

The glazed expressions returned.

"He swore he'd never ever go inside again, but my

grandpa told me what he did when he went in. So, if I want to continue the family tradition and be a real Injun like my grandpa, I'll have to do it. And I'll have to go alone." He checked himself. "I mean, I'm giving you a chance to go with me so I can show you around. And it'll only cost you a quarter."

The others looked upset. Several mouthed, "Gee, Charlie, I don't have any quarters."

Charlie looked thoughtful. "Spoke card?"

The others brightened and nodded.

"Each?"

"As soon as we come back."

"Deal. And we can't waste any more time now because we can't be there after dark. That's something else Grandpa warned me about. Never go to the Round House after dark."

"Yeah," said Iggy. "We're outta time."

They exchanged glances. As one, they rubbernecked to see if anyone was watching, and a minute later, three kamikaze destructos sped up the alley leading to the old train station. Crossing the tracks, they were surprised to see the mere girl's bike press ahead. Charlie, Sam, and Iggy redoubled their efforts, and as they left the last beat-up shack behind, managed to catch up to Lori.

They paused in a dusty field. Dismounting, they pushed their bikes to the top of the gentle ridge that dominated the western reach of Okwalla. Beyond lay a wilderness of eroded ridges, sheer cliffs, and winding valleys choked with dense thickets that stretched, it was rumored, all the way to the next state. With a last furtive look to check for grown-ups, they remounted and let the pull of the earth propel them down the far side, picking up speed until they had advanced far into the winding valley along a neglected dirt path.

At last, they slowed to a crawl.

Sam was breathless. “That was great.”

“Yeah. We went as fast as a car.”

“Enough of that.” Charlie glanced up. “We have to hurry.”

The others looked at the dark tangle of brush crowding either side of the narrow valley and swallowed. Charlie set his jaw and pedaled forward. Sam and Iggy followed, this time easily distancing Lori, who gazed wide-eyed, her head jerking at each unfamiliar sound that rose from the shadows.

For what seemed hours, they penetrated the woody arcade, pedaling without respite. The cliffs rose higher, and the dirt path became increasingly split with crevasses and sinks, forcing them to dismount more and more often and walk their bikes across to firmer tracts where the dirt mixed with shell and gritty limestone.

Sam paused to inspect a lump. “Hey, I found a fossil.”

Lori broke into a smile as she looked. She batted her eyelashes at Sam.

Charlie frowned. “Look later, will ya?” He glanced again at the sky where the sun was touching the farthest cliff-face. “We have to hurry.”

“How much farther?” Lori whined. “I’m tired.”

“Yeah, tired,” Iggy added, whizzing shells into the wood.

Their leader twisted his handgrip again. “Then go back, *wuss*. Both of you. I told you we can’t waste any time.”

“Oh, alright.” Iggy spun another shell. He remounted and he and Charlie pedaled forward.

Glancing at Lori, Sam followed the others.

Lori sighed and hurried to catch up. “Why are we doing this, anyway? I’m scared, guys. The woods are getting dark. Did anyone bring a flashlight?”

Charlie snorted. “Isn’t that just like a girl? Afraid of a little dark. Of course, no one brought a *girlie* flashlight.” He put his foot on one pedal again and turned his haughtiest stare on the others. “Well, are you comin? Or not?”

“I guess so.”

All together, they resumed pedaling.

The sun crept inch by inch behind the hills, the shadows in the woods stealthily lengthening as if another world watched, waiting to emerge.

A rusty fence with multiple strands of barbed wire blocked their path. Without a word, they maneuvered their bikes into the brush to a spot where the wires had been flattened by a fallen tree. They carried their bikes across and rejoined the dirt path.

Within a short time, Lori halted again. “I can’t go on, guys. Club or no club, I’m tired. And thirsty. I wanna go home.” No one answered and she looked around. “Guys?”

At the edge of the woods, they stood, staring silently upward. Above rose a vast limestone cliff jagged with outcrops and dark holes suggestive of caves. At the top of a slope of crumbled rocks and detritus, just beneath the top-most layer of stone, loomed a vertical cylinder of ancient stone bricks, shaped in a tapering dome. The outer face was smooth and gave no hint of means of entry. The last rays of the sun illuminated the tower redly; as they watched, the reflected light narrowed, the lower reaches of the pylon turning gray.

“There it is.” Sam stared. “The Round House.”

“Yeah,” echoed Iggy. He found himself eyeing the cliffs all around, no longer looking for grown-ups but for something less tangible but more threatening. “Hey. Ya know what? It looks like a stone teepee.”

“I don’t like this place, guys,” Lori said. “I don't

like it here."

"Ha. You've only been here once. And you've never been inside." Charlie tried to puff out his chest again but found it more difficult than before. "I've been here three times, including today. And it's not a teepee. It's a pueblo. That's what my grandpa calls it. A very special pueblo. That's why there's a fence. There used to be a sign by the fence, warning people away...'til it disappeared."

Another layer of stone turned from red to gray.

Sam turned to Charlie. "So, what do we do?"

"You see that flat rock on top, right beside the highest part of the pueblo, almost at the top of the cliff? We have to climb up there."

Brows lifted.

"Way up there?" Sam shook his head in disbelief.

Charlie glanced at Sam's leg. "What's the matter? Is your *cub-foot* in the way?"

"*Club*-foot, Charlie. I've had it since I was born."

"Aw, you can do it. Anyone can. I climbed up there last time I was here. I'll show you how." Charlie took a step, then paused to see if the others would follow. Three sets of feet followed behind him, and, reassured, Charlie commenced climbing the broken stone.

Several minutes passed as they struggled up the slope, Sam, prickling at Charlie's comments, taking the lead, his partial club-foot stumbling but not preventing his climb. Halfway up, Iggy lost his grip and slid back down amid a crush of boulders and broken shell. He caught a sprig of mesquite that checked his descent. After much effort, he managed to scramble back up again to rejoin the others, Sam lending a hand to help him.

Charlie reached the base of the pueblo. Here lay a narrow shelf, and in another minute, all four sat along its edge. They inspected patchworks of bruises and minor cuts.

"Gee. We're really high up."

"Look how small our bikes are," Lori added. "They look like doll bikes from here."

Charlie sniffed. "That's nothing. Wait 'til we get up there." He turned and looked up. The others dropped their jaws.

"Way up there? It's too dangerous."

"Besides, how will we climb up?"

"Are you chicken again? I told you what we need to do. We have to climb up there on top of that flat rock and stand on the very top of the pueblo." Charlie stood up and looked at Sam. He flapped his elbows. "Pu-cuuuck." Turning, Charlie clung to protrusions in the structure. "See? There are handholds here, just like a ladder. This is how the Injuns got in."

The others watched wide-eyed as Charlie climbed vertically, one hand and foot negotiating pits in the sheer cliff-face on his left, his other hand and foot locating depressions in the structure on his right. Within two minutes, he stood triumphantly on the flat rock at the peak. "Pu-cuuuck." He flapped his elbows again while grinning at them.

Not willing to take this, even if Charlie was older by two months, Sam screwed up his courage and started after. He soon had joined the club's leader and chief instigator, and he too grinned. "Pu-cuuck." Sam yelled down at Iggy and Lori.

To their surprise, Lori was the next to climb. More agile than them, she made it to the top in one minute.

The three stared down at Iggy.

"Well, what's the matter?" Charlie called to Iggy. "Chicken got your tongue?"

"It-it's my glasses, guys. I dropped them when I rolled down the slope. They...uh, they don't fit right no more." Iggy stared up. He made no move to join them.

"You know what? I think I heard somethin in the bushes. I'd better wait here and watch the bikes. Yeah, that's what I'll do, I'll watch the bikes to make sure no rustlers run off with them."

"We're not playin rustlers anymore, Ig."

"I'm not playing. It's for real. I think I heard someone in the bushes. It could be rustlers."

Charlie put his hands into his armpits again, but Sam put a hand on his shoulder. He looked back at Iggy. "Okay, Ig, you do that. We'll be back soon." Looked at Charlie. "He's just a kid, Charlie. After all, he's a whole three months younger than me. We don't need him for this."

Charlie shrugged. He turned and paused. Swallowing hard, he wiped both hands on his shirt. He glanced once at Sam and Lori, then, shielding his eyes from the bright glare of the setting sun, he led the way along the parapet for about twenty feet to where the last brilliant sunrays ignited the white roof of the pueblo. Here, in the exact center of a ring of painstakingly shaped ancient capstones loomed a four-foot-wide aperture, its blackness yielding nothing to the sun's dying efforts to deliver warmth and light to the interior.

Inching to the edge, Charlie peered into the blackness.

Sam and Lori joined him.

Sam leaned to look. "What do you see?"

Charlie continued staring in silence.

"Charlie?" Sam glanced at Lori. He nudged Charlie. "*Charlie*?"

As if awakening from a trance, Charlie shook himself. He looked up. "It's down here. Inside."

"What's down there?"

Charlie took a deep breath. For a moment he stood quietly, staring into the pit. "Nothing. And everything."

He pointed at a slit in the side of one rock. “There’s the first handhold.”

“But it’s too dark, Charlie,” Lori said. “How can you see where to go?”

He forced a mirthless grin. “Whadaya think this is for?” He brandished a flashlight from his pocket.

“You mean you had that all along?”

“Sure. You don’t think I was gonna waste it on a scared girl, do ya?”

Sam looked straight ahead, brows raised.

For a moment, Lori looked indignant. Then she too found herself staring into the black abyss. The beam of the flashlight shot forth, and she caught her breath.

“There. See? More handholds.” Charlie put one foot on the first slit in the hole, then paused. He needed both hands to descend.

“I’ll hold it while you climb down,” Sam suggested.

Charlie breathed deep. He surrendered the light. “Be sure to shine it right on me...or rather right on the wall while I’m climbing down.”

Sam nodded. “Alright. On the wall.”

Charlie put his leg into the abyss, found a slit. His body began to slide into the darkness, which was now lit by an unsteady needle of light flickering over an endless series of roughly cut stones. “Hold it still. How am I supposed to see the way down?”

“Okay, whatever you say. What do ya see, Charlie?”

“Nothin. Just you jerkin the light... Now I can see the ground.”

A minute passed with only the rasp of cloth on rock measuring the progress of Charlie’s descent.

“There.” Charlie’s voice echoed up from below. “I’m on the floor. But I can’t see a damn thing. Throw me the flashlight.”

Sam and Lori exchanged glances. The sun was gone, and the entire cliff-face had turned gray. "Are you sure?"

"Yeah, dammit. Throw me the light. But don't turn it off, leave it on so I can find it."

"But that's crazy. It'll break." Sam and Lori stared into the pit where a small circle illuminated Charlie's upturned face. His wide eyes shifted and his cheeks shined with sweat.

"You got a better idea?" His voice echoed.

"Would this help?" Lori pulled some string from a pocket.

"Super. That'll work." Sam looked back at Charlie. He cupped his mouth to yell. "We found some string. How about we lower the flashlight to you?"

"Fine. But hurry up." Charlie's voice echoed.

Lori unspooled a length of string and Sam tied one end to the flashlight. He breathed deep. "Okay. Here goes." Slowly Sam lowered the light, the spiraling beam tracing a corkscrew, until it lit on Charlie's upturned face. A stream of sweat poured down his neck. Clasping the light in his hand, he eased.

"Okay. Now Sam." Shining the beam on the handholds, Charlie watched Sam slowly clamber down.

"Your turn, Lori," Charlie called up.

In a few minutes, Lori stood next to them.

Charlie shined the light in her face, angry. "Why didn't you tell me you had some string before I came down?"

She pursed her lips and turned up her nose. "And waste it on a mere boy? *Hmph.*"

Charlie glared at Sam.

Sam shrugged.

The beam shone behind Sam, and Charlie and Lori caught their breath.

"Lookit."

He flicked the beam rapidly over the interior of the structure to reveal a series of red ocher pictographs.

"Well, I'll be..."

Charlie grinned. "I told you. Injuns."

Sam stepped closer, placing his hand on Charlie's arm to help guide the flashlight. Images appeared in its bright circle, a collection of primitively drawn stick-figures. Some ran after buffalo, others brandished bows and arrows, and others stood gazing skyward.

"What are those there—"

A flurry of wings rushed into the chamber.

They scrambled.

"It's in my hair," Lori yelled. "Get it out!"

"Goddam bats," Sam said. Grabbing Lori's hair, he helped untangle one, and they retreated to a wall. Charlie's light swung wildly about the interior as he swatted his arms and legs.

"It's just goddam bats." Sam laughed. "They won't bite. They're going out...now that it's...nighttime."

He and Charlie exchanged worried torchlit looks.

Charlie took a breath. Standing before Sam, he shined the light under his chin so that his face lit up like a ghost's. He transferred the beam to Sam's face. "Just bats to you. But this is a special place. My grandpa told me. Nothing down here is what you think it is."

Lori had stepped farther in the darkness, and after she finally calmed, she leaned against one side of the structure. "You know, it's not completely dark down here. Some light is still coming in from above—"

A crack sounded.

Sam and Charlie glanced up. "What was that?"

The crack grew to a rattle, and Lori sprang back from the wall. With a roar that reverberated through the chamber, the wall collapsed. She stumbled out of a cloud of dust into the flashlight beam, coughing.

Sam and Charlie stepped closer. The beam of the

flashlight illuminated a gaping hole that led into the cliff. "Well, how do ya like that?" Open-mouthed, they left Lori coughing in the darkness and stepped through the aperture and into another chamber, much larger than the first.

Charlie moved the light. Here were more figures—but executed with more precision and thought than the stickmen in the outer chamber. In one panel, hunters with carefully drawn hide trousers and feather headdresses stalked buffalo. In another, warriors with obsidian-tipped clubs and antique feather and jaguar headdresses challenged each other to combat. One lay decapitated. Beside them stood several figures wrapped in buffalo hide with arms raised skyward; their eyes too large for their faces; on each of these a mop of hair, or something like hair, stood on end. A look at the other friezes revealed a large-eyed cloaked figure standing in the midst of each, seemingly leading or commanding the others. The circle of light moved again and lit on a confused tangle of sticks from which smoke or fumes seemed to rise, more large-eyed figures standing in the center, half sunk in the tangled mass.

They slowly closed their jaws.

"What's it all mean?" Sam asked.

"Aw, who cares?" Charlie rearranged pieces of wall with his shoe. He lowered the light to inspect them.

"Wow," Sam continued. "This is awesome. We should tell someone about this."

Lori recovered her breath and followed them into the chamber. She came alongside, similarly entranced. "It's like we're explorers. We found something new."

"Get ahold, guys." Charlie lowered the beam of light again to rest on the floor. "These pieces are bricks. Someone was here before us. And they walled this room up. Grown-ups."

They breathed deep and, for a minute, were lost in thought.

"Well, what do we do next? What did your grampa say?"

Charlie looked serious. "I have to kiss the Midnight Sun."

Sam and Lori exchanged puzzled looks.

"He said it may not be easy to find, but I'll know it when I see it." He shined the light into a tunnel that exited the far side of the inner chamber. "We have to go in there."

The others shivered.

"*In there?*" Sam stared, his eyes following the beam of light. "But that goes into the cliff. It's like going under a mountain. Or somewhere else..."

Charlie inspected the ground. "It's not hard. And someone's carved out a path. The way is smooth."

They gulped.

"Spoke card?" Charlie looked less confident than the tone of his voice suggested.

Sam blew out his cheeks to calm his heart. "Double spoke cards. For us."

"Deal." Charlie breathed more easily and wiped his palms again.

They stepped in.

The path wound for some distance leading in and downward, and before long, the smooth path gave way to rocky outcroppings and embryonic stalagmites. The dim light from the far-away sun vanished, leaving them hanging on the feeble ray from their single torch. In the infinite blackness an occasional spray of luminescent minerals shone forth like distant stars from another dimension. Patches of deeper darkness on either side suggested other corridors, other chambers.

From behind, in the direction of the collapsed brickwork, a crack echoed, and in response a flurry of wings again whipped the air.

Lori screamed.

"Bats again," Sam called. "It's only more bats. It's okay. They've gone now." Sam thrust his hands in his pockets, still reluctant to accept her embrace for how it might make him look, while Lori stood next to him, shivering.

Another moment passed, and they picked their way forward again. Soon the flashlight limned a crevasse that plunged between two stalagmite-crowned ridges paralleling the abyss like guardians. Together, they edged forward.

"See? More handholds."

Sam placed one hand on Charlie's arm. "You're going down *there*?"

Charlie nodded. He took a step and halted. In the beam of light, more illustrations took shape on the live stone, with more detail than before. The bed of sticks were now clearly a pile of bones, and the figures with their hair on end displayed an unmistakable look of horror as they stood within its midst, flames and smoke engulfing them.

A hand settled on Sam's shoulder. He jumped. The others caught their breath.

Lori gulped. "It's me, Sam. Just me. I'm sca—" she stammered, "scared—scared—scared..." Lori moved close to Sam and gripped his arm. He made no attempt to dislodge her, but planted his feet more firmly, and took quick breaths until she stepped back.

The flashlight dimmed. Charlie shook it and the light strengthened again. For the moment.

"It's d-, d-, down here, Sam... Lori..." Charlie whispered. He looked into the crevasse, then back to them. "Pu-cuuck?" he said weakly.

Sam shook his head.

The sweat dripped again from Charlie's cheeks.

"*Triple* spoke cards?"

Sam and Lori looked at each other, breathed deeply, and once more edged forward.

Using the handholds, they descended carefully to the next level. Here, at the bottom of the crevasse, the hand-slits abruptly ended. A floor of undulating limestone stretched away into a darkness that seemed suddenly less complete.

"See...see that?" Charlie aimed the beam to the far side where a wide crack had ripped the floor, opening the way to still greater depths. "Wa-watch." Before the others could protest, he switched off the light.

They sucked their breath.

From within the crevice shone a barely visible luminescence, its dull rays exiting to pulse against the jagged roof overhead.

Sam looked askance at Charlie. A mixture of triumph and terror lay on the older boy's face, far beyond what one should expect in a boy of his age, and Sam found himself wondering if they had just become grown-ups.

"We-we found it. Th-th-this is the last step." The beam of light flickered. Sweat poured from Charlie's temples and down his chest. He stepped forward.

No one followed.

Charlie halted. He spoke without turning. "Guys, *puh-leeze* come with me." His hand shook, imparting a quiver to the beam of light. "We're almost done. Just one more minute, and we can leave."

"Tell you what, Ch-Ch-Charlie. We-we'll wait here. And we'll ho-hold the fla-flashlight for you."

Taking a deep breath, Charlie slowly let it out. "Okay. But d-don't leave. And don't lose the light. We don't need it here, so you can turn it off, but we c-can't find our way back w-without it." He clenched his jaw to stop stuttering.

Handing the flashlight to Sam, Charlie placed one leg over the edge to inch downward into the crevasse.

Lori stayed back, and Sam took a step in her direction. Her lips trembled as she smiled at him, and Sam turned and risked flicking off the light—he was unsure which was more responsible for his goosebumps, their solitude and isolation, or the weird lights that played about the mouth of the pit and the roof of the chamber, and he realized he was glad that Lori had come with them. The possibility that she might again sidle up to him and cuddle, the assurance that she liked him despite the deformity of his partial clubfoot, gave him confidence and helped calm his fears. But he said nothing, leaving the choice to her. After all, that's what Charlie would do. And Charlie was tough. But, beyond reason, and although the soft glow from the crevice rendered the darkness in the cavern less than pitch-black, something about the strangeness of the glow impressed him with a need to remain quiet and inconspicuous.

A hand fell on Sam's shoulder. A familiar warmth traveled through his body, and he felt relief and gratitude that Lori had approached and again wanted to embrace, and he decided that he cared not a whit for Charlie's attitude, and that in the future he would gladly receive not only Lori's hugs but her kisses as well. He started to turn. The hand on his shoulder tightened and began to hurt.

"Ouch," Sam squirmed. "Not so hard, Lori. Man, I didn't know you had such a grip."

Sam twisted round—and froze. The flashlight fell to the ground as Sam stared upward into two grinning faces lit by automobile night-sticks.

"You punks made my sister Josey cry. Now I'm gonna *pound meat.*"

CHAPTER 4

"Get on, faggot." Sun-golden skin entirely free of the usual afflictions of adolescence framed hazel eyes under sandy hair, lines of humor etching either temple. A green Suzuki 300 buzzed, then slowed to a purr. "Ya got our shit?"

"Wow. You really did it. You got a motorbike." Steven nodded and brandished a large black plastic bag.

"Good," golden boy said. "You can sit behind me. But if you mess up my new bike, you won't live to see tomorrow."

"No problem, Ro—"

The first let loose a glare that cut him short. "Say it and die."

"Edwin. That's what I was gonna say."

"Eddie," he corrected.

"*Eddie.*"

"That's better." Eddie grinned. "I've got the matches. You got the shit. And it's Fourth of July." He gunned the bike again, louder, and shouted over the roar, "Poppa's gonna have some fun tonight."

Steven grinned and said nothing, the bright sun of a summer morning lighting his facc. Hc climbed on behind Eddie, carefully placing a boot on each rest.

Unzipping one pocket of his leather jacket, Eddie removed a comb and ran it through a peach-fur mustache. Steven, older but still clean-faced, watched with envy. "When I lean, you lean," Eddie instructed, aware of the effect his precocious maturity had on his peer. "And don't put your arms around me. I have a rep to maintain, you know."

"Sure thing, Eddie. Well, I'm ready."

Eddie broke into a mocking grin. He whipped out a cigarette and lit it with an expensive engraved lighter and strapped on new goggles and a shiny black and green helmet. "Eddie's steady and ready, and Steven's even. And the whole stinkin town is away at the festival. Say bye to your old lady, Steve-O. It's time to raise some hell."

"Yeah!"

The motorbike buzzed like an angry hornet and lurched out of a yard strewn with auto parts and broken lawn furniture. It peeled away, leaving a long carbon smudge on the concrete. Racing down a series of side streets, they avoided the main thoroughfare of Okwalla. Although the Fourth of July festival was in Eastside Park, and Main Street would have even less traffic than usual, Eddie stopped at the entrance to an alleyway several streets away.

He glanced behind him at his partner. "Let's take the back roads. We don't want to run into your-friend-and-mine."

The wheels spun. Bursting from the opposite end of the alley, they raced through several stop signs and pulled onto the southern turnpike. Steven pointed at a couple of houses and began to open his sack.

"Not yet," Eddie yelled over the noise of the motorbike. "We gotta get gas first."

Speeding down the mostly empty turnpike, they joined the main highway that channeled traffic into Okwalla, or, according to some, steered it away. In a few minutes, they arrived at an older but still well-maintained filling station.

Eddie ditched the cigarette, pulled in, and ran over

the bell-hose.

A minute passed. A dour face appeared at the window.

“Move it, Mr. Monkey Wrench,” Eddie yelled. “You got a customer.”

Thirty seconds passed, and a thin elderly man eased out the door and shuffled toward them.

“Ya got molasses for blood or somethin?” added Steve. “Step on it, baldy. Time’s a wastin.”

The older man creeped up and passed a crusty gaze over the motorbike. Squinting to see, he finally grunted. He rippled his lips and slowly began to unhook the pump handle while Eddie and Steven dismounted.

Eddie snatched the handle. “Hey, Len, what’s this?” Eddie touched a button on the old man’s work-shirt, and Len looked down. Eddie snapped his hand up and popped him on the nose. “Gotcha.”

“Ya little shit—”

“Calm down, grandpa. Here ya go.” Eddie thrust a crisp twenty into Len’s hand, and the old man quieted. Eddie smirked at Steven. “Nobody argues with Jackson. He’s everybody’s friend.”

In a minute, the tank was filled, and Len noted the amount. He began the long journey back inside to make change. After he stepped inside, Eddie produced a plastic bottle, unhooked the pump again and drained the hose. Len returned, inching across the pavement, and Eddie accepted his change. As the old man drifted back to his office, Eddie winked at Steven. He started the engine and rolled a short distance as if preparing to exit the station, then killed it.

With a mischievous grin, Eddie nodded for Steven to open the black plastic bag. Extracting one of the smaller white bags, Steven brandished it. Eddie waved him forward. The two crept to the door to Len’s office, taking care not to be seen through the window.

With a last look to ensure no car was approaching, Steven opened the bag and deposited its smelly contents on the concrete porch. Eddie sprinkled gasoline on top, carefully re-closed the bottle, tucked it away, and lit the mess with his lighter. Quickly they sneaked back to the motorbike. Digging in his pocket, Eddie extracted a clutch of firecrackers and handed several to Steven.

Eddie ran the bike over the bell-hose.

Len peered out the window and Eddie, struggling valiantly to control a grin, waved him out a second time.

At the door: "What the goddamhell you want now, punks? You got your gas, and you got your change. Now get the hell off my property, or I'll—" He looked down. His shoes, encased in dogshit, leapt with flames.

Together, and in rapid order, Eddie and Steven flung the firecrackers, which exploded like a military bombardment and rewarded them with the sight of Len pirouetting with the gracefulness of a ballet dancer. His dance soon deteriorated into the leaping of a hamstrung frog.

"Yaaaa!" Len disappeared inside. His cries echoed through the station.

"Haw!" Eddie twisted the bike-handle, and they jerked away. *"Yeeee-haaaa!"*

In another moment, Steady Eddie and Even Steven were back on the highway, looking for their next victim. At the exit to the turnpike, they pulled behind a billboard. Eddie pulled off his goggles.

Five minutes later a police car sped past, lights flashing.

"Okwalla's best." Eddie smirked. He wiped a tear from one eye and glanced at Steven. "*Life*...is good." Cranking the handle, they re-entered the turnpike and sped back toward town. Eddie inserted one hand into a jacket side pocket and pulled out a cigarette pack. He slowly braked. In another alleyway he halted.

"Only two left. How about you?"

Steven searched his pockets and came up empty.

"Well, give me a beer."

"I thought *you* brought the beer, Eddie. Where am I gonna put it, in here with the dogshit?"

Eddie shrugged and handed him one of the cigarettes.

He gunned the motor again. "Look's like it's time to make another donation to our favorite charity."

Steven grinned. "Righto, mate. Let's go see Mr. Mexico."

Away they lurched. Soon they sighted a large Minit Mart sign and rolled into the parking lot. Eddie stopped in the alley where the bike would be invisible from the entrance and they deposited the black bag a few feet away.

Pulling baseball caps low over their foreheads, Steven entered the Mart. Eddie followed a minute later as if they had not arrived together. A few moments of affectedly casual browsing, and Eddie approached the front counter. "How's it goin, Pablo? Ya got any new mags in?"

A short pudgy man with a red vest and a broom mustache gave him a hard look. "No, not for you. You gotta be eighteen for that. How many times I gotta tell you, *mon*. No cigarettes. No beer. And no Lotto."

"Aw, I know all about that. But that's not what I'm askin about. I'm askin about magazines."

"Magazines too. No Playboy. No Hustler. I can't do it, mon. And I tol' you, it's not Pablo. My name is Enrico. See the nametag?"

"Oh, don't pop a fuse, José, I'm just askin. You see, I've been waitin for the latest *Cycle World*. Gonna buy me a new Suzuki 300 as soon as I can, and I want to read up on 'em." Eddie pulled out a ten-spot and grinned. "See? I'm ready, willing and able." Eddie glanced in the convex mirror above the counter. On the other side of the store, Steven shuffled the other way down an aisle. "*Cycle World*. Check for it, will ya?"

"Look on the magazine rack, mon."

"I did that already." Eddie craned his neck to peer into a back room behind the counter. "Come on, bro. Look in the back and see if you got any new ones in."

"No, there ain't no new magazines—"

"How do you know if you don't check?"

Enrico let out his breath in irritation. "Un momento." He disappeared into the back room.

Snapping his cap even lower to block cameras, Eddie stretched over the counter and reached below and under. Straightening, he tossed a carton of cigarettes to Steven who caught it like a football star. The carton disappeared under his coat.

Eddie thrust his hands in his pockets as Enrico returned. The cashier shook his head. "Like I tol' you, I got no new mags. Maybe mañana. Come back tomorrow, mon."

Looking up and past him to where single packages of cigarettes were displayed, Eddie looked inquiringly once more at the cashier. "What kinda cartons you got below, Pablo?"

Enrico shook his head. "Forget it, mon. I can sell you Twinkies and comic books. I can't sell you beer, smokes or porn."

Behind Eddie, Steven exited the store without approaching the counter. Eddie put the ten back in his pocket. "Well, let me know when the new *Cycle World* gets in, will ya? That's all I wanted, honest." He took a step away, paused. "Course, I do have Jacksons too..."

Enrico paused a moment as if weighing potential

profit against possible jail time. He shook his head again. “Can’t do it, amigo. Come back when you're eighteen.”

Eddie shrugged. “Your loss, Mr. Mexico. Don’t say I didn’t try to cross your palm with silver.” Eddie struck his chest with his fist in a mock gang salute. “Mañana, bro. When my *Cycle World* gets in, keep it in the back for me, will ya, on account-a I’m your A-Number-One customer.”

Enrico shrugged.

Eddie walked out. Strolling slowly, he approached the corner of the store. Turning the corner, he tossed the baseball cap into a dumpster then jumped on the Suzuki. Steven leapt on behind; his coat bulged with parcels. Eddie glanced back. Grinned. “I tol’ you, *mon.* You can’t have no beer or cigs ‘til you ees eighteen.”

“Ha!” Steven laughed. “We got him again. This is even easier with the motorbike.”

The bike roared, and a few minutes later, they zig-zagged through a maze of alleyways. “*Yaaa-haaah!”* In a park, they paused behind some children’s play equipment. Steven laid out a six-pack, a half-dozen Twinkies, two burritos, and the carton of menthols Eddie had tossed him.

“What a haul.” In minutes they had downed the beer, and for the next half hour hooted at each other’s antics trying to smoke a dozen cigarettes at once.

“Enough of this scene,” Eddie finally said, suddenly serious. “Here. Eat the Twinkies and burritos, they’ll soak up the beer and sober you up.” While Steven gorged Twinkies, Eddie stood and fished in his pockets. He pulled out the remaining firecrackers and counted them. “Ya still got the crapola?”

Steven nodded.

“Get on, faggot. It’s time to show this burg who’s boss.”

"Righto, bwana."

Exiting the park, they buzzed toward town center, one eye alert for the next target, the other for your-friend-and-mine, careful to avoid the east side where preparations for the evening's Fourth of July fireworks would be in progress. A stop sign loomed and they sailed through, exultant at the falling away of every restriction.

Eddie slowed, the bike momentarily careening. He regained control and halted.

"Main Street." He pointed to Steve, one brow rising.

Steve looked cautious. "Maybe we should go around, Ro—"

The *look* cut him off again. "Not gonna tell you again, bro. I hate that name. My parents were jerks when they hung that around my neck. I go by my middle name now...*Edwin*."

Steve sniggered. "You mean Eddie, don't you?"

Eddie eased up. He chuckled. "Yeah, that's right. I almost forgot. Eddie." He peered ahead. "Let's make the Drag, Steve-O. My little sister had summer school this morning, and she was going to the library afterward. I wanna show off my new bike to somebody. I'll bet Main Street's empty. Everyone else is scarfing chicken legs and lemonade in Eastside Park."

Steve-O snickered. "Chicken legs and lemonade." He took another long drag on his menthol. "What a bunch of losers."

"Ya got that right. Let's roll." Eddie wrenched the accelerator, and the front wheel popped. The wheels ate up the road, and they approached Main Street. Here the buildings fronted the streets without any setbacks except for aged sidewalks, and true to Eddie's prediction, the traffic was even less than before. Only a beat-up pickup truck coasted by.

They paused. The pickup turned and vanished.

"There's the library," Steve pointed.

"Lookit. Even the police station's empty." Eddie tightened his helmet. "I always wanted to spin some dust in those assholes' faces. And City Hall, too. Show my jerk of a dad what I think of him for dumping me on my wino mom and her dickhead boyfriend."

"Go for it, dude."

He jerked the handle, and the back tire squealed. Up they lurched. As they picked up speed, Eddie let loose with his favorite salute in the direction of both civic institutions, middle finger extended.

Out of a side street appeared a young kid, pedaling nonchalantly; he turned onto Main Street and headed west.

Eddie slowed, stopped. Glanced at Steve again. "Are you thinkin what I'm thinkin?"

"If you're thinkin he's got bulls-eyes all over him, I am."

"Got your ammo?"

"Yo, bro!"

With a spin, the bike leapt forward. In another moment they were riding alongside the kid on the bike.

Eddie slowed down; the engine quieted to a purr. He spat a loogie in front of the kid and got one leg. "Hey, Ralphie, baby. What's the news, squirt?"

Ten-year-old Ralph, astride a bike that was too big for him, glanced once, nervously, and tried to speed up.

"Why ain't you at the Park with all the other losers? What's the matter, punk? They run out of chickens and lemonade?"

"Leave me alone. I'm trying to find Lori. I'm going with her to a secret place."

Steve sniggered. "Secret place? Like where, squirt?"

"The Round House. But it's none of your business.

Just leave me alone."

"What was that? You tryin to tell me my business, punk?" Eddie gunned the motor, kicking the front tire an inch off the ground. "You know what we do to little punk kids who try to tell us what to do?"

Ralph looked stricken. A tear leaked from one eye and he sped up.

"Show him, Steve-O."

Fishing in Eddie's saddlebag, Steve produced a lighter in one hand and a string of firecrackers in the other. He lit three and tossed them in Ralph's path.

Bang! Pop! Bang!

"Haw!"

Eddie turned his eyes back to the street just in time to see the red light. He braked.

Eyes fixed on his pursuers, Ralph sailed through the light just as the pickup returned from the side street.

The truck hit—broadside. Ralph's body flew to a crumpled rest beneath his shattered bicycle.

With a screech, the truck halted. A bearded rancher with a wide-brim hat jumped out and ran frantically to the boy. In another moment, the rancher leaped up and ran toward the police station.

Eddie and Steve traded looks. Eddie gunned the motorbike, lurched forward, then stopped with a jerk.

Red and blue lights burst upon them from the opposite side street. A cop with pale blue eyes and bull neck jumped out, trailing sunglasses in one hand. He rushed to Ralphie. Felt and prodded. A moment later a second cruiser appeared and a policewoman with short trimmed dark hair tumbled out.

Brant inspected the damage. "Time to put your EMS training to use, Marla."

Marla glanced at Ralph's crumpled form. "Oh my god." Rushing back to the police car, she snatched bandages and began carefully inspecting Ralph's broken body while Brant hurried to the station. In moments, a white-coated attendant came running from the police station with the rancher in tow.

Eddie nudged Steve and turned off his bike. Casually, while no one was looking, Steve tossed the black bag into a storm drain along with the cigarettes and firecrackers. His lighter followed.

Brant straightened. Sighted them. He approached with a frown, Marla following close behind.

"Evening, Officer Brant. Too bad Mr. McReynolds wasn't watchin where he was goin. They let anybody have a driver's license these days, don't they?"

Brant halted in front of them. "Shut up. Get off the bike."

"Yessir, officer sir." Eddie and Steve got off and stood quietly, hands in pockets.

Turning to Ralph, Brant saw the EMS worker get to his feet and nod in Brant's direction. Another attendant arrived with a long body-board, and he and Marla gently placed Ralph on top and carried him into the side entrance to the police station, which doubled as Okwalla's emergency treatment center.

Brant returned to the two teenagers. He sniffed their breath, sneered, gripped both by an arm. "Get your asses inside."

They marched forward.

Inside the police station, Brant escorted the boys into a small, featureless, white-painted room with a blank table and several folding chairs. He exited, shutting the door behind him.

For what seemed an eternity they waited.

Finally, the door re-opened. An older man in gray suit with mustache to match entered, Officers Brant and Marla tagging behind. For a moment, the three regarded the teenagers in stony silence.

At last, the older man spoke. “Rose Edwin Alexander.” For a moment he stood quietly as if his statement required a response. He took a breath. “Officer Brant tells me he found you at the scene of a serious accident. You want to tell me what happened?”

Steve and Eddie exchanged cautious glances. Eddie looked up. “It’s like this, judge—”

The judge interrupted. “I’m your *father*, Rose. You can at least call me that.”

“Yeah, well, it’s like this, *father*, sir. Stevie and I were on my new bike and we were heading for the Park to join in with the Fourth of July party over there—you know, Mom’s there now with...well, you know...then we saw Ralphie on his bike. He wasn’t lookin where he was goin too good, so we tried to tell him to watch out, but he just pedaled right on through the light when Mr. McReynolds came from the other direction. He wasn’t lookin too good where he was goin either, and he just smacked right into poor little Ralphie.” A half-tear seemed to form in Eddie's eye. “He’s okay, isn’t he? I mean, Mr. McReynolds didn’t...” He looked at Steve. “Didn’t...”

“No, Rose. He’ll live. But he’s had a serious injury. There’s some question as to how serious. He’s being taken to the hospital in Alton. We’ll find out later what the story is there.”

Brant looked at Judge Alexander. “I got a call from Len Squires, Judge. Seems someone did a little number on him soon after he gassed up a *new* motorbike. A Suzuki 300.” Brant looked back at the boys. “Two teenage boys that may answer to the names of Rose and Steve.”

“We’re truly sorry for that, sir, I don’t know what came over us, and we’ll never do it again.” He looked up at his father. “It would be too bad if a little infraction like that messed up our lives, seein as how we’re just a couple of young kids with our whole lives ahead of us." The tear dried and was replaced by a look of self-pity.

The gray man motioned to Brant, and the two left the room, leaving Officer Marla inside with the two boys. Once outside, Judge Alexander stopped and looked carefully around, glancing at Marla through the one-way glass, who kept a scolding glare on the boys with her arms folded. His eye traveled the length of two intersecting hallways, both empty.

"What do you have, Brant?"

"They were at the scene, Judge. The bike checks out as Eddie's. Sir...were you aware that he was getting a motorbike?"

Judge Alexander nodded. "He just got his license. His mother told me last week that she had bought him the motorcycle. Over my objections, I might add."

Brant moved his lips, his grey-streaked mustache twitching.

"Anything else?"

"Squires phoned in a complaint but says he doesn't have time to swear out anything. I also got a call from the Minit Mart. The clerk thinks someone stole something around noon. But he wasn't sure who did it, or what exactly was stolen. He says his camera only got coats and baseball caps."

"I mean what do you have about this Ralph Drumond kid, Brant. You should see the kid's legs. They say he may never walk." The judge took a breath. "I need to know if my son is going to jail. Having just turned seventeen, he could be tried as an adult." Although he was shorter than Brant, he stared with such august dignity that he seemed to gaze down on the policeman. "You know. It's not easy being a kid. Especially in today's world."

Brant shrugged. "Rose was clean. But he was at the scene, and he was the one driving. McReynolds says he thinks the boys were chasing the kid and drove him through the red light. I know he's your kid, Judge, but...well, it looks like we had almost a crime wave today, and Rose may have been part of it."

"Now, now, Brant." Judge Alexander smiled and put his arm around the officer and glanced up and down the still empty hallways. "You don't know that. What you've told me doesn't amount to a damned thing, nothing that will hold up in a court of law. So what if Rose *was* at the scene? He's got a license and he's entitled to drive. And what does McReynolds know? He could just be trying to cover his own butt. And Rose did say he tried to stop the kid but couldn't do it. We can't prove otherwise."

"But Judge..."

The Judge looked around again. Sidled closer. They both glanced at Marla through the glass who was still glaring silently at Rose and Steve inside the detention room. "Look Brant. I didn't want to mention this, but you remember when you had that DUI?"

Brant nodded a slow nod.

"Well, you know how pesky those things are. They never really go away. The best you can do is just hope the court is too busy for matters like that and keeps it off the docket. And, of course, you know that the mayor and I are due to get together next month to discuss Okwalla's rehiring list." He squeezed Brant's arm and smiled broader. "And since Marla is new to Okwalla, you're at the top of the list. You're the best darn police officer this town ever had...and we want to keep it that way." The Judge poked Brant's shoulder every few syllables. "And you know how hard it is to get those annual COLAs pushed through City Council. Besides, you also know how it might look for my reelection campaign if my only son were to end up in Okwalla's only court."

Brant pursed his lips. Took a deep breath. "Well, you are right, Judge. Rose did have a license. And McReynolds says he didn't actually see anything. And he's the one who actually hit the Drumond kid. And we don't have a witness who says otherwise. And Squires said he doesn't have time to file a report." Brant shrugged, nervously. "I don't see how I can hold either one."

Alexander patted Brant's back. "*That's* my Brant. You know, my daughter's in school this summer, and I asked Rose to check on her each day and make sure she gets home all right. I'm a busy man. Can't do it myself. It's a chance for Rose to show some responsibility."

A moment passed. Brant blinked. Turning, he walked into the detention room. He opened the door, swinging it wide. He invited Officer Marla out, and once she had left, threw the bike's keys on the table.

"You're outta here. Both of you."

Flashing grins wider than Okwalla Valley, Eddie and Steve leaped to their feet. "Thank you, sir, Officer Brant, sir."

They sauntered out the entrance. Outside the police station they turned and waved. When the station doors had closed and no one any longer watched, their five fingers turned to one. The middle one.

Within minutes they were puttering at a moderate clip down Main Street, both tires carefully on the ground. Eddie maneuvered behind the library and parked properly in a space.

"Hang loose for a minute. I gotta check on Josey."

"Nanny duty, bro? How lame is that?"

"Shut your trap, jerk. She's my kid sister, even if she does live with my jerk-off Dad. I'm gonna take good care of her. Not like how my dad did with me. I'm gonna be better than that."

Steve-O shrugged. He withdrew a cigarette out of

a hidden pocket in his jacket, lit it, and settled back.

Eddie strolled through the front door of the library.

Five minutes passed.

He reappeared. He slammed the front door to the library so it banged against the wall, a sullen look darkening his face.

Steve sat up. “What’s eatin ya, bro?”

Eddie placed one boot on Steve’s leg and pushed him off the bike. Eddie jumped on. He glanced at his friend. “Somethin happened to Josey.” He looked at the sky where the sun was approaching the horizon. “She’s been cryin all day because of what some punk kids did. She even has a bump on her head.”

“Yeah? Like who?” He spat. “We’ll fuckin kick some ass.” Steve looked scornful. “What’s wrong with this burg that they can’t control a few stupid kids.”

Eddie gunned the engine. “I’ll tell you one thing, Steve-O. If they don’t, I will. Those punks just messed with the wrong guy.” He strapped on his shiny new helmet. “And that piss-ant Ralphie told us *exactly* where to find ‘em.”

“Huh?”

“The Round House.”

“The Round House...” Steve nodded, then looked worried. “But that’s off limits, bro. Haven’t you heard what old Injun Willie says about that? He told everyone to stay away, and the owner fenced it off. That’s what my mom says, too. They closed it before we were even born.”

Eddie turned and stared him down. “I don’t give a flying *fuck* what some senile old fart said. Someone hurt my sister. And no one can do that...” He revved the motor while Steven tightened his own helmet. “And expect to keep breathing. Get on, faggot.”

Bucking air, the bike sped away. In moments, the

old train station with its crumbling weed-grown tracks flashed by, followed by a series of dusty fields, mesquite, and strewn tumbleweeds. Leaving the road, Eddie raced up a gentle ridge, and down the far side. The western extension of the turnpike appeared, and Eddie guided the bike back onto the road. He let the throttle run. Cop or no cop, the open road was too inviting to putter along at any posted speed limit.

The road curved gently to the north, bypassing the tangle of ridges and wilderness that lay along the town's northwest side. Soon it began to wind through hills. As the sun touched the farthest ridge, they at last halted. On the left, the turnpike continued through open prairie to the next county. On the right, an old track split off and plunged into hills and wilderness.

Eddie looked at Steve. Steve nodded. The bike sped onto the path, spinning dirt. The path avoided the canyons with their dense brush but traced a continuous ridge along its peak, a longer route than through the valleys below, but laid long ago with motor vehicles in mind—until, for reasons now obscure, the road expansion plans had been canceled.

As the last light began to die, they arrived on a high cliff free of clinging vegetation. An eight-foot-high wooden fence blocked their approach, studded with broken nails and barbed wire.

Eddie kicked it. A ten-foot section promptly collapsed, snapping the old, rusted barbs. Together, they pushed the motorbike across and through, halting to view a steep cliff that stretched below and disappeared in thick woods. At the very peak stood an old weathered sign, with only one beat-up board remaining, on which could barely be made out the word *Mystery*, and just below: *Pueblo*.

Steve nudged Eddie. He pointed. Far below, within the tangle of trees stood three children's bicycles. Immediately below Steve and Eddie rested a wide flat stone leading to an open pit set in an artificial conical-shaped structure. Turning to his motorbike, Eddie withdrew two automobile night sticks from the bike's saddlebag. He tapped Steve and together they dropped to the flat stone. Stepping to the yawning gap, they broke the sticks, and in the light of their glow, lowered themselves within.

CHAPTER 5

Its energy exhausted, the sun had long since sunk beneath the hills to rest and renew, and the globe that was the Earth turned once more upon itself, and the other world that was present during the day—patiently waiting if unsuspected—moved to reclaim its right. Slowly its shadows spread from each nook and crevice. From deep below, a low humming oscillated and dull lights flickered. Eyes opened. Blinked. They directed their pale stare upward as if the exhaustion of heaven left them suddenly free to look, to do more than watch, to ride the growing tendrils of darkness, and seek a way to make themselves known. Voices echoed and the eyes turned toward the sound, and slowly, stealthily moved.

"In here." Eddie pulled Steve by a forearm.

Together they stepped across a carpet of broken bricks and entered a second chamber.

"Is that..." Steve halted and stared at the walls.

Holding high his night-stick, Eddie peered upward. He sniffed. "Just a bunch of old graffiti. My kid sister can draw better than that."

Steve hmphed.

"This way," Eddie called.

Into the cliff thcy picked their way, entering a tangle of catacombs.

After a few minutes, Steve hesitated. "I'm not sure this is such a good idea, Eddie. There are other tunnels down here. Are you sure those punk kids came this way?"

"Damn sure." Eddie held up his night-stick in an effort to cast a glow, but the light extended no more than a few feet.

"I mean, they could go around us," Steve peered into the darkness, "and then we'd be in here alone...just the two of us." He swallowed.

"Don't be such a pussy. Hold up your night-stick and keep looking. I didn't come all this way just to gawk at scratches in the rocks like some stupid tourist."

Steve took a deep breath and let it out. He followed Eddie as they felt their way down a wider path.

A gentle wind blew on Eddie's cheek. "Cut it out, Steve."

Steve said nothing.

"I said cut it out. Back off and give me some room." Eddie turned.

From a dozen paces back, Steve raised his night-stick. "Wha'd ya say?"

Eddie frowned. "Nothin. Let's just get on with it." He blinked and stepped forward.

A crack sounded, sending a whirl of wings spinning through the darkness. Steve froze. Glancing at Eddie and seeing unrattled toughness, Steve regained control.

The path again descended and, before long, opened up in a chamber larger than the others, followed by another larger cave.

Eddie elbowed Steve, whispered: "Bingo."

Before the two a thin beam of light flicked about the chamber, and two high voices echoed–kids' voices. Eddie and Steve hid the wands behind their backs and approached in silence. One kid faced away and inched toward a stony ridge. The other remained standing, looking away. He took a step backward, toward Eddie and Steve.

They didn't know.

Grinning with pleasure, Eddie laid one hand on the shoulder of the nearest kid—and squeezed. "You punks made my sister Josey cry. Now I'm gonna *pound meat.*"

The kid spun round, his face draining of color even in the darkness.

"Struggling won't help, Sammy." Eddie dropped his night-stick and grabbed Sam's other shoulder and lifted him off the ground so the boy's legs kicked air. "To think it was *you* who did that bad thing to my kid sister." Eddie grinned in Sam's face. "But ya know, I'm kinda glad ya did. Cause now I got the perfect excuse to pound the ever-livin crap outta you, just like I've been meanin to do for some time." He dropped Sam to the ground.

Sam stared open-mouthed. He dropped his flashlight.

At the sound of Eddie's voice, Charlie halted. He paused with one leg over the ridge, mid-step, preparing to descend.

"And where do you think *you're* goin?" Steve stepped quickly to Charlie and grabbed him by one arm. "You ain't goin nowhere, Johnny Appleseed." Steve jerked him and Charlie fell off the outcropping and stumbled at his feet.

Eddie laughed. "Appleseed. That's good, Steve-O." Gripping Sam's shoulder with one hand, Eddie picked up the boys' flashlight with the other. He clicked it and it came on, strong as ever. Shining it under his own chin, he tittered.

Steve dragged Charlie back from the outcropping and with some effort propped him up beside Sam.

"Well, don't this beat all?" Eddie grinned, vastly amused. "Little Sammy the cripple, and Grade-A Chuck the half-breed." He glanced at Steve. "What do ya think, Steve-O? Don't that beat all?"

Steve snorted. He curled his hands into fists and drove one into his palm.

Eddie cackled. "Who woulda thought that a couple of little punk creeps like these had such balls? Can you imagine that they would cause us this kind of trouble? Making us come all the way inside the Round House and *trespass on private property*, which could get us in trouble with *the police*." He leered at Sam. "Is that what you wanted? For us to get in trouble with *the police?* How dumb is that, when everybody knows my old man is the judge, so no cop will ever do jack-shit to me." Eddie grinned. "I mean, they musta known what we would do to 'em when we found 'em." Eddie looked at Steve again, mocking. "You think maybe they were just stupid? Surely, they didn't think they could get away with that shit?"

Sam glared. He opened his mouth to speak. Eddie grabbed him by the throat, forcing a gurgle.

"What do you think we should do with 'em, Eddie?" Steve sneered. "Kill 'em now or kill 'em later?"

"I don't know, bro. I've been thinkin about this all the way over here. And now that I found out who it was that thought they had the guts to mess with us, I think we should make sure they never bother us again. I say, let's teach 'em a lesson they ain't never gonna forget."

"Yeah, bwana," Steve grinned. "If they think they're gonna get away with this, we'll fix it so they don't never forget."

"Especially seein as how it's just a couple of loser punks." Eddie watched Sam struggle to catch his breath. "Little Sammy So-So, crippled little boy who lives with his stinkin drunken uncle after his ma and pa had the bad taste to *die* on him."

Steve-O snickered.

Eddie shifted his gaze to Charlie. "And little Charlie Fremont, snot-nosed kid who spouts off to everybody who'll listen that he's half Injun...as if that's something to be proud of...and whose grandpa is that senile old fart Injun Willie. You have the nerve to spread *that* all over town? What a beast."

Eddie and Steve exchanged smirks.

"Shut up," Charlie yelled. He gripped his hands into fists. "You can't talk about my grandpa like that."

Eddie glared at him with mock seriousness. The circle of light settled on Charlie's defiant face. "Did little Charlie say something, Steve-O?"

"I'm not sure, Eddie. I don't think he's that stupid. Not when we have him holed up here in this cave. And not when I've got a knife...and he doesn't."

The light shined back on Charlie's face. He looked crestfallen, but the defiance remained.

Eddie finally let Sammy's throat go.

While Sam gasped for breath, Steve pulled out a pocketknife and snicked out the blade.

"What about you, Sammy boy? Are you ready to say *uncle*?" Eddie sniggered to Steve, chuckling at his cleverness.

Sam had a tear in his eye; he coughed but resumed his defiant glare.

"You got the knife, Steve-O. But I got the heat." In answer to the wide-eyed stares of Sam and Charlie, Eddie pulled out his cigarette lighter.

"Here's the deal, punks. First, we're gonna pound the both of you. Then, I'm gonna give you each a cigarette. You're gonna take some puffs so you get 'em real hot. Then you're gonna burn each other. Whoever hurts his friend the most gets to go free; but whoever turns out to be the pussy is gonna get cut. And I mean cut good. And don't think you can get away, either, because there's only one way outta here, and we're blockin it. And whoever tries to get past us is gonna get beat up, and disappear...*permanent*. And ain't nobody ever gonna find any part of you down here where you're not supposed to be anyway."

"Yeah! That'll do it," Steve yelled.

Steve grabbed Sam by a shoulder, while Eddie took hold of Charlie. "Ya ready, punks? Are ya ready to take your licking?" Retrieving his night-stick from the ground, Eddie placed it on a flat rock beside him and motioned for Steve to do the same, then put the flashlight beside the sticks so its beam shined eerily. Sam and Charlie cast exaggerated shadows across the cave.

Letting loose his fist, Eddie planted it in Sam's stomach.

Sam bent over. Groaned.

Steve followed with a backward slap across Charlie's face. A bizarre play of chiaroscuro flashed on the side of the cavern as their fists landed.

Charlie collapsed.

Nudging Steve, Eddie murmured, "Not the face, Steve-O." Steve nodded and plunged his fist into Charlie's midriff, then spun him around and planted a boot on his backside.

After a minute, the shadow-play paused. Reaching into his boot, Eddie extracted two cigarettes that had escaped the pat-down in a hidden compartment on the motorbike. He lit both. "Well, that was fun, but I'm outta breath. It's time to play games." Eddie brandished the two lit cigarettes. "Hold 'em, Steve. I'm gonna burn the both of 'em just so they get a good taste of what they got comin."

Steve propped up Sam and Charlie and stepped back.

Eddie advanced, a leer on his face, glowing cigarette in each hand.

"Ohhh!" Eddie doubled over.

"Uncle *this,*" Sam yelled. Letting loose with his

good foot a second time, he landed a second blow between Eddie's legs. Steve looked away from Charlie. In a flash, Charlie scooped up a handful of dust and flung it in Steve's face. Steve shouted in pain, his face peppered with rocks.

"This way," Charlie hissed. He grabbed Sam and pulled him toward a patch in the cavern wall where complete darkness loomed. They vanished within.

"Goddammit!" Steve cleared his eyes and snatched up the flashlight. He shined it on his friend. "You okay, Rose?"

Eddie stood up and groaned. Erect, Eddie kicked his friend's leg. "How many times I gotta tell ya, faggot?"

"Oh, yeah. Eddie."

Dropping the cigarettes, Eddie retrieved the night-sticks. "That's it," he called out in a singsong voice. "Oh, kids...guess what? No more Mr. Nice Guy. Now we're gonna take you apart and leave your bones behind." Echoes of his threats reverberated through the caverns, and they plunged into the darkness in pursuit.

Hurrying through pitch black, Sam and Charlie soon slowed. Limping on his clubfoot, Sam tripped. He struggled to his feet and they picked their way forward more slowly, glancing often behind. Within moments, they glimpsed the night-sticks floating like ghosts in the air. The ghosts grew larger. A thin pencil of light joined the night-sticks. Another patch of darkness loomed and they slid within the patch just in time to avoid being caught in the twisting circle of light.

"Nope," drifted a harsh voice from behind the beam. "They didn't come this way."

"What other way, dickhead?" echoed the reply. "They must be up ahead."

Sam nudged Charlie. "This path goes down," he

whispered.

Charlie shook his head. “It’s after dark...but we can still kiss the Midnight Sun. It’s not too late.”

Sam looked incredulous. “You’re kidding. I mean, that’s all pretend, right? But Eddie and Steve...they’re real. And we’ll be real dead if they find us.” Sam elbowed Charlie and whispered again. “They’re coming. The only other way is down. Down there.”

Charlie felt his stomach churn, feeling the imprints of Steve’s fists. He looked back at Sam. “What about Lori? Do you think she’s okay?”

“Lori.” Sam pulled up short. “Damn. You think she’s still in this cave...with *them?*”

“I don’t know. I don’t remember seeing her after they showed up.”

“And what about Iggy? You think they got him, too?”

“Don’t know that either.”

The wall above glimmered with a circle of light. They gulped and moved quietly down the path into more complete darkness.

Except it wasn’t complete. The circle of light passed over their heads and moved on, and Charlie and Sam again glimpsed the eerie flickering of lights on the ceiling above, the lights they had glimpsed when they had first approached the crevasse. Slowly they ventured out of the passage and descended into another cave. The dull lights grew stronger.

“It’s here,” Charlie hissed.

“And we’re back,” replied Sam. “Back in the same chamber. But below the ridge you were about to climb down into when Eddie and Steve got us.” As in confirmation of their suspicions, the flashlight’s beam reappeared above the stony ridge and shined briefly on the ceiling, obscuring the pale flickering that emanated from the crevice that yawned a scant twenty feet away.

Caught between, the two boys huddled.

"What do we do?" Sam whispered.

Charlie shook his head.

Over their heads reappeared the ghostly wands floating as if disembodied. "Where the hell did those punks go?" Steve's voice drifted. "Just wait 'til I get 'em this time," Eddie echoed. "I'm gonna leave their skeletons behind. Try to make a monkey outta me, will they? Goddam punk kids..." The voices grew distant but the night-sticks and flashlight continued to penetrate the upper chamber.

Sam and Charlie peered about. "We can't get out. Not as long as they're up there."

"Yeah. And let's hope they stay up there. There's no place else left for us to run. Except..." Charlie looked at Sam. The sweat had reappeared on his cheeks, and his hand resumed shaking.

The luminous flickering from the crevice came again, stronger. With a jerk, Charlie swiveled and stared. From somewhere they heard a low humming.

Charlie froze. The sweat burst from his face like a faucet. He rocked back and forth on his heels. "The Midnight Sun," he mumbled, "I still have to kiss the Midnight Sun."

Sam lost his cool. "Stop it, will you. That's just a kid's game. There's probably nothing in there but an old broken mirror anyway."

Charlie said nothing but continued to rock on his heels. He wrapped himself in his arms.

Above them, the voices grew more distant, and Sam inspected the ceiling for the tell-tale signs of their searching. Soon he breathed more easily, seeing no more quivering searchlight, and no more floating wands. From the far side of the cave he heard the distant echoes of an angry exchange—Eddie and Steve arguing. Their sticks were no longer visible.

Silence followed.

Sam began to relax. Looked at Charlie who sat on his haunches and rocked, oblivious, arms wrapped.

Noise returned—Sam jerked. He raised his head to peer upward toward the rocky mezzanine where Eddie and Steve had attacked them, expecting to see the two older boys again, expecting to again glimpse the pursuing arcs of light.

He froze.

Slowly turned.

Suddenly Sam wondered why he had bothered worrying about teenagers at all, who shrank suddenly to insignificance. With an electric humming in his ears that oscillated now softer, now louder, but already seeming to deafen, he stared at an enormous black sphere eight feet in diameter as it emerged above the lip of the crevice. Etched with patches of light shifting like soft pustules, it arrived like the first glimmerings of a dawn, but not the sun of day, but of a midnight sun, emitting black rays that, mixed with feeble glimmers of light, alternately illuminated and enshadowed the cavern in hypnotic spirals. No, Sam decided, not light. But a putrid imitation of light, fit only to emphasize and outline the more forceful rays of darkness stretching to seize them.

"Charlie?...*CHARLIE!*" Sam shook him.

Charlie snapped out of his trance.

"They're gone. Up there. Eddie and Steve. They've left." He looked upward and stood. "We have to go."

Ignoring him, Charlie stared into the black sphere, his eyes saucered.

"Forget kissing it, Charlie," Sam yelled over the humming. "It's too late. You can't."

Charlie stepped forward. Of its own accord, his mouth opened, ten years of old-folk's-tales working within.

Sam clambered away, climbed up the ladder of handholds. Halfway up he paused. "Charlie. Don't do it. Come back." Tears burst. "Don't you remember what your grampa said? Not after dark."

Charlie shook. Again was himself. Once more he gazed at the sphere. The midnight sun continued to spiral, enthralling with its intricate patterns, rising, constantly rising, growing stronger. Its equator rose above the lip of the floor and exposed a dark abyss beneath. Charlie stepped closer; he reached out and touched the pulsating surface.

He peered under.

For a moment he stared. Then—as if struck—leaped back. Sweat burst from his face, and he turned and ran toward Sam.

At the top of the ladder of handholds, Sam succeeded in climbing out and over the ridge. Turning, he covered his eyes. "Don't look at it, Charlie. Don't look. Take my hand."

Below, Charlie scrambled up. Dissonant sounds emerged from the humming, and, his face twisted, Charlie again looked back. With a shudder, he slipped and slid down the handholds to the bottom. A second time he climbed—almost reached the top.

"That's it. Grab my hand."

Clammy with sweat, Charlie stared at Sam and gripped it.

Sam breathed easier, pulled.

Halfway over the stony ridge, Charlie let a brief smile settle on his face—he stopped moving. His eyes widened. "Something's got me, Sam. Pull...*PULL!*"

Sam dug in his heels, pulled with all his strength.

Charlie's mouth opened. Face ashen, he was suddenly yanked back over the ridge. His hands gripped the outcropping as his body flapped and jerked. "Help me, Sam. Don't let me go."

Sam threw himself forward. He thrust his hands down to Charlie's wrists, pulled with the strength of desperation. He felt a tingle. Opening his eyes, Sam sucked a breath. Charlie's face glowed with the same loathsome light that permeated the sphere, his eyes and mouth giving forth an expansive impulse, which, even as Sam watched, spread like a contagion to the rest of Charlie's body.

Sam looked at his own hands. With a quiver, they commenced to shine with the same midnight light that possessed Charlie.

The light moved up Sam's arms.

To his shoulders.

His chest.

His neck.

The world turned black. Sam felt his knees give way and his body collapse. "Don't let them take me," echoed in his ears as if from a great distance, mixing inexplicably with dull sounds as of Fourth of July firecrackers and rockets.

CHAPTER 6

From somewhere throbbed a persistent hum, low but penetrating, bearing him on its surface like a jellyfish on the ocean. The waves lapped gently, rocking him to and fro in time to the throbbing, cradling him in its protective embrace. Turning him. Round and round he turned, a circle of light growing ever larger, ever brighter. A distant memory of danger that had once accompanied such a circle of light emerged briefly, then vanished, to be replaced by soothing comfort, as if he were afloat in a cocoon. The light grew clearer, and a foreign object intruded. He blinked. A bird took shape, perched on round arch-stones, and Sam was suddenly aware that he lay on the floor of the first chamber of the Round House, staring upward through the narrow aperture at bright blue sky.

He jerked upright.

Peering, he saw no sign of any other person. He glanced at the walls. The pictographs were there. Recalling a flashlight and two grinning faces lit by glow-sticks, he shivered. He had not expected to survive after Steve pulled out his knife.

He stood. Lifted his shirt. The shirt was torn and the pummeling fists of the night before rushed back to mind, having inflicted deep bruises. The pain had been intense, and Sam touched his stomach where he had received the worst of the beating, and felt...*nothing*. In surprise, he felt again, delicately probed.

No pain.

He removed his shirt. In the direct rays of the noontide sun, he examined his body and found no bruises, no injuries. Only dirt and fatigue. That the events of the night before had occurred he had no doubt. At one side even now the second chamber loomed, with its open gap where Lori had collapsed the wall of bricks. He was certain that if he were to re-enter the lower catacombs, he would find Charlie's flashlight on the floor, burned out.

But not Charlie. Somehow, someway, he felt that Charlie had not exited, and that no search would locate him. Just as he felt that Iggy had left before Eddie and Steve showed up. Lori, however, was another matter: she was unharmed, that he also felt, but there was something more, something he did not understand. He could not detect what was at work about her—*or himself.*

Sam shook his head. These were mere feelings, vague impressions. What were these new feelings? Where were they coming from? He shook the sleep from his body and took a step.

Halted.

The strangest sensation he had ever experienced washed over him, so strong as to make him almost dizzy, and he put out his hands to steady himself. Feelings of hope, relief, and disbelief. Disbelief that such fortune could have come his way, from whatever source. Sam removed his special shoe and slowly lifted his pant leg.

His foot was normal.

He looked closer. Reaching down, he passed his fingers over the shin, the ankle, the outer edge, the inner stretch, the heel and toes. He stood straight and gazed wildly in confusion. Again, he inspected. His congenital clubfoot, the affliction which, though no more than a slight deformity, had caused him such pain in his few short years, making him shy and introspective, was gone.

No utterance could express his joy. He walked weakly at first, then boldly, and Sam broke into a grin. Tackling the handholds, he soon stood on top of the Round House bathed in light, this time the clean light of a healthy yellow sun.

He had changed.

Abandoning his shoes, including the one made special for his clubfoot, he climbed the flat rock with confidence, and slid quickly down the slope to the floor of the canyon, marveling at his lack of hesitance, his new balance. His bicycle was still there, though spokes were broken as if someone had stomped them. The same as Charlie's bike, a fact that he had also somehow known while still inside the pueblo. And Iggy's bike was gone, also confirming what he had felt.

He picked up his bike and rolled it.

As he struggled back to town with his twisted bike in tow, he whistled at first, eventually fell silent. With the onrush of the sun's illuminating rays came a series of impressions. Some were warm and embracing, others were menacing and offensive, but all were strange and inexplicable. How had he known beforehand that Charlie's bike had been damaged by Eddie and Steve? How did he know that the two bullies were alive and back in Okwalla? How did he know that Charlie had vanished?

Pushing on, he became aware of an image taking shape in the clouds. It was the image of a buffalo-skin-clad medicine man whose hair stood on end. Sam shook his head. The day was warm—too warm. Two pennies jingled in one pocket. He removed one penny and placed it in the other pocket and instantly felt cooler, and proceeded back to town with a smile, though he wondered what he would tell Injun Willie about his missing grandson, Charlie.

It was past noon when a tired Sam finally wheeled his dented bike into the yard of an old but well-tended patio. He slid the glass door to one side. Seeing no one, he threw himself onto a sweat-stained couch as only a twelve-year-old boy who had labored beyond his strength could do. Momentarily, an urge that was already becoming familiar prompted him, and he rolled onto his back on the couch and re-positioned himself precisely in the middle.

He slept.

He awakened to a rasp as the front door opened.

"Well, *I'll* be." An elderly, unshaven man with splotched skin shuffled in. Bending over Sam, he feebly stretched a soiled blanket over the boy. The old man looked behind where noises indicated another person. He called out, "I guess that fixes that. I don't know where the goddamhell this kid's been, officer, but he's back home now." He finished stretching out the blanket over Sam. "Puts me through hell, he does. Look. He's even lost his shoes."

Behind him, a policeman stepped off the wooden porch and entered the house. The policeman removed his cap and smoothed his thick dark hair. "I'm glad that's settled. At least we won't have to comb the woods." Officer Brant replaced his cap and scribbled something in a notebook. "You did the right thing, though, by calling us when you found him missing. It's what we're here for."

Uncle Roy nodded. Briefly his lips attempted to form a smile, then lapsed into their usual sullen grumpiness.

"But let me give you a word of advice, Mr. Trencher."

Through bleary eyes, Sam's uncle looked at the cop.

"I hear your boy's been hanging around with old man Willie's kid...name of..."

"Ya mean Charlie?"

"Yeah, that's him. He's a problem kid. You might want to put a little distance between them, if you know what I mean. Just to keep yours out of trouble."

Roy nodded.

"FYI...Judge Alexander's boy tried to file assault charges today against Sam and Charlie. He claims they attacked him and Steven Rundle while they were picnicking in the woods."

Roy snorted. "Attacked? Ridiculous. Sam's practically a cripple. He can't walk more'n a few blocks. And can't run worth a damn."

"We didn't accept the charges, but your boy has been missing since last night. Sam's back, and that's good, but we still can't find Willie's kid. We've had our run-ins with that Charlie in the past. I just came from Willie's house. Charlie's been missing since yesterday. Maybe he skipped town for parts unknown. Wouldn't be the first time such a thing happened." Brant recrossed the threshold. "I suggest you let things calm down a while. And keep your boy out of trouble. The Minit Mart says two kids stole some cigarettes yesterday, and Sam and Charlie aren't a bad match for the description. I wouldn't want to think that your Sam is starting down the wrong road too."

"*Goddamittohell.* That's what I get for takin on my brother's problems and playin the Good Samaritan." Roy wiped his bristly mouth. "I'll take care of it, Officer Brant sir, don't you worry."

Brant nodded and shut the door. Out the window, the police car turned once into the drive, then drove off.

The afternoon wore on.

Finally, Sam groaned. He sat up. "Uncle Roy?"

No answer.

Sliding his legs off the couch, Sam paused. Again, he lifted one pant leg and inspected his foot. It was no illusion after all; the change was real. He stood. Stepped slowly about the room. His muscles ached from the long walk home, but the old pain that he had known so well had vanished. Grinning, he skipped into Roy's bedroom—skipped for the first time in his young life.

Roy lay inert on the bed covers, a bottle of Old Crow spilled on the floor beside him. He snored to wake the dead. On a bed table stood an assortment of plastic film containers and prescription bottles, long neglected, several also tipped over with their contents strewn. With the familiarity of habit, Sam pulled another bed cover from the closet and unfolded it over Roy, who turned over and let out a quiet burp. In Sam's eye, a tear formed; Sam flicked it aside.

***

Across town, a lanky figure with long gray hair in a ponytail stood in a doorway, watching Officer Brant enter a police car and exit the driveway of the decrepit hovel he called home. The old man resumed gathering several items, which the policeman's visit had interrupted, and stuffed them in a duffel bag. When he was done, he also exited and walked to a beatup truck parked twenty feet from the house entrance, leaving the door to his ramshackle house ajar.

The pickup door clicked shut. A key turned, and after a moment of uncertain grinding, the motor leaped to life. Gently depressing the accelerator, as if concerned that the aged vehicle might fail, the driver slowly picked up speed, turned onto Main Street, and cruised past Okwalla's noblest institutions: the library, City Hall, the police station with its attached makeshift medical clinic, and farther down, the Bronco Diner, with a dentist's office and a window displaying *Rose E. Alexander, Sr., P.C.* across the street.

The day was typical, boasting a moderate crowd of strollers, yet more than one might expect for the day after Okwalla's annual Fourth of July extravaganza. For all the attention the strollers received from the driver of the pickup, they may as well have not existed.

Leaving Main Street, the pickup entered the southern turnpike, bypassing the Minit Mart and soon thereafter bypassing the highway entryway. Len Squire's gas station and Mr. Patel's new Haven Motel, both short of patrons, drifted past. The western turnpike appeared, and the lanky driver with the gray ponytail entered.

North he drove along the gentle curve, circumventing the tangle of valleys of the western wilderness. Turning onto a dirt path, the truck followed a long bumpy back road to at last reach a cliff free of vegetation, an eight-foot wooden fence blocking the approach. The mottled wood was partly collapsed.

The pickup halted; the motor stopped.

The old man stepped out. Intricately engraved snake-skin boots planted in the dirt. Walking to the collapsed fence, the boots stepped over the rusted barbs and nails and the weather-beaten sign with the words: *Mystery* and *Pueblo* still visible upon it, striding forward until he stood at the top of the cliff where the valley and its woods stretched out in gorgeous panorama. A cone of rocks in the shape of a teepee rested below.

Unbuttoning his casual light-colored jacket, he tossed it on the ground. His store-bought Western-style shirt landed on top. Next off were the boots, which he propped next to the clothing. He removed his jeans and placed them by the boots. Then his socks and underwear came off. Finally, he removed his factory-made wide-brim hat and let it fall with the rest.

Free at last.

He raised his head, his gray hair braided and tied in the old style and stared into the late afternoon sun as it raced toward its daily rendezvous with night.

Stepping back to his truck, he reached in and withdrew a heavy buffalo skin cloak. He shook off layers of dust, and with some difficulty, as if no longer familiar with its fit, managed to drape it over his shoulders and slide his arms into two slots. He next produced a pair of feathers. These he inserted in his hair. Finally, a knife slid free of its sheath. The old man hesitated. He steeled himself. Taking his long hair-braid in one hand, he cut it off with a single clean stroke of the knife. He placed the braid on the ground and again gazed at the sky.

He began to dance.

"Hi-ya, ay-ya, ha-ya, ee-ya..."

Without a break, the chant continued through the rest of the afternoon, the ancient ritual of harmony he had learned from his father and grandfather, continuing so long as the sun remained visible.

When the sun had entirely disappeared below the horizon cliff, the old man finally stopped. As the darkness of the netherworld awoke and spread its shadows, he sat. From several buffalo-hide packets, he withdrew paint and applied red and white smears to his face.

He stood.

From the back of the pickup, he lifted a coil of stout rope and a primitive wooden torch with pitch smeared on one end. With flicks of a match, he lit the torch. Like a flag in a strong wind, the flame crackled, and he smiled at the life-affirming sound. Raising the brand aloft, he walked to the edge of the cliff and lowered himself onto the flat rock that led to the pueblo. He carefully traveled its length. Over the entrance, he paused. The sun was gone; the shadows seemed to reach forth as if desiring to enfold him within their grasp. From within the chambers below, a low moan seemed to drift. Securing one end of the rope to a projection of blunt stone, he dropped the coil into the abyss, and without a backward glance, Injun Willie climbed down the rope into darkness.

***

Weeks passed. Summer was over, and twelve-year old Sam resumed his annual trudge into dilapidated classrooms to listen to horn-rimmed school-marms drone about their trips to Orlando, sisters in Seattle, and proper posture. The final bell had rung and Sam was crossing the esplanade when he saw Iggy.

Sam rushed to his side and stood staring at Iggy as if at an apparition. "You're alive."

Iggy sniveled back mucus and stared back through coke-bottle glasses. "Oh, hi, Sammy. What's up?"

Sam was dumbstruck. "What's up?" He raised both hands in the air. "Don't you remember what happened..." he peered about—then whispered, "at the *Round House*?"

Iggy looked stealthily right and left. "Sam...I can't talk about that. My mom and dad came down hard on me for going there. The police even came to our house, asking about it. I was grounded for two weeks."

"Grounded? Is that all you can say?" Sam looked stricken. "What about Charlie? What about Lori? Don't you know that Charlic is gone?"

"Oh, yeah. I heard he and his grandpa moved away."

"Moved away?" Sam shook his head. Again, those strange indefinable feelings. They said otherwise. "I don't think so..."

"Well, that's what my mom says." Iggy stared at him without expression.

"And what about..."

Sam stared above Iggy. Over his head had appeared what seemed to be dirt, or flakes. No, he thought as it coalesced into the shape of a cigarette. It was embers. Burned out cigarette ashes to be exact. He puzzled over the image.

A half minute passed, and Iggy eyed him oddly. "Sam? What are you doing?"

"Huh? Nothing." He looked back at his friend. "Look, Ig. Charlie did not move away. He's gone. The Round House took him."

Iggy cocked his head.

"Don't you remember? Eddie and Steve. Didn't they stomp your bike like they stomped mine and Charlie's?"

He shook his head. "Eddie and Steve? No, my bike is okay, and I didn't see anyone but you guys. Anyway, I left as soon as the sun went down. You know I have to be back home before dark." He sniveled mucus. "Weren't you guys right behind me?"

For a moment, Sam felt relief that Iggy had not suffered at the hands of the bullies as he and Charlie had. Strangely, however, his relief was mixed with resentment that Iggy's good fortune left him unable to comprehend Sam. He found that he resented his own resentment, and then resented this as well. *I guess this is what grownups mean when they say they're having a bad day.*

"And you can't see Lori anymore."

"What? Says who?"

Iggy looked right and left again. "Her mom says you're bad. The police came to see her too. They think you robbed the Minit Mart."

"But...but that's nuts."

"That's just what they said."

"Well, I have to see Lori."

"I'm not supposed to talk to you either."

"Look, Iggy. You live close to her. Stop by her house on your way home. Tell Lori I'm coming by tonight at nine o'clock. I'll tap on her window. Tell her I have to talk to her."

He shrugged. "Okay." Shouldering his books, Iggy started down the street, flashing a confused but friendly smile in Sam's direction.

The next few hours drained away. Finally, nine o'clock neared, and Sam energized himself. It was a simple matter to trick Uncle Roy into thinking he had retired for the night. Once the door was shut, the window slid open. Within twenty minutes, Sam stood in a side-yard a half-mile away, among clothes pinned to a wire for drying, watching a second-story window in a house of yellow clapboards, the yellow shrouded in darkness. He had walked the distance only once before, preferring to bike. Until his foot healed in the cave, walking this distance had been hard—now it was easy. Striding the distance, he felt less upset over the loss of his bike.

Picking up a pebble, he hurled it. The window clicked, and after a few moments a small light came on. A dark-haired girl thrust her head through and peered down.

"Lori. Lori. Over here," he hissed.

She looked. Her brows raised.

"Come down."

Her head shook.

"Why not?"

"I can't talk to you, Sam," she whispered. She looked behind her, then held up a just-a-minute finger...then disappeared.

Around the corner of the house, Sam waited. He

let his weight rest on one foot. He shifted his weight to the other. Then decided to balance equally on both feet, now that each had become the same. His hands found their way into his pockets and he noted, with a sense of relief that remained inexplicable, that the coins in his left pocket exactly matched the coins in his right: one nickel and one penny each.

Moments more, and a shadow slid close. The skinny girl with the dark hair appeared before him, smiling, and with the moonlight glimmering on her pretty face, Sam felt strange, previously unsuspected emotions stir.

"Lori, are you all right?"

She looked puzzled. "Of course. Why wouldn't I be, Sam?"

"Because...due to...you know why. Because of Eddie and Steve."

"Who?"

"You know...you were there...at the Round House."

She shook her head. "I heard that something strange happened to you, Sam. But how would I know since I went back with Iggy."

"Iggy? But that's wrong. You went in with Charlie and me...into the second chamber. And the other rooms beyond that. You were there when Eddie and Steve beat up Charlie and me, when they pulled the knife, and when.. when the Midnight Sun..."

She leveled a steady stare at Sam. "Other rooms? What other rooms?"

"Don't you remember? You leaned on the wall. And went in with us when it fell down."

"What wall? I saw only a single room. We looked at the pictographs, and when it got dark, I left, and Iggy and I took our bikes and went home. You and Charlie just sat there and wouldn't answer me. That's when I left. I thought you were coming right behind us." She shook her head again. "Are you okay, Sam? The other kids say you're...seeing things...saying things."

"But what about Charlie? Have you seen Charlie since then?"

"Of course not. He moved away with his grandpa. Everyone knows that. They moved to the next state, on account of...on account of Charlie robbed the Minit Mart. That's what my mom says. And I'm not supposed to see you either because...well, because you were with him." She looked back at her house for signs of outraged grownups.

Sam gripped one hand into a fist. Conscious that his other hand was open, he clenched it also to keep an even match. Then opened them together. He felt dizzy. Stared skyward where clouds roiled.

"Sam? Sam," she whispered.

"Huh?"

"What are you staring at?"

He blew out his cheeks. He settled and stared straight at Lori. "I love you, Lori. I always have."

She stepped back, eyes wide. Lori dropped her face in her hands. "Now you tell me." She looked up again. "I can't talk about that night, Sam. I didn't see anything except a few old drawings, and...and that day was hard on me, and on my family."

"Your family?"

She nodded. "Ralphie is back from the hospital. He's crippled. They're saying he'll never walk again. That old man McReynolds..." She buried her face in her hands again and softly cried. "All my parents do now is argue."

Sam couldn't reply. His gaze was transfixed by an image of hair standing on end above a bed, smoke spilling into the sky, somewhere beyond Lori, or behind her, or over her. He wondered again what it all meant.

She stopped crying. "Sam...Sam. You're doing it again."

"Sorry. I don't know what's come over me. But I'm not the kid you knew when summer started. And our club is no more. And look..." He took a few steps to show her his new physical capacity. "My clubfoot. It's okay. It all happened that night..."

Her brows raised in a so-what manner. "I heard it was better. I just thought you went to the doctor and got it fixed."

He let out his breath. "Yeah. Fixed."

Again, she glanced behind. "I have to go, Sam. I'm sorry, but I don't know anything about what happened to you. And I don't remember anything else, and I don't want to talk about that night. I just can't. I don't want to talk about this whole summer. I just want to forget everything. I'll see you at school. You can't come here anymore. My parents won't let you in, and if they see us together, they'll ground me for the rest of the year." She leaned forward to plant a kiss.

Surprising himself, Sam lurched back and avoided it.

A brief uncertain smile from Lori. She blew the kiss into the air. "You're still my boyfriend."

Again the smile, and she was gone.

CHAPTER 7

Where do the years go? How long does it take to adjust to a truly life-changing experience? Sam eyed the mirror in his bedroom, contemplating things and notions far beyond what he could have imagined in his prior life. His life had become divided in two: *Before* the Event—and *After*. Five years earlier his only concerns had been water balloon fights, spoke cards, and whether Roy was bringing ice cream home for dessert. Now, with his seventeenth birthday nearing, his mind was occupied with coins, tightropes, an on-again-off-again flirtation, and a preoccupation with deciphering a parade of mysterious images. Which were the normal urgings of growing up? And which were the abnormal consequences of that night at the Round House? How to tell? Who to ask?

Sam peered in the mirror at the reflection of his uncle standing behind him. Roy had unexpectedly improved in the year after Sam's cure, as if Sam's change in health had boosted his uncle's psyche, giving him the faith to try again to properly raise his kid brother's son, after the accident that had deprived Sam of both his parents while still an infant. An infant afflicted with a clubfoot.

Then Roy had worsened. The doctors had fancy words that grew longer with each visit: adenohypertrophy; borderline diabetes; hysterical conversion syndrome. The words hardly mattered—Roy could barely read and couldn't sleep without a bottle in his hand. On occasion, Roy seemed to spontaneously recover and launch himself into projects around the house for days, all amid an acrid smell of medicine; these always ended the same, in collapse in a filthy bed for even longer periods. Sam soon learned to get himself up and off to school. Which he sometimes failed to do on time—or failed entirely—prompting more visits from a glaring Officer Brant doubling as truant officer.

But tonight, Sam was happy. His love interest was on-again. The previous night, he and Lori had made up, talked into the wee hours, promised themselves to each other until time should end, and made a date for the morrow, she having accepted his strange but persistent refusal to be touched. With the passage of time, the past had been forgotten, and her parents had at last relented and allowed Lori to meet him for breakfasts before school at the Bronco Grill. And, finally, her parents had agreed to allow them to go together to the upcoming school dance, the last of the season, the anxious parents comforted to learn that Sam touched absolutely no one. Roy had even promised to let Sam rent a tuxedo the following day in preparation. Sam stood with a smile, adjusting an imaginary bowtie in the reflection.

Dreaming of a future he could barely conceive, Sam sat on his bed. Shuffling his legs, Roy approached and sat a short distance from him and smiled his best ersatz hope-this-is-convincing-enough-to-work smile. Roy leaned closer and attempted to drape one arm over Sam's shoulders and Sam again felt the urge to surrender and embrace him—but again withdrew, as always, Roy, having long since accepted Sam's peculiar withdrawal, as open affection was unnatural for the older man, anyway. Their mutual affection, however, was genuine. The gaping hole in Roy's own life, due to lack of a family of his own, had been filled by his brother's son, so much so that neither could any longer imagine a life without the other, despite the pictures of Sam's dead parents that filled the house.

Empty faces.

Roy shifted his jaw. "Tell me again, Sammy." He peered with red-rimmed eyes, focusing on the only topic that could induce him to summon his limited powers of concentration.

"Yeah?"

"Yeah, boy. Once more."

Shrugging, Sam prepared once more to describe the night of The Happening. How much Roy believed, Sam could not tell. He did not know how much of it he himself believed. But there was one fact that was indisputable and remained the focus of Roy's fixed attention—Sam could walk. So, Roy listened.

"Don't know why you keep wanting to hear it, Uncle Roy. But..." As Sam recounted the events, Roy leaned back, shifting his weight onto his hands outstretched on the bed behind him. Today he had stirred himself not only to speak, but to shave, as Sam noticed with surprise. When he finished his recitation, Roy pointed to Sam's leg, motioned. When Sam raised his pant leg, Roy observed again, stared at his foot one more time, grunted in surprise as always.

When Sam finished, Roy stood. He contemplated the ceiling, again retreating to that silent realm that increasingly absorbed him. He nodded as he looked about Sam's room, at the stacks of pennies in orderly rows, the shoe boxes stacked precisely three abreast, the perfectly made bed, the freshly painted walls entirely bare of pictures, the stack of perfectly folded towels for use during the night when the sweats came to his nephew. Roy burped. Trudging out of Sam's room, he rejoined the soiled chaos of his own.

Next day, after Sam had left for school, a small noise gritted at the door. Roy emerged from the desolation of his bedroom. Kicking bottles and papers, he grabbed some buttermilk in yet another attempt to ease his ulcer and took the day's letters from the mailbox. He spread them on a table formerly engulfed in the same chaos as his room, but recently cleared and cleaned by Sam.

Roy grunted. Uncertain of his own feelings in this regard, he casually, deliberately, pushed aside the buttermilk to make way for a new bottle of Old Crow, taking a silent measure of satisfaction in spilling some. Most of the mail he tossed on the floor, including anything that looked like a bill, as he missed the trashcan by a yard.

He paused. This one he decided to open. "Medical Center," he slowly read aloud. Clumsily he ripped open the envelope, haltingly inspected its contents. His bleary eyes gradually focused. He pieced through the unfamiliar words and finally, slowly, his red eyes rose to look at the ceiling. His soiled fingers tore it up.

Roy lurched to full height. The mirror in his own room was cracked and too caked with dust to return a realistic image, and he walked into Sam's room and peered into his nephew's conspicuosly clean mirror. For a long moment he stared, the words of the medical center letter, insofar as he could read them, circling in his mind. At length, he turned and consulted the clock. The day was still young.

He could remember a time when he himself was young; it wasn't that long ago. A time when there had been no bottles, no ailments, no diabetes, and—none of the new ailment that the letter had informed him of: *c-a-n-c-e-r*. Who could tell now that he had once ridden a simple street bike from one coast to the other, vigorous, youthful, and proudly independent? Or worked on tramp steamers from the Orient to Africa, making strange contacts in stranger alien lands. The marvels he had seen. The plans he had made. Now—to end like this... He shook his head.

Still, hope remained. Or rather had returned, and from a wholly unguessed source. An opportunity had arisen, a chance to turn things around, to regain his life with all its former promises and rewards. He had seen it with his own eyes, flawed as they were.

Staggering to his room, he rummaged until he located two flashlights. Made certain the batteries were good. Roy walked onto the porch. Propping scratched sunshades over his eyes, he stumbled to the green Cadillac that had once been a source of pride and flopped into the driver's seat. The speedometer presented itself through his Old Crow haze as two divagating images, but from a lifetime spent in Okwalla he knew the back roads, the best ways to avoid ticket ambushes. The motor rumbled to life. Turning into the road, he headed west.

The watchful sun slowly crossed...

When Roy at last returned, hours later, it was dark. Opening the door to the Cadillac, he ambled into his house. His clothes were stained and torn—more than before. The kitchen table had been cleared and cleaned, which meant Sam was back from school. Walking from room to room, Roy paused to stare as if each represented something unseen, unsuspected, the newness of all impinging on his mind with the force of the former exotic voyages that he had loved so much.

The front door creaked.

When Sam walked in, Roy was sitting on his favorite lean-back staring at the ceiling. "Hi. Hi there, Sam. Sammy boy."

"'Lo, Uncle." Seventeen year old Sam spoke in a voice deepened by adolescence. He headed for the kitchen, carrying a small sack of groceries.

"Sammy, Sammy, Sammy boy."

Sam paused. He cast an inquisitive look at Roy, then started forward again and deposited the sacks on the cleaned kitchen table. He returned to the living room.

Roy dropped his gaze; a wild look was in his eyes.

"Are you okay, Uncle?"

Roy wiped saliva from his mouth. "Think so. Can't tell for sure."

"You feel okay?"

"Fine. Feel fine." One hand wandered to his side where a lump had recently appeared. The hand searched as if puzzled to find it missing. "I think."

Sam smiled. "I did my homework already."

"That's nice, boy. That's nice." Roy's eyes wandered to the ceiling as if preoccupied with patterns in the paint.

"And I cleaned the front room. Are you ready for me to start on yours? Remember, you promised to let me clean it up."

The eyes lowered. "Nope. Can't do that, Sammy. I like it just the way it is. I can't have you messin with my med...uh, with my things so I can't find what I need when I need 'em."

"I was gonna go see Lori tonight, Uncle. I promised her last night that—"

Roy jerked erect. He swiveled his torso as if stretching for calisthenics.

Sam stared.

"Nope. Don't feel fine. Feel *great*." He lifted his knees as if about to join a marching band. "Ha-ha. I feel great."

Sam sat at the front table and watched. He had seen his uncle's manic episodes before, but this was something new. From habit, Sam started to rearrange the remaining letters and envelopes into orderly piles while Roy strode about in time to a silent drum.

"Uncle Roy, did you...go anywhere today? Did the doctor give you something? Your clothes look...like yesterday's..." He hesitated. In truth, Roy's clothes always looked slept in, always looked like yesterday's.

"Nope. No medicine. And no juice. Not this time. But I did just get back from...the doctor. Yep, the doctor..." Roy chuckled as if at a hidden joke. "That's right, I went to see the doctor...and I feel *great*."

"Are you sure I shouldn't call him?"

"Touch the phone and die." Roy halted and flopped into his armchair. Reaching behind and under, his hands located a glass bottleneck. A half a fifth appeared, and he noisily took a swig. "You know what? Things are gonna be different this time. I can tell. I'm starting a new life. Gonna start over and do it right this time." He leaned back, grinning.

"You gonna watch some TV now, Uncle Roy?"

"Yeah. Turn it on. Right now, I'm gonna enjoy a bottle of my very best to celebrate my new life." He breathed deep—smiled a genuine, life-engaging smile. "My new life... Now get me my blanket, will ya? Just throw it here."

Sam walked into the hallway and extracted a well-worn bed comforter from the closet. He brought it to Roy and spread it over him, taking care to avoid touching.

"Thanks. Now don't wait up for me. You go ahead with whatever you have to do, and I'm gonna just sit here and relax. I gotta think."

Sam knew what *relax* meant. He watched as Roy took another swig. Sam glanced at the front door then back to his uncle. This was extreme even for Roy. Sam looked at the clock. Lori was waiting. Frowning, he pursed his lips. Uncle Roy needed watching. What difference would it make if he skipped tonight and saw Lori tomorrow after school at the Bronco Grill? Sam glanced at the phone—then at Roy. Not yet. Best to wait for Roy to fall asleep before calling Lori to tell her he can't make it.

"Oh, before you turn in, bring me my cigarettes, will ya?"

Sam fetched a half-carton from Roy's room.

"Atta boy, Sammy. My Sammy boy. Say, Sammy, did I ever tell you about the time when I jumped ship in Hamburg?" The armchair ceased rocking.

Sam stared as Roy interrupted himself.

"Gettin warm in here. Why do you suppose that is? Must be the blanket." Roy pushed it down. "This Greek ship captain had..." Roy sat up. "Look, there's that goddam jerk of a politician."

"Don't throw the bottle at the TV again, please Uncle. We can't afford another one."

Roy eased back. Looked serious. "Right. Okay." Roy frowned again. "Relax, will ya? I said I won't." He sank into a sullen silence as the politician vanished. A moment passed. "Say, is the AC broke?"

"No, Uncle."

"Turn down the stat. I'm hot."

"That happens to me sometimes. But I rearrange things, or stand in the center of the room, and that helps. And sometimes I think touching people will help—but I don't think that's a good idea."

"That's *you*. I'm *me*."

"Yes, Uncle, I know. That's just me."

"I have my own way to stay cool." Roy took another drink, grinned again.

Sam said nothing. Entering the hall, he turned down the stat. Yes, he had better stick around. He glanced at the pin board by the phone and again wished that Roy would relent and get them a couple of cell phones.

"Off to bed now," Roy called after him. "You have your school in the morning, and I'm gonna sit here and enjoy my smokes and my TV and a well-earned rest. Besides, I have plans to make." The bottle found his mouth again and was followed by a series of smoke rings.

"Okay. G'night, Unc," Sam called from the hallway.

Sam's door shut. Lori could wait.

Roy sank deeper into the chair. He was truly relaxed; deeply happy. He sucked a long toke on his cigarette and blew it out with more relish than he could remember. He smiled broadly. Today was more than something special—it was the dawn of a new age, a new epoch. Tomorrow he would begin again, start anew, be proud once more, silence his critics and the whole damn town. Show them all where to get off.

His hand wandered to his side where that very morning there had been a lump and was reassured to find that nothing could now be found. It was *true*. Sammy had been right, after all. The lump had vanished the moment his lips had touched the *Thing*, and had not, would not, return. The last few years with Sam had convinced him of that. He had been reborn and was determined not to lose his chance—equally determined to tell no one of the source of the New Roy. The *Thing* must never be mentioned. No, not even to Sam because young lips talk and this secret was for no one but himself and, who knows, he may have need of it again one day, and he cannot take the chance that someone, whether an owner or even the goddam Feds, might prevent him from getting what he needed. Let his Fountain of Youth lie quiet—until needed.

So, what to do? What to attempt? What plans should he make? His failed life, the self-destructive spiral that had consumed him for so long, had become a glorious renaissance. Suddenly he had time—health—energy. An unsuspecting world would react with shock when he launched himself upon it...*tomorrow*. For now, he leaned back in his chair, mesmerized by the endless series of possibilities that presented themselves to his inflamed mind.

First, he would learn to read better. The little bugs on the page that crawled and shifted so elusively would be tamed, brought under control. A week should suffice for that. Next, he would renovate his Cadillac. Maybe paint it red. That should take a day. Then he would start jogging and lift weights again, get his body back into shape. Another week at most. Next, buy a bike and ride it across the country as he had done when he was eighteen. Two days more.

And what about Sammy? Roy shook his head. Not to worry, he was almost an adult; Roy had done his job, done more than his duty required, and now Sam would have to take care of himself. This was Roy's time, his chance for happiness, and no one would be allowed to interfere—not even Sammy. He relaxed further, smiled more, and blew another huge puff across the room.

He glanced at the TV. The images flicked by with their usual relentless assault of the irrelevant and superficial on a programmed and credulous audience—but not to Roy. Roy watched with endless fascination, taking mental notes as to what to use, what to deal with, what to change now that the Power was once more his. His body felt great. No pain could he feel, no fatigue, no lethargy. He peered, sat upright, relaxed again, shifted. But to his surprise he was always comfortable. His least favorite politico reappeared on the TV, and he stirred momentarily out of his laying of mental plans for a grandiose and spectacular comeback to shake one fist at him. For a moment he entertained plans for an assassination that would careen the country in a fresh direction. He reached for the bottle to celebrate. Recalling what he had promised Sam, however, he refrained from tossing it at the screen and instead downed another swig.

He glanced up and behind. “Getting damned hot in here.”

Tossing the blanket to the floor, he spread-eagled on the armchair. Jerked upright again. “What the heck?” He stared at the TV and was transfixed to see the politician in the midst of a conversation on the air, speaking with his hair standing on end. Roy shook his head at the spectacle. “Humph. The asshole must be managing boxers now.”

He changed the channel and found some music. *It’s gettin really hot in here*, he thought, and paused to strip off his shirt. He grunted and switched back to the politician. His image was gone. Roy glanced back toward Sammy’s room. Although the house was Roy’s, he realized he had become hyper-sensitive to the constant admonitions and almost feminine-like corrections of his nephew regarding his housekeeping, or rather lack of it. The couch had become a casualty of Roy’s slovenliness long ago; Roy saw no reason why his chair should not join it. This house was *his* and no one else’s. And he would do as he pleased while under *his* roof. He removed his shoes and socks and leaned back, his sweat drenching the cloth of the chair.

The heat increased yet again and he sat up.

“Dammit. That boy did not turn down the stat like I asked him.” He lurched up, propped himself on his feet, and strode to the hallway. His energy was still flowing, and he paused at the entrance to his own bedroom, a picture of a plastic film cartridge container coming to mind. He hesitated. *No*, he thought, *not this time*. He had found something better. And far cheaper—free in fact. Roy stopped before the thermostat. In surprise he saw that it read sixty-four degrees. With a pluck of his thumb, he lowered it still further. "Can't be no goddamned sixty-four degrees in here," he muttered. "Must be broke." He lifted a fist to vent his frustration on the thermostat, then glanced at Sammy's door...and lowered his hand.

Roy entered the kitchen and helped himself to a glass of ice. In the front room, he poured a scotch and soda and watched the ice pop. He tasted it and felt instantly cooler. Exhaling, he was surprised to see his breath crystallize in the cold air that filled the house. He shrugged. "That's better," he whispered as the cold alcohol trickled down his throat. He resumed his sentry-like duty on the armchair, prepared to fling insults if his cherished enemy dared reappear. He lit another cigarette. As the rings crossed the room, creating a miniature smog-bank near the ceiling, he sank back, feeling fatigue for the first time that day. Briefly he closed his eyes. *Yes*, he sighed, the satisfied smile fixed on his face. *Tomorrow...tomorrow...*

He jerked.

Through the dull alcoholic haze, an utterly strange sensation crept over his scalp and neck. At a loss as to what may be causing it, he slowly raised himself upright and for once forgot to reach for his bottle. The TV blared incoherencies and for a moment he contemplated entering his room to inspect his mirror. *Forget it*, he thought. *X-rays couldn't get an image from that hunk of glass*.

An idea flashed. Using the remote, Roy flicked off the TV and stared into the blank screen, seeking his reflection.

His jaw dropped. Before him, ensconced in an undersized, over-patched, lean-back armchair sat a round-mouthed scarecrow whose hair stood on end.

Slowly, one hand wandered to his head and touched the strands, and an electric tingle filtered through his fingers and down his arm. Visible on the screen, sparks popped at his hairs' end. Not even the double vision induced by Kentucky's finest could disguise the weird sensation and weirder image.

He lowered his arm—stared at it in shock. His arm had turned pale.

Or, more precisely, been painted white. Shaking his head in a futile effort to clear it, Roy had the eerie experience of not knowing whether his reaction to his hair had caused him to turn an unprecedented shade of white, or whether the extreme paleness of his skin was causing his mind to exaggerate. Doubt evaporated when a moment later his skin shined with an effulgent, putrid exudence, beginning with patches that erupted from within like a plague, but inverse to plague in its color, an *anti-plague* that rendered his arm whiter than a death shroud waiting to enfold them. The patches merged and melded, spreading from his arm to the rest of his body—hastily Roy stripped off the rest of his clothing. An effulgence crept, which entirely failed to suggest the healthy rays of a yellow sun, followed by purple and violet. Sinking further into the armchair, Roy glimpsed the image in the TV expel smoke, turning the smog-bank near the ceiling into an impenetrable haze.

"IA! Aaagajabah!" Roy leapt to his feet, stiff as a ramrod. Snapping his head left then right, slaver spilled from his mouth. His wild eyes scanned the room and lit on Sam's door. His hands clutched and jerked. Flinging himself out of the chair, Roy lurched into the hallway—halted before Sam's room—banged on the door, fist after fist.

"Uncle Roy?" Muffled surprise leaked through the thick wood.

"Iiiiiiyaaaaa!"

For a moment Roy fumbled with the lock. Paused. He unleashed another barrage of pounding. Roy backed up—grabbed his head with his hands. He rushed back toward his chair and snatched the glass of ice.

Flames burst.

Roy's body erupted, pregnant with the energy of a sun, fires rushing forth with a roar. Falling backwards into his chair, the chair joined the conflagration, which spread to the carpeted floor and furniture, then hurtled to encompass the ceiling. "I look best in my white tie and tails," blared the TV. Then exploded.

Smoke pouring beneath the sill under his door, Sam threw on his pants. He changed his mind and rushed to the door to undo the lock and reach the phone in the hallway.

He halted.

With a crash, the door thundered from its hinges to fall warped at his feet, sending Sam fleeing across his bed. He rolled onto his knees—was swept aside by a bright tongue of flame. Behind him his bedroom window beckoned. He snapped open the window lock and hurtled through.

He landed on his shoulder where he lay groaning.

Sam struggled to his feet. Turning, he stumbled backward, and from the sidewalk he watched the flames as they engulfed Roy's house. A minute passed as the fire spread. Lights flashed; red and blue and yellow. Before his stunned gaze, the yard filled with fire truck, red ambulance, blue and white police cars. Firemen snapped free a fat hose and plugged it into a hydrant, and water finally appeared and soon drenched him and everything else except, seemingly, the house, which continued to erupt and roar.

Out of the chaos hurried a sweaty Officer Brant.

Catching sight of Sam as he stood massaging his arm, Brant jogged up to him. He thrust in Sam's face a plastic bag with several black plastic film cylinders, one spilling a dirty substance. "Found this below your window, Trencher." Stuffing the plastic bag into his police jacket, Brant folded his arms. "Crack cocaine. You want to explain it here? Or downtown?"

CHAPTER 8

A grown-up Sam hesitated before the glass door of the Bronco Grill and stared at his reflection, one hand fingering a pebble in his pocket. He had somehow misplaced a penny. He decided to attempt a substitute. Wasn't sure it would work. He suspected his temperature was rising, but it was too soon to tell, and once more Sam pondered whether his entire life was really all in his mind, after all, no more than a dark dream from which he could not awake. His mind went back six years to the death of Roy, the pebble reminding him of the crack cocaine that had brought him down, destroyed his reputation, booted him out of school, out of town, and out of Lori's life. He could not explain it; he had never seen the drug, or suspected its presence. He could only suppose that someone—perhaps even Uncle Roy—had procured it and somehow, for an unknown reason, placed it in Sam's room by the window. That wasn't the feeling he got from his uncle from the other side, though.

Maybe the talk was right. *Crazy*.

Except that there had been *others*—ashes, flames.

His interrogation by the Okwalla police had failed to reveal the source, and with Roy dead, Officer Brant and Judge Alexander had given him a choice: join the Army or face prosecution. How could he refuse? He enlisted that very day and soon moved in with his new uncle—Uncle Sam—his success in avoiding physical contact with the recruiters a minor miracle in itself.

Too embarrassed to tell Lori what had happened, not wishing to harm Roy's reputation any more than had already occurred, and recalling Roy's strange behavior the night of the accident, Sam had left Okwalla with his tail between his legs and vanished.

Now he was back. The wheel had turned. The glass door was opening. And *she* smiled at him from within the Bronco Grill. He approached the entrance for more eggs and bacon, nodding to Ralph in his wheelchair on the sidewalk under the overhang. Others nodded as well, dropping coins and dollars into Ralph's tin cup as with a trusted valet. Ralph rattled the change and with a smile and pass of the hand, the money disappeared. Onlookers clapped. *The town mascot*, Sam thought. *He entertains them*. Sam eyed Ralph as he walked by his wheelchair, still apprehensive as to whether Ralph might have some other sleight of hand waiting in ambush, but Sam slowed just long enough to drop a whole twenty in his cup. A little goodwill never hurt—especially where Lori was concerned.

"Morning, Sam," Lori greeted him as he entered. Customers were sparse, and Sam sidled to the same booth as before.

She looked behind to a balding man with black walrus mustache, tan formal sport coat and white name tag. "On break," she called to the sport coat.

Sam felt a sharp pain in his chest. Was surprised that his jealousy was that strong, surprised to learn that a mere feeling could cause physical pain. He would not have believed it from others. Didn't want to believe it in himself.

She sat at the booth seat across from him.

"Lovely to see you, Lori." He was relieved that the man in tan was merely her supervisor. No other feelings, no other signs appeared in his vicinity. Sam relaxed. Because the images had not yet time to appear, he liked his first morning encounters with people. For the first few minutes at least he was normal, the slate clean, his conversations like everyone else's.

She was dressed for work, and Sam decided the Grill was due a compliment as his eyes again passed over her cleavage. Her uniform was more entertaining than the pantsuit she had worn the previous evening, and it took some effort to re-direct his gaze to her face. "Lovely," he said, smiling. He glanced at her shirt's front pocket where he had seen a small red rose when he first sat down, and hesitated. The rose was gone. Confused, and fearing that Lori would again accuse him of spacing out, he sat for a moment, his smile frozen, waiting for her to speak. The images typically appeared or disappeared gradually. Rarely out of the blue. The rose meant they were strong. And he still had no idea what it meant.

"Today's a big day." Lori's smile seemed genuine. "Ralph's application to Social Security came through, and he can finally get his own special van, with a chairlift. Tomorrow, I take him for his first driving lesson." The smile faded. "It's been hard, Sam. Not just for him, but for me."

Sam pouted as he realized she would have no time for him on her only day off. "I was wondering how the two of you managed."

"I'm looking forward to not having to take care of him. I have a right to my own life, too, you know."

Sam slowly nodded. It was coming again.

"That's why I'm getting married...to get away." She looked at him with her head cocked. "Is that wrong?"

He shrugged. "I'm no one to judge."

Several people entered the Grill, and the bald man with walrus mustache looked sharply at Lori, cowboy hat in hand.

She glanced at him, then back to Sam. "Break's

over." She stood. "My fiance's in town. He's kind of jealous, Sam. It's really best if he doesn't see you here. But come by my house again tomorrow night and we can talk then."

Sam recoiled. Petals had appeared around Lori's feet and for a moment Sam wondered how she could walk without slipping. The petals grew tendrils that connected to form a net of gorgeous red and purple hues. They entwined her feet and wound about her legs. He had known it would come, had been avoiding it. Still, he wished it would just go away. Another glance revealed sharp thorns on the tendrils.

"This person...your fiancé. He sells flowers. He scatters petals everywhere he goes, but the flowers bring pain and hurt people. And once he has them, they can't escape. Including you."

Lori stood in place, frowning. "Sam, I told you. It's not fair for you to interfere. Not after leaving me alone for six years. Besides, Rose has changed. He's not the same person you knew before. I know the two of you didn't get along. But all that's changed. You should let bygones be bygones. He's really an okay guy. And he sells real estate, not flowers."

Sam breathed deeply.

For a long moment he sat, his eyes unwavering, his gaze directed at Lori as if transformed into a mannequin. The shock of her fiance's name was greater than he had expected, more devastating than he had feared. Momentarily he doubted what he had heard, again doubted his own sanity. Wondered whether he really sat in his teenage haunt The Bronco Grill in a sleepy town called Okwalla on a backwater planet called Earth counting the hours that remained in his life like a prisoner on death row.

His mind reasserted itself. He knew—had known all along—though his conscious mind had refused to see the obvious. Perhaps his psychic skills were not so off after all; perhaps it was just his insecurities and subconscious resistance that interfered with his readings.

Who else?

Roses. Rose Edwin Alexander. And behind him the tightrope, smoke, and flame. It was impossible, but Lori's presence, her earnest look standing over him beside the booth, sorrow and worry on her face, convinced him of the truth of the nightmare.

Lori was engaged to marry *Rose.*

A smile returned to Lori's face. "Tomorrow, then," she said. "See you about six."

***

The red rim of the sun turned orange where it touched the dry ridges to the west as Ralphie's wheelchair ground concrete on the downtown walkway. The rims of the wheels were also red, also due to atmosphere, but the red of oxygenated iron rather than prismed sunrays. Red streaked the hair of the wheelchair's occupant. Not from nature in his case, but from late hour attempts to impart a non-conformist mood to his appearance by staining his hair with henna, reflected also in the red daggers he had painted on its metal frame, to match the red daggers tattooed on his arms and shoulders. *Like Brando,* he thought. Maybe others would notice the signs of rebellion. He had also let his hair grow long—not from an empty wallet unable to afford haircuts—but from a deliberate attempt to promote his new bad-boy image. *To hell with life's rules. What good had they done me?*

Ralph gripped the rusted rims of his small purchase of freedom—or his tool for marginal non-confinement as he preferred to think of it—and his muscular arms thrust him forward another half dozen feet. A protuberance in the sidewalk appeared. Though no more than an inch in height, for a cripple in a wheelchair it towered like Mount Everest, potentially blocking him not only from the next few feet but from the progress of his life. For a moment, he panicked. *Fuck this life, goddammit! Fuck you, fuck me, fuck God, fuck above all the stupid fucks who run this town and should have helped me when I needed it...when I still need it.* Sidling up to the tiny ridge at an angle, he slid one wheel backward over the ridge and barely made it to the other side.

His rage subsided.

God, I need it today. He glanced at the zipped pocket to his right which held today's take. A small jingle reassured him as the wheelchair hit another bump. The heat lessened, but the day's sweat still drenched him.

Fifteen minutes and an exhausting two blocks later he wheeled in front of a glass door. A stenciled sign read "Rose Realty." A visitor exited and held the door open with a smile.

Fake, silently breathed Ralph, though he smiled.

A clean-cut young man in his late twenties emerged from a back room dressed as if interviewing for a Greek fraternity except for a fringed Western-style jacket and a knock-off Stetson hat pushed back to reveal a stretch of sandy curled hair. One lip twisted.

"'Lo, Ralphie boy." Rose pulled up a chair behind a handsome desk and flopped into it, pausing to massage an elbow where a door had recently struck it.

Ralph forced a smile. "I'm back, Rose. Just like I said I would be."

"Course. I never doubted you, buddy." Rose glanced around to make sure no one else was in the room. "You always have been a *stand-up* guy."

"That's me, Rose. That's me." He smiled broadly

as Rose got up and walked to the front door. With a swift movement he locked it and pulled the shades, then returned.

"Can I get you a drink? It must be hot out there...on the street."

The smile turned sheepish. "Uh, if it's okay with you, Rose."

"Not at all...just watch the dirt, will you." Rose eyed Ralph's sweaty shoulders. "I can't have dirt on the carpet. You know what I mean."

"Yeah. Sure."

Rose poured some lukewarm tap water into a dentist's paper cup with a picture of a tooth on the side and handed the cup to Ralph. Ralph gulped it like a castaway on a desert isle.

Rose smirked. He removed his hat and jacket and placed them on the desk. Sitting behind the desk, he adjusted a gold ring and fiddled with a small safe built into the floor.

Ralph's smile turned earnest.

The hand paused. Ralph sucked a breath.

"Time for business, then, Ralphie." He held out a palm. "Seein as how you're such a good customer, I'll let you pay in arrears again. But that means you gotta pay now...for last time." Rose peered at Ralph's zipped pocket. "What was the take today?"

"Five Jacksons. Same as yesterday."

Rose frowned. "Just five?"

"Uh...yeah...but I got a bunch of Hamiltons and Lincolns too. And some change." Ralph looked nervous. He blurted, "I almost pulled off the insurance trick this time. I know you said to keep trying, so I keep trying just like you said."

Rose moved closer, staring hard. "Well, what the hell went wrong? I told you, you gotta slide under the car and smack it good with a metal pipe. I even gave you the pipe."

"Officer Brant—"

Rose turned beet-red. Rising from the desk, he abruptly leaned forward and grabbed Ralph by the throat. "Goddammit. I told you not to worry about that piss-ant Brant. I'll take care of City Hall. You just do your goddam job."

Ralph stopped breathing and turned white.

Rose released his grip. He sat down again, calmed, and straightened his rattlesnake tie. "I just gotta put the spin on it, is all."

Ralph coughed. "I'll do it, Rose. I swear I will." He glanced at the floor.

The smirk returned. "Ralphie boy, Ralphie boy...what am I gonna *do* with you? You can't do nothin right. I oughta cut you off cold turkey."

Ralph caught his breath. "No—"

Rose smiled. "But not today." He held out his palm again. "Okay, then. Pony up."

Unzipping the bag, Ralph dumped its contents into Rose's hand.

"See? Five twenties."

Rose counted the bills. He grabbed the bag and shook it upside down, and some quarters slipped out. Ralph paled. But Rose kept smiling. "Don't worry. You got it covered, buddy. For today at least." He swept all the money into his drawer and shut it.

Leaning to one side, Rose opened the floor safe and extracted two black, old-fashioned, photo cartridge containers sealed with plastic tops. He placed an oblong ceramic platter on the desk, and carefully removing the tops, positioned the two cartridges on the platter.

Ralph inched forward, eyes bugging.

"Dab of meth," Rose recited, "with a hint of horse." He tapped a small portion from each open film container on the ceramic. Blue snowflakes interspersed with white powder. Using a straw, he mixed the two into a single concoction, then scooped minute amounts of each drug into a new paper cup. “No syringes here, bro. Got to clean or burn every trace.”

Ralph nodded. “Rose, how about...do you think you could make it...*two* hits?”

For a moment Rose frowned and Ralph paled again. Rose’s lip twisted. “Sure, Ralphie boy, why not? After all, you’re one of my triple-A customers.”

“Thanks.”

“But take it now.” He glanced behind Ralph at the locked front door. “Can’t have you strip-searched by Okwalla’s finest the moment you hit the sidewalk.” Rose touched the straw to the ceramic platter again and scooped more residue into the paper cup. In a few seconds, both cartridge containers were securely locked up again and the platter removed and rinsed in a back sink.

Shivering with anticipation, Ralph glanced behind him at the door. *The doctor is in*, Ralph thought. *Or should I say the dentist?* Using the straw, he snorted the concoction and handed the empty dentist’s cup back to Rose.

Rising, Rose burned cup and straw over the sink then cleaned the top of the safe and washed his hands. Returning to the desk, Rose watched as Ralph closed his eyes and turned all his senses inward to enjoy the gradually spreading ecstasy.

All I’ve got, thought Ralph. *All I’ve got. This and a three-by-three foot of concrete in front of the Bronco Grill in this fucking dead-beat town.*

Rose tapped the desktop with his fingers. “So, we’re done for today, *kamerad.*” Rose stood and crossed the room. Unlocking the door to the street, he threw the door wide for Ralph and said, “I’ll bet that wheelchair's gonna feel a whole lot lighter for the next day or two. Hell..." Rose grinned, his fringed hat back on his head, "I'll bet I see you pullin wheelies like for Guinness World Records."

Ralph swung his wheelchair around. He thought of the new van waiting to be picked up, and his hand began to shake. He had never driven a car, and the last person he wanted to know about it was Rose. As he neared the door, a rush of ecstasy washed over him.

"Uhhh..." Ralph's jaw opened and Greek came out. "Yeah...wold...lecords...." He too grinned. "Sam...Sam Trencher," he mouthed.

Rose paused, hand on door. A long slow look into the distance transformed the tightly-curled-hair-cropped face into stone.

"Bunco Grill," Ralph mouthed under half-closed eyelids, "One hour 'go. Gave it me...a Jackson."

Rose continued to hold the door as Ralph slowly wheeled himself out. As the wheelchair bumped to the end of the block, Rose drummed his fingers then looked at his watch. Stepping out, he locked the door to his real estate office from the outside. On the sidewalk, he stood and rocked on his heels contemplating a swiftly growing darkness relieved by two desultory streetlights. Downtown Okwalla had yet to catch up with the development on the turnpike.

His hand wandered to his elbow, which had still not recovered from the impact of the swinging door the day before, and he massaged it with his other hand. Slowly he nodded.

A new Escalade jerked to a halt before him, its brights and radio blaring, defiant of cross traffic and the angled parking stripes.

Rose stepped to the driver's side. He hissed, "Move over, faggot. We've got a problem."

CHAPTER 9

"Sure thing, Eddie."

A hand lurched toward the driver's throat. "You moron. It's *Rose* now, I told you." Rose stared Steve down. "Rose Realty. How many times do I have to tell you?"

Steve gulped. "Uh, sorry, Ed...I mean *Rose*." Steve began to shift seats to let Rose drive.

Ignoring his own instruction, Rose circled the Escalade and flopped in the passenger seat next to Steve. He sighted a parcel wrapped in clear plastic lying between the seats. Rose snatched it. He stabbed paranoid glances out both windows. "Are you crazy? How much attention are you trying to draw to us? Why don't you just take out a front-page ad?"

"Oh, yeah." Steve laughed. He turned off the brights. While Rose tossed the package on the floor, Steve gunned the engine and traced a one-eighty across several lanes and lapsed into a boring straight-arrow road trip toward the edge of town, lighter on the pedal and eyeing the speedometer.

"But it's not real, you know."

Rose glared at Steve. "Of course, I know. I'm the one sent you to our friends in Tucson to get the best counterfeit ever made. And it still cost me a bundle. Pull in there."

Following Rose's direction, Steve pulled up a side street, and kept going until Rose signaled him to break into a cul-de-sac between two warehouses.

"The Dead District," Steve intoned.

Pausing a minute to make certain no one followed, Rose switched on a portable lamp and tore open the plastic on one of the bundles. He carefully inspected several hundred-dollar notes.

"I told you they were the best," Steve said.

Rose whistled. "You were right, Steve-O. Our friends definitely came through." He looked out the car window at the warehouse.

Steve followed his stare and sighted a red plastic can in the growing darkness behind a dumpster. He glanced inquiringly at Rose.

Rose half-smiled. "It's payday again."

One last glance left and right to make certain they were alone, then Steve slid out of the Escalade. The warehouse door was unlocked, and he carried the can inside, reappearing two minutes later with the can upside down, empty. Steve put the car in gear, and a few minutes later, the Escalade rolled to the main road.

A mile sped beneath the car's tires and Steve turned onto the turnpike. High sirens and flashing lights leaped upon them. A fire truck sped past in the opposite direction escorted by two police cars, racing in the direction of the Dead District. Rose laughed. "Okwalla's finest."

They drove toward the West Loop. Another mile and they curled into the back lot of a large structure. A neon sign flashed: Haven Motel: *VACANCY*.

Rose turned on a burner cell phone, rarely used, and texted a brief message. A few minutes passed.

Finally, a dark face thrust from the delivery entrance. Spying the Escalade, it withdrew, and the dim light extinguished, followed a few moments later by the delivery door swinging open.

Rose and Steve glanced behind them at the turnpike for one last cautionary look.

"Let's move."

At a nod from Rose, Steve took the plastic-wrapped bundle, placed it in a dark canvas bag, and with the red can in the other hand, slowly sauntered to one side of the parking lot where he tossed the empty red can into the Haven Motel's dumpster. When Steve was in position, Rose strode to the door as if alone.

The dark visage thrust out again.

"Is that being you, Rose?" the face asked in a thick East Indian accent.

"Yah, it's being me." Rose mocked him. He stopped smiling. "And my name is *Ben* as far as you're concerned. Got that?"

A toothy smile in need of a dentist flashed, reflecting pale light. "Are you alone, *Ben*?"

"No, I'm not alone," Rose snapped. "Just making sure *you* are."

"Oh, I am alone. Completely alone, sir, except for my hard-working wife at the front desk. Please to come in."

Rose stepped into the darkened back room, glanced around. Then he motioned to Steve. Emerging out of the darkness with bag in tow, Steve followed them into the motel's kitchen.

With the back door closed and locked and blacked out with voluminous padding, Mr. Patel switched on the kitchen lights, and he locked the door separating the kitchen from the rest of the motel to make sure no one might interrupt them.

"There is news?" Patel asked.

Rose answered while Steve emptied the canvas bag. "Our friends in Reynosa...they can keep supplying horse, but things are getting hot there. They want us to step up our meth production here in Okwalla. On account of, we have protection."

"But we are short on epi—"

Steve ripped open a package and dumped hundreds of white pills on the stainless steel of the largest kitchen table. “Not no more.” He grinned. “Wholesale batch.”

“Ooooh, sir,” Patel crooned. He ran his fingers through the pills as if through silken hair. “There is enough pseudoephedrine here to make gallons.”

“You got the idea,” Rose interjected. “We’re going big time. We’ll put your chemistry degree to work again, but with ten times as much quantity as before.”

“And here’s the horse.” With a nod from Rose, Steve threw down a large plastic-wrapped white brick. “One kilo. Our brand specialty. I want you to mix it with meth to make speedballs. Our latest test subject is in High Heaven as we speak, with no ill effects. And if my plans work out, we can graduate to fentanyl.”

Patel looked up and peered once more at the bag, then back to Rose, inquiringly.

Rose smiled. He nodded once more to Steve. “Bring it on, *Jerry*.”

“Yeah, *Ben*,” Steve said. He pulled out the Tucson cash that he had rewrapped in plastic. It plopped next to the heroin and the pseudoephedrine.

Crooked teeth beamed to blind both of them. “Ahhh.” Patel orgasmed, snapped it up and tore away the plastic. He began to count it, then paused as if committing a faux pas.

“Not to worry, Mr. Delhi.” Rose grinned right back. “Ten thousand even. Payment for your last batch of meth. And your next dividend will be five times that.”

“I’m rich.” Patel sighed.

“Get used to it, brother,” Rose said.

Steve added, “*I* already have.”

“But we’re gonna update our product to fentanyl, bro. No more crack cocaine. The street price of crack has dropped through the floor. So let me have the rest of your stuff and we'll unload it on our contacts in the north-east."

Patel stood erect—hesitated.

Reading Rose's mood, Steve stepped closer to Patel to get his attention.

"Don't get tight on us, Mr. India," Rose said. "This ain't no game."

Patel stopped smiling and exhaled. He turned and opened a lock on an old disused commercial oven. He pulled out a smaller package of dirty white material wrapped in see-through plastic and handed it to Steve, who stuffed it in his canvas bag.

Steve pointed to the back door. Patel unlocked it. Jerking his hand in a mock salute to Patel, Steve turned on a heel and exited into the night, taking the bag.

After relatching the door, Patel turned to Rose. Now that Rose wanted something from him, his backbone had returned. "And...my five percent?"

Rose stared hard. Softened. "Of course." He grinned and gathered Patel into his embrace. "Thank you, brother. There's enough money and good times coming to make all of us happy." He smoothed the fringe on his Western jacket. "*After* it's sold."

Patel stopped smiling, but said nothing.

Out the door, Rose followed Steve's path to the Escalade. As he approached the car, a waft of acrid smoke struck him. He jerked open the door to the darkened auto and watched open-mouthed as Steve feebly attempted to hide a crack pipe. "Dammit, Steve-O. I told you we don't need to sample the shit. Just sell it."

He gulped. "Sorry, Eddie-"

Rose began a slow burn.

"I mean, *Rose*."

"The stuff's old inventory. It's no good. We gotta

get rid of it."

Steve was already high. He snorted defiance. "It was good enough to frame that punk kid Trencher six years ago, wasn't it?"

For a moment, Rose seemed about to explode. He suddenly calmed and laughed. "Yeah. That's right. We ran that punk kid Trencher right out of town..."

Steve and Rose laughed together long and hard.

Rose grew suddenly serious. "'Til today."

Steve's eyebrows raised as he and Rose locked glances—in low tones they continued to talk.

***

On its way to a remote destination, the red wheel of a wheelchair rolled past the plate-glass window of a street-side office. Seemingly of its own accord, the office's metal-framed glass door opened, and a clean-shaven thinnish man in his sixties with a shock of white hair sauntered in from Main Street.

A bright smile greeted him.

"G'afternoon, Sue Ann."

"Morning, Mayor." At her desk, Sue Ann smiled wider.

The glass door closed, displaying 'Redy Insurance' in stencils.

Before entering his back office, the older man paused. "Oh, Sue Ann, can you bring me the files for those new accounts, please? I need to make sure everything is in order before I submit them to the carriers."

"Yes, Daddy Jack." She flipped her expansive hair smartly from one side of her neck to the other, then leaned over a desk drawer, her backside out-thrust.

Jack lingered longer than necessary, watching. He straightened to receive the files. Smiled broader than he needed to at his secretary's addition of "Daddy" to his name and retreated to the comfort of a leather chair strategically positioned so as not to miss any of the scenery, his back-office door half open. As usual. He soon lost himself in paper and missed her next twist and bend.

The yellow wheel turned and the sharp black hand on the antique Art Deco clock on the wall approached five.

"Sue Ann. Can you come here, please?"

The bright smile hurried to obey.

He opened a dull stack of papers, pointed to an unfilled blank. "Two more signatures. Pages nine and ten."

She mouthed an O of surprise.

"How many times, my dear? How many times?" He sighed. "Really. If I hadn't checked your license twice, I would wonder if it was real."

She pouted, radiating sincere remorse.

"But not to worry." He smiled. "Chase down Tom and get him to sign...I must admit, you do bring in the business like no one else. I don't know how you do it, but since you came to Okwalla, you've been the best rainmaker Redy Insurance ever had."

"Just a smile. And UV light." Sue Ann flashed her brights once more. Taking the pages, she swirled and headed out the door.

Jack called after her. "Tom's a tough customer. Maybe you should call him first, make an appointment."

She paused; flashed a look of confidence. She twirled her hair and said in a girlish voice, "He'll never know what hit him." The door swung open, shut behind her.

Eyes on her derriere as it dwindled across the crosswalk, Jack stood at the door breathing deeply. He shook his head as if coming out of a trance and smiled wide, glanced once apprehensively down the street in the direction of his home where his wife would be.

Drawing the shades, he locked the door and retreated through his office to a back room, where, after checking that the lights were off throughout the office suite, he opened a back door and exited and locked it. Crossing to a Ford pickup that was far from new but that he could never quite part with, he crawled into the driver's seat. In another moment, his tie and jacket exchanged for a nondescript windbreaker, he was tooling along the western loop.

A tasteful sign equipped with quiet lighting in good repair appeared over his truck: Haven Motel: *VACANCY*. Another minute and he approached the front desk, sunglasses and cap failing to cover his surreptitious glances at the only other customers in the place, a tired trucker in green, soiled jacket and a swarthy mustachioed vacationer in tank top and shorts, their eyes fixed on a large flat-screen hanging in the motel lobby.

The front desk was vacant.

Jack stood and waited. He leaned and peered. At last, a hint of movement rewarded him.

A toothy smile showed around the corner. "Oh, sir, please excuse me." Patel put down chopsticks and a paper box of cashew special from a local Chinese eatery and stepped forward. He wiped his mouth with his bare hands. "Excellent fare, despite the price. I just cannot get enough."

"Evening, Pete."

Patel peered as if confused. "Is that *you*, Mayor Jack?" His eyes grew wide in mock recognition. "I would never have *known* it was you, sir."

"Don't worry 'bout it." Jack glanced about again and spoke quieter. "Just the usual room again, please, Pete."

The motel owner accepted a hundred dollar bill and offered a plastic keycard but pulled it back just as Jack reached to accept it. Another quick sidelong glance and Jack, feeling perspiration beneath his clothing, threw down a fiver. "And your five percent...in advance."

Grinning, Patel slid it into a pocket. The plastic key slid across the desk into the mayor's hand.

"Room 155."

Patel started to point, but Jack nodded and walked off. He knew the way.

Thirty minutes later—the perspiration now grown to wetness—the mayor of Okwalla still stood within Room 155. He jerked at a loud knock on the door.

He cracked it and let one eye peer out. Exhaling, he opened the door wide as the newcomer entered.

"Can't you at least put on dark glasses?" Jack said.

The newcomer glanced about the room. "What do you want, a rubber nose too?" He nodded. "Relax. Nobody visits this place. I don't see how this motel even stays in business." Judge Alexander removed his formal jacket and draped it on the bed.

"Okay, Edwin," Jack said. "What's the big emergency? When you ask to meet me here, it means you want something."

"Jack, Jack...you are such a worrier. And in case no one has ever told you to your face, a negative nabob." The Judge stepped close and put an arm around him. "How long we've known each other? Thirty years? Forty? In all that time all you could do is look gift horses in the mouth."

Jack grew skeptical. "How is insuring fire traps a *gift horse*, Ed? Especially when those fire traps have a habit of burning down."

The Judge shook his head. "Oh, I'm not here for that, Jack. I'm actually here to do *you* a favor...that favor you asked me about just last month, in fact."

Jack brightened. "Yeah?"

"I know you need cash for your reelection campaign, even if the mayor's job is only part-time. And you know it's much simpler to receive that cash outside of City Hall where no one will ask where it came from and where it's going. Christ. It's unbelievable how the government floods us with goddam forms. Life is too short for such crap." Judge Alexander screwed together two ends of an electronic cigarette and frantically puffed. "Next time I'll spring for the high-nicotine brand. I haven't been the same since City Council made the court non-smoking."

"You know I tried to stop that measure, Edwin—"

"I know."

Jack breathed more easily. The sweat beneath his windbreaker receded a bit. "Ed, if I hadn't covered those last two fires, I would be sitting pretty by now. You know they don't just write a fat check these days. I get penalized for every policy that goes bad." He glanced out the window. "I heard sirens earlier."

"Yes...Ferguson's warehouse. That old rat trap. Been empty for years."

Eyes widening, the mayor caught his breath. "*Another* one?" Jack blurted. He stepped back. "Dammit, Edwin. You'll put us both in State prison."

"Federal, actually."

Hand to forehead. "That's even worse."

"Not really. It's actually better." Edwin smiled and extended the reassuring arm again. The Judge's gray mustache twitched. "I'm sorry, buddy. Should have kept my mouth shut. Just relax. It's not a problem. I got it covered."

The mayor calmed but kept looking through the curtained window as if blue and whites were about to appear, with a SWAT team in tow.

"Jim Ferguson owed me after I got him out of that jam. That wife of his was a real shrew. I gave her the worst in their divorce so it's only fair he pay me back. He owned nothing but that junk heap in the Dead District. This was the only way he could."

"And your own hands stay clean, of course."

"Of course."

Resigned, Jack let it all out. "Alright, Edwin. But I need the full $10,000 you promised."

"Not a problem, Jackie Lantern."

The mayor winced at his old nickname.

Judge Alexander stared at him. "Just don't forget who put you in the mayor's chair...and who can take you out."

Jack's gaze flicked to the window again. He almost wished a SWAT team *would* come crashing in and end his misery.

"After I leave, sit quietly for five minutes and wait for the phone to ring. Not the room phone by the bed...your cell phone."

Jack directed a puzzled look. He sat on the bed.

"What can I say?" Edwin added. "You've got *my* vote."

Jack forced a clearly insincere smile.

The Judge either did not notice, or did not care. Retrieving his jacket, the Judge donned it and disappeared down the motel hallway.

Ten minutes later the phone rang. A male voice Jack did not recognize spoke. "Go to Room 156. The door is open. Look under the bed." The voice hung up.

With sunglasses and golf cap back on, Mayor Jack looked out the door. He peered up and down the hallway. Empty. He crept next door. With a gentle push, the door swung open. Entering, he fell to his knees and glanced under the bed. Spying a package that looked like freshly cleaned clothes, he pulled it out.

Through clear plastic that was torn at one end, glinting in the dull overhead light of the motel room, shined what appeared to be a large stack of crisp hundred-dollar bills. He again breathed a sigh of relief. Still, he sweated. Even in a podunk town like Okwalla, mayoral campaigns were not cheap, and due to the fires, his insurance business was barely breaking even. Thank goodness for his new secretary's avalanche of clients; he needed her help now more than ever.

***

Pete Patel stared as the mayor's Ford pickup exited the parking area of the Haven Hotel to vanish on the ramp to the West Loop, creeping carefully like a man with little to gain and everything to lose.

He had hardly gone when a couple sauntered in the main entrance and approached the front desk. The woman was young and wore her smile like a marquee, the natural curves of her body accentuated by a tight-fitting single-piece purple dress, bulky black folder in one hand. Older than the woman by at least twenty years, the man removed his Western hat to reveal a pate that had lost most of its hair. A dark mustache compensated to some degree, its uncut length entirely obscuring his lips.

"Evening, dear guests." Patel's face was wooden-Indian stoic.

"Just one night, please."

A single furtive glance took in the lack of luggage. "Sign here, please."

The broad mustache failed to hide the growing smile beneath.

"Room 156," Patel said.

"Thank you." The couple skipped off like schoolkids, his large masculine hand on her derriere squeezing a giggle out of the woman.

Down the hall, Room 156 appeared.

They hurried in. As the door closed behind them, the man pressed forward, catching Purple Dress against the wall, her legs lifting off the floor to cross behind his back.

He buried his face in her neck and let out a laugh. "Smart fer sure, Sue Ann. Smart fer sure."

She giggled again. The balls of her feet dug into his lower back. "Careful, Miiister Boorger," she rolled every syllable. "You're gonna need a saddle if you want *me* to ride you."

Growling, he pretended to thrust.

"Down, boy. Oh, you are such a *dog*." She laughed.

"I couldn't wait to get you here. Promises, promises. That's all you ever do is make promises."

"What else, Miiister Boorger, sir?" He let her down and she stepped toward the motel room's large window and gazed through the flimsy curtains toward distant lights. Turning her back toward him, she glanced over her shoulder and winked.

He enfolded her again, this time from behind. "*Tom*, Sue Ann. You can call me Tom, can't you?"

She removed his arms and placed his hands on her buttocks. "Don't know, Miiister Borger, sir. What should I call you? You haven't done *nothin* for me yet." She turned and winked again over her shoulder seductively.

"Nothin?" Tom fondled her buttocks and kissed the back of her neck. "Nothin? Just let you drive me crazy is all."

"Oh *darlin*. You're not even half-way there..." She smiled up at him. "But you're on the right road and drivin fast."

His hands wandered to a zipper on the back of her dress, twitched and fumbled while his face turned red with eagerness.

Sue Ann escaped his grip. She turned to face him. "You're still not quite there, Miiister Tom."

Tossing the black folder on the bed, Sue Ann slowly unzipped the binding that enclosed three sides, watching Tom squirm, despite himself, at the seductive action of the zipper. She withdrew several papers and a pen and spread them over the bed until there was no place to lie down.

Tom stared, breathing hard.

An adolescent pout transformed her lips. "You know I simply have to get this finished, Tom. I'd love to play with you, but that mean boss of mine said if I don't get this policy done then he'll fire me. He was mad as a bull that lost its balls."

Tom thrust the papers aside and flopped his bulk on the bed next to her. "That don't cover me no way a'tall, Sue Ann." His hands reached for her again.

She thrust a pen into one of his hands. "You know that, and I know that. But mean ol' Mayor Jack *don't* know that." She pouted again. "Don't you want me to keep my job, Miiister Borger, sir?" Her finger stroked his bald head then wandered down his chest toward his midriff.

"I...I ain't sure 'bout that, Sue Ann. Jack is more expensive than hay in winter, and I signed his insurance policy already. If I sign this supplement, I'll be way over-insured."

"That's nothin, dear boy. We'll just fix it so you get a little of that money back right up front."

A look of confusion came over Tom.

Sue Ann's hand moved to the back of her neck. She moaned, "Oh, I'm getting so hot." She turned her upper back toward him. "Do you think you can loosen my zipper just a bit?"

Still holding the pen, he almost stabbed her in his haste. Then paused as the papers suddenly reappeared with several hundred-dollar bills on top. Crumbling, he followed where she pointed and signed in two places. The papers vanished into the black folder and were zipped away, leaving the money on the bed. She smiled as her eyes flicked between the money and Tom.

He snatched up the bills and stuffed them in a pants pocket.

The giggle returned. She proceeded to unbutton him again. He caught his breath. Grabbing his shirt, he popped the last two buttons and threw it aside. In another moment he had unzipped her purple dress and thrown it after his shirt on the floor.

Their passion exploded, and a half hour later, both exhausted, Tom proceeded to put his clothes back on as Sue Ann traced happy tattoos on his skull.

"My, my, *my,* Miiister Borger. You do put those bulls to shame." She smiled.

He kissed her again, hard. "Smart fer sure, Sue Ann. You're smart fer sure." He glanced at the window as if expecting an unwelcome visitor. "And you won't tell my wife, will you?"

"Hope to die and Scout's Honor, Miister Tom. I would never tell your wife. Now you rush on home. And don't worry. Your insurance agent will be right here the next time you need any little thing at all..." She laughed and buttoned his remaining shirt buttons for him and wriggled back into her purple dress. Standing before him, she felt Tom between his legs. "You're in good hands, Tom."

He caught his breath, then exhaled loudly. "I can't stay, Sue Ann. I'll be missed." Another kiss. "Next time." He stepped out the door and paused to put on his hat and flash a grin. "Smart fer sure."

The door shut.

Sue Ann unzipped her folder, inspected her paperwork, and zipped it up again. Pausing, she glanced in the mirror, adjusted the dress and dabbed at her makeup. “Never knew what hit him.”

Another minute, and the room was empty.

Striding quickly past the front desk, Sue Ann exited the Haven Motel and entered the parking lot. As she approached her new silver Jaguar, a figure appeared out of the growing darkness. She stopped and stared but said nothing.

“How did it go?” a man’s voice said.

“Mission accomplished.” She tapped her folder. “He grabbed that cash like it was fresh steak.”

“That’s nice, Sue Ann. That’s real nice. I knew you were the right person for the job.” Stepping forward, he grabbed her in his arms and planted a passionate kiss on her lips. He let her go.

“When?” she asked. “When can we cash in our chips and leave this backwater dump? I hear Rio calling.”

“Patience, my love. Our plans are moving swiftly, but it’s gonna be a bit longer. I’ll let you know when it’s time to buy the tickets.” Headlights from the loop briefly shined in his direction and the man stepped quickly into darkness.

She giggled while unlocking the Jaguar. Entering, she sped away.

***

At the front desk, Pete Patel watched as the woman in the purple dress strode quickly out the door.

Five minutes passed.

Nodding to his wife, who responded by silently taking his place behind the front desk, Pete retreated to the still empty kitchen. He tested the lock on the back door and listened at the door to the hallway.

No one.

He tapped on the door to his office and it swung

open.

Judge Alexander stepped into the bright light of the kitchen. "Did you get it?"

"Oh, yes sir, Judge, yes sir." Patel gazed at the Judge. He handed him a small flash drive. "This is being Mr. Tom Borger."

The Judge smiled at the device. "Tom swore he would never sell the Bronco Grill to me. I think he's about to change his mind. If he doesn't, *no more Bronco Grill.*"

"As you say, Mr. Judge." Patel sucked a breath and looked about him. "Your Honor, sir...I'm losing money every month. When will it be *my* turn?"

The Judge sucked another e-cig. "Soon, Pete, soon." He peered more closely at Patel. "And Mayor Jack?"

"Oh, yes." Patel pulled a second flash drive out of his pocket and handed it to the Judge. "Room 156. I was put the money under the bed for Mr Jack. He took it off before he left. Ten thousand..." He cocked his head and stared at the Judge at a peculiar angle. "That's being a lot of cash for me to pay, Your Honor."

"Not to worry, Pete. Tonight you did your civic duty by recording an insurance agent giving kickbacks to a client, and the mayor of Okwalla accepting a ten thousand dollar bribe."

"You will using the mayor's recording, then?" Pete looked suddenly nervous and his eye wandered to the flash drive still in Alexander's hand. "But the ten thousand dollars was *mine*."

"It's nothing at all for you to worry about, Pete. I got it covered." The Judge headed for the door, then paused. "But if I ever hear that you recorded anything else than what I told you to record...you'll get a visit from some very special friends of mine." He shook his head, smiled, and left by the side door he had entered.

As the Judge's state-of-the-wallet Audi turned the corner out of the parking lot and tooled onto the West Loop, a figure emerged from behind the motel and lowered a camera. After a quick inspection verified the photos, the figure backed around the corner and disappeared in the back lot.

CHAPTER 10

Black squares formed a checkerboard against the faded yellow clapboard of the aging wooden house, the pattern crawling across the wood to halt at intervals like a stone skipping on water. The black burst tan and the yellow burst white and the squares enlarged and, like a marquee, flashed on and off. This wasn't part of those distant sweet memories of standing beneath these same trees, watching hungrily for a sign from the object of fascination in the upstairs window. Maybe a view of the street would restore sanity...

Tan with white trim, the Voyager van appeared around the corner, and in the growing dusk alternately glided and jerked down Southmore Street, jabbing to a halt in front of the Drumond house. The passenger door flew open, and a pale Lori Drumond spilled out.

For a moment she stood, trying to catch her breath.

"The ramp," a rough voice called from the driver's seat. "Is it...is it positioned over the front walk?" The van jerked forward another inch.

Lori put her hand over her chest to calm herself. "Yes," she called.

"Good." The motor died. Inside the van, Ralph released the hand brakes that the auto dealer had installed for him, jiggled his body from the driver's seat into his adjacent wheelchair, wheeled it into position at the top of the raised ramp, then flipped a lever inside the van. With a clang, the side door slid back. Slowly and painfully the ramp lowered, emitting beeps like a five-a.m. trash truck until his chair was level with the front walk. The noise stopped and he rolled off the metal platform onto concrete.

Ralph stared ahead, ignoring the looks of several neighbors who stood and frowned, annoyed by the beeping. "Made it," he muttered. Though lifelong neighbors, the wheelchair had made Ralphie, the former neighborhood paperboy, into something alien, something to be tolerated only when convenient.

"I don't know how I survived," Lori said. She managed a smile as Ralph spun a wheelie, his arms bulging as if training for the Special Olympics. He entered the bottom leg of the new wooden L ramp that led to their front door while Lori approached the first front concreted step.

A figure stepped from the thick trees that shadowed the porch.

"Omigod, *Sam*." Lori lurched and clutched her chest again.

Sam stared, fingering thirty-seven cents in each pocket, aware exactly which coins were where. He had recently begun to place a penny in each back pocket beneath his wallets in addition to the loose change that he kept in the front pockets. Even then he felt his temperature rise. For a moment, he glanced at the overarching branches of the trees lit by the late afternoon sun, and he moved a foot to place himself precisely between two shadowing branches of equal size.

"Didn't mean to startle you."

She dropped her hand. The smile returned, surprise turning to relief. Then to engagement. The smile was real—perhaps too real. "What are you doing here at my house?" Lori said.

"Don't you remember? You said to meet you

tonight. After you took Ralph to get his new van and his first driving lesson."

"Oh. Yes." The work clothes were gone, replaced by the formal pantsuit. Obviously new. Like her new cell phone, new car, new furniture, far more than a waitress serving blue-plate specials could afford. Another red rose materialized above and behind her, soon joined by a flurry of imaginary petals. Sam disciplined himself to ignore them but could not resist a quick glance up the street. Only the sinking sun and deepening shadows were visible.

"Would you like some tea?"

Despite the shade, Sam felt hot. He answered quickly. "Yeah, Lori. Tea. The coldest you got."

At the threshold, the wheelchair paused, and Ralph glanced up from his preoccupation with propelling the rubber wheels on his wheelchair. Contrary to what Sam expected from someone whose mobility had just taken a giant leap forward, Ralph's expression was far from happy. He directed a frown at Sam.

"She's leaving me, you know."

Taken aback, Sam glanced at Lori, who returned the same sad expression.

"We've had this talk, Ralph. I'm not going to stand here on the porch and have it again."

"She's leaving you, too." Ralph looked up at his sister. "She's marrying...*him*."

Lori waxed indignant. "And who do you think bought us all our stuff, Ralph? He helps you, too."

Ralph looked at Sam "Yeah. *Helps* me. If you only knew."

"Inside," she commanded.

Climbing the mountain of a threshold, the wheelchair sailed across the wooden floor, stalled briefly on a new rug, then rattled into the kitchen where

Ralph banged around, hurrying to prepare two cold drinks.

Lori followed then she and Sam sat on the sofa, listening to Ralph rattle cups. She whispered to Sam. “I’ll get yours. It’s too hard for him to carry them. You know, he refused a motorized chair because he wanted muscles.”

Lori stood. Entering the kitchen, she reached for the ready glass of tea, but Ralph snatched it, ignoring what he spilled. For a moment, it appeared they would wrestle over the remainder. But he handed the glass to her with a look that went suddenly blank.

“Thank you, brother dear.” Returning to the couch, Lori handed it to Sam who grabbed it greedily. Within seconds, he drank half the glass while Lori’s eyebrows lifted in surprise, and then Sam put the half empty glass on her new coffee table.

Her mouth opened but she was distracted by more noise from the kitchen. “Lovebirds alone...I’ll leave you lovebirds alone.” The wheelchair squeaked into the hallway and vanished behind a door that shut with a thump at the end of the hall.

Lori looked back at Sam. He retrieved the glass of iced tea. Another moment and his tea was drained. He felt cooler and wondered how long it would last. Visions of ice baths came to mind, deliciously cool.

She moved closer. From long habit, due to fear—or was it paranoia?—he slid away. It would relieve him of some heat, as touching anyone would, but who knew where that might lead? He shuddered. His *gift* was like a loaded gun that could never be unloaded and had no safety.

“Damn,” she said, looking down.

He jerked from his reverie.

“Tea on my new pantsuit.” Lori jumped up and stamped a foot. “*Damn!*”

Surprised at her emotion, Sam also stood. He had never seen Lori lose her temper.

She put her own glass down. "The only new clothes I've had all year." A tear appeared.

Involuntarily, his gaze wandered back to his own clothes: old worn jeans, but at least recently washed.

She whispered, struggling to suppress her anger. "I'll be back in a moment."

"I'll be here."

She glanced at him reprovingly as if to say: "this time" and disappeared down the hallway.

He suppressed his own urge to break into a smile, remembering the stimulating attire she had previously appeared in. He knew Lori well—perhaps too well—but six years was still a very long time. And though he knew they still had feelings for each other, he did not want to trade on those feelings, assume anything, especially since she was clearly committed, and since he himself was...*not normal.* How else could he put it? How else admit it to himself?

Alone in the room, Sam stood with his hands in his pockets. Not as usual—as *always.* He must be sure. The coins *must* balance. Even now the cool contents of the glass of tea had already transformed, already transmuted into fuel for the flame, the heat in his spine rising. A wisp of air raised stray hairs on the back of his head. He had felt that before; it had been a while, but he knew what it portended. Stiff straight hair was a warning.

There was something wrong.

He counted the change again. It matched. He repositioned the coins into exact mirror locations in each front pocket. Risking a momentary leap in temperature, he withdrew both hands and checked the pennies in his back pockets, made certain they were also in mirrored locations at the corner of each wallet.

What else could he do? His wallets were identical and both empty. There were no tree branches inside Lori's house; inside, he could not stand between twin branches or sit between matching car windows.

His eye wandered to the pictures on the walls. Maybe that was it. One picture was off kilter. The nature scene in the frame tilted counter-clockwise. Sam glanced toward the hallway. His feelings were not always rational; even when they were, he did not have the energy or inclination to explain himself, it was simpler just not to be seen. He stepped across the room and adjusted the picture. *Clockwise.* He stepped back and felt instantly better. Clockwise demanded counter-clockwise, like counter-clockwise demanded clockwise. And down demanded up. And up demanded down. He leaned forward, hands on knees, then straightened. He adjusted the angle of the coffee table, then threw himself down on the rug and lay prone as if praying to Mecca and beyond, ignoring the dirt that Ralph had tracked in. As suddenly, stood straight again.

He felt a degree cooler. He sat on the couch just as Lori reentered the room.

She sat again and smiled. "Why, Sam. You have dirt on your face." She wore the same short pants as the night he had first arrived, which alone seemed to raise his temperature a notch, but in place of the revealing T-shirt, this time she wore a more covering blouse. Speculating silently, he could not help but wonder if her dress reflected more than her moods, reflected her own conflicted motives, one day throwing the gates of paradise wide open, as it were, the next revealing them to the world but still locking them against him. A subtle anger stirred. Locked to *him*—of all people.

Sam blinked. A vine had appeared behind Lori, its tentacles growing from either side to meet over her chest. For a moment he wondered if his *gift* had suddenly extended to X-ray vision as her blouse seemed to evaporate leaving her breasts exposed but tied with woody vines.

She leaned forward, crooning, her lips puckering for a kiss, her full breasts pushing forward inviting to be touched...

"Sam."

He recoiled, almost sliding off the couch.

"Sam."

The vision vanished. Lori sat where she was, modest blouse still covering her. "There you go again."

Shaking his head, Sam looked tired. "I'm sorry, Lori. Maybe I need another glass of tea."

Her look of concern turned again into that enigmatic smile. "Won't take but a moment."

She soon returned. Just as quickly as before, Sam drained the glass. For a moment he stood in front of her, eyes closed, hands thrust in pockets, immobile as a Greek statue, his brain calculating degrees of Fahrenheit.

"I...I saw you move the picture, Sam."

Sam opened his eyes. He looked at her and lowered his gaze. His shoulders squirmed, not daring to relinquish his grip on the pocket change. "I feel ashamed."

She angled her gaze. "Why? I still don't understand."

He sat again, sat closer, looking into her eyes. "Don't you remember, Lori? Did you really forget everything about *that day*? It changed my life completely. Did nothing at all change in *your* life?"

She stared hard. Sam had withdrawn his hands from his pockets to lean forward, and she glanced at them as if to take them in hers. He yanked his hands back violently without touching her and thrust them again into his pockets. She inhaled and caught her breath as if an impulse to speak had surfaced. Now she too lowered her gaze. “I do remember.” She stared at the floor.

Sam now caught his breath. “You...you *do?*”

“I didn’t want to. I wanted it gone. I couldn’t deal with it. Just like I couldn’t deal with my parents’ problems. Or Ralphie’s accident. Or my...my fucking lousy job. My fucking lousy life...even at ten years old. Do you understand?” A new hardness that Sam had not suspected shone from her dark eyes. “I still can’t deal with it...with my fucking lousy life.”

He stared. Her emotion only made her more beautiful. “What do you remember from the Round House?”

“The cavern. The drawings on the wall. The bricked-up room that collapsed.”

Open-mouthed, Sam absorbed her words.

“I remember we went down the rocky path into a larger cavern, where Charlie climbed down deeper.” She grew confused. Shook her head. “It was a long time ago. I don’t remember anything else.” Looked up. “But I lost the two of you. I called you and Charlie for what seemed forever, and you never called back. You never returned. I got scared and finally climbed out. Iggy had his bike. It had broken spokes, and he was wheeling it away on foot as fast as he could go. My bike was broken also, so I grabbed it and followed him.” She shrugged. “It couldn’t go far. I left it in the woods and I never saw it again. Just like I never saw Charlie after that.”

“But your parents said Charlie moved away. I knew he didn’t. He never came out. And then Injun Willie disappeared. And I’m sure he never left Okwalla.”

She nodded. “I believe you.”

“But don’t you see, Lori? Don’t you see what this means?” A wild look seized him. “It means we *did* see the same things that night. It means I did not imagine everything. It means that everything that's happened to me since is *not* all in my mind. That I'm not..."

She blinked.

"You know...*crazy*."

Her head shook. "But I didn't see everything that you say happened. And why didn't I come back changed like you?"

"I'm not sure. But maybe... When Charlie came back after Rose and Steve chased him, when he tried to climb back up from the deep... Charlie touched me. Something strange happened. A glow rose up my arm, spread over my body. He did what his grandpa had told him. He kissed the Midnight Sun. Then he touched me. Grabbed me with his hands and wouldn't let go." Sam stood again, gripping his coins. "And everything changed."

"But changed *how*, Sam?" An earnest look took hold. "Why do you jingle coins and...move pictures?" She shook her head again. "Why do you act so...strange?"

"Act?" He stepped back, stared wildly again. "Act? What is acting compared to being? What is acting and feeling compared to bones and flesh? I was transformed on that night. Made special. Given powers that no other human alive possesses." He suddenly turned sad. "Wasted on me, I should say. Because after all these years, I still don't know how to control it, how to use it." Sam brightened. "But my foot speaks for itself. There is no confusing that. No way to explain it away, impossible to dismiss *this* as a dream. This is *real*."

He pulled off his shoe, tore off the sock, and stared approvingly at his foot.

"But you had an operation...you got it fixed."

"Fixed? No, Lori. No doctor touched me...ever."

He drilled her with his stare. “Fixed? Do you see any scars? Signs of an operation? No. I stumbled in a cripple...and I walked out in perfect health...on both feet.” He felt the back of his head tingle as hairs raised, and he quickly replaced the sock and shoe. He stood again. Balancing on one foot, he switched to the other, the one that had once been afflicted with the clubfoot deformity. “In balance. Always. Maybe that's why. Perfect is balanced. Balanced is perfect. The thing requires balance, and if it finds you imperfect, it makes you perfect because there can be no balance if you’re not perfect. Since that day, I’ve never experienced an ailment...not even a cold.” He looked sad again. “Only fevers...always fevers.”

Wondering, she listened quietly.

He sat again. “I *know* it was real.” He extended both hands simultaneously, made fists of both. “I know that one day I was a cripple. And I know just as certain that I am sitting in a house on Southmore Street in a slum called Okwalla on a spinning rock called Earth that I walked out gifted as no one before me has ever been gifted. I was no longer a cripple. No longer. All I had to do was kiss the Midnight Sun...or touch someone who had, someone with the Glow still upon him.”

Her eye wandered to the picture, wandered briefly in the meadow of the nature scene. Her smile returned, wider and whiter than before. For a moment, the ten-year-old skinny girl returned, listening again to her first and best love as he proudly boasted of his adventures with spoke cards and bikes.

Tears burst. She crumpled inward seeking to make herself smaller. “Sammy...you’re still my boyfriend.”

Sam caught his breath, jerked his shoulders back.

She buried her face in her hands. “But I’m still getting married.”

He looked at his shoes. “I know. I knew before my car came to a stop when I first came back to town.”

She looked up. “But you don’t know more than that. You can’t know more.” His shoes continued to attract his gaze as she spoke. “You don’t know Rose like I do. He’s friendly. And funny. He helps me and Ralph. He’s successful, has a good business. With his father, the Judge, it’s like he’s—”

“Lord of Far and Wide.”

She bent her head, eyes closed.

“I’m sorry,” Sam said. “I’ve no right to rain on your parade.”

“Then don’t.”

From somewhere a smear of cobalt blue materialized over a bare portion of wooden floor to the right of Lori’s couch. For a moment, Sam mistook it for a balloon and wondered how he had missed it when he entered the room. He blinked. He had not missed it; it had appeared from nowhere and now resided comfortably defying him to give significance to its inexplicable presence. He glanced as something materialized to Lori’s left, a matching smear of bright red like a cold pitcher of fruity Kool-Aid. Both colors solidified, took on sharp edges and remained suspended in air, defying gravity and explanation, increasingly well-defined angular translucent objects suspended in air without visible support.

He slowly looked back to Lori.

“Don’t say it, Sam.” The hard look had returned. “I don’t want to hear your crazy ideas on how I’m doing to die.”

Continuing his gaze upward, he suppressed a tear. Forced a good mood. “Dancing shoes.”

“Uh. *What?*”

“I have dancing shoes.” He shrugged. “Folk dancing. Balkan styles are the hardest, especially if you dance alone like me. Before the Midnight Sun, I could hardly walk. Now...I have dancing shoes."

Lori caught her breath. "Crazy. I can't hear any more. No more, today, Sam. That's enough for one day. I just can't take any more." She buried her face in her hands again while Sam walked backward to the door. With a sigh, he turned the knob.

She spoke again. "Will you be here tomorrow? You...you're not leaving Okwalla for a while, are you?"

"No, Lori." He looked at her matter-of-factly, hands thrust into pockets, fingering identical coins in identical fashion in identical pockets. "I won't be leaving Okwalla again. Not for a long, long time."

The door shut him out.

Ten feet away in the unlit hallway a young man in a wheelchair listened as quiet sobs sounded from the invisible couch. Like an aroma, the sobs' vibrations rose to waft through the undisturbed air and settle quietly on his eardrums, where they evoked as little reaction from him as from the wheelchair and the other items of furniture that clogged the house of the dead. His gaze was elsewhere, gliding from his sturdy strong arms down the length of his crippled body to his thin legs to rest on his feet, legs that were capable of movement but whose strength years of therapy had been unable to restore. One hand felt a withered foot, stroking it as if to impart life where it once had lived but where life had long since departed. His gaze lifted and a quiet voice repeated. "*I stumbled in a cripple and walked out in perfect health. Before Charlie kissed the Midnight Sun, I could hardly walk. Now, I have dancing shoes.*"

CHAPTER 11

Morning came. Hues, lit orange by miles of dust to distant mountains, turned to yellow as the sun's rim ascended, every minute growing harsher to eye and skin. The entrance to the Haven Motel opened, and a man in plaid shirt and green vest that were only a bit less soiled than the previous evening, despite its immersion in thin soap and half-hearted scrubbing by Mrs. Patel and her Mexicana concierge, politely held the door for an entering customer.

Crossing to an 18-wheeler parked crosswise in the motel's expansive, mostly empty parking lot, green vest placed a white cap over his tousled head. He gave no thought to the *Duval St.* insignia on the cap, which might have aroused more than casual interest among certain people had they been there to notice, or to the *Vaya Gonzalez* sign on the side of the truck, which had often been noticed, but not by anyone who cared.

Climbing by stages into the driver's canopy, he began the process of triggering the engine and checking for signs of tampering during the night. He was used to sleeping in the truck-cab itself. Staying the night in an actual bed was sufficiently rare that he could not rid himself of concern for a break-in until he inspected every window and every door in the large truck. Satisfied, he jerked the monster into gear and cratered onto the Loop.

Fifteen minutes later, he was traversing Okwalla's East Loop and approaching the turnoff to the Dead

District. Traffic was light. Decrepit adobe shacks sped by, their inhabitants staring dully at the arrival of modernity in their unchanging lives. A pair of warehouses loomed, one cerulean, the other tan, flanked by a desultory auto junkyard gleaming rust-red. With a loud exhalation, the truck slowed in front of the auto yard and ground to a stop in front of the cerulean structure.

Two short men in oil-stained overalls hurried from a wood shack set in the middle of the auto yard to the warehouse. There they unlocked a small door and closed it behind them. Moments later, the truck died, and the man in the soiled green vest climbed down. He walked casually into the warehouse behind them.

Speeding from the opposite direction, a black Escalade approached and jerked to a stop by the same warehouse door, cutting off the truck. Two Anglo men in cowboy jeans and hats knocked on the small door. After it opened, they entered and closed it. An audible lock sounded.

A minute passed.

The windows to the adobe shack closest to the warehouse were shut from the inside, the dull faces retreating to the interior.

Another minute passed.

From behind the blue shack a blue uniform appeared, overlaid with a black bullet-proof jacket stenciled: *SWAT*. An AR-15 cocked. More blue-black uniforms emerged left and right of the warehouse. More minutes passed and two more uniforms quietly hurried across the interval between the adjoining warehouses.

Two Okwalla cruisers rolled in from opposite ends, converging slowly on the small door, their silence almost complete. They coasted to a stop. The door of one cruiser slowly opened, and an officer cautiously emerged, using the car door as a shield as he aimed his rifle at the warehouse door.

The second cruiser halted. A woman in blue and black put a rifle sight to one sun-shaded eye and similarly sheltered behind a car door. Two more SWAT officers approached the warehouse door from either side, clutching an iron battering ram.

From behind her cruiser door, Marla nodded to Officer Brant—Brant made one hefty swing with the ram and the warehouse door sprang from its hinges. It seemed to hover. Then struck the concrete floor inside the warehouse with a bang.

"Police. Get on your face, you fucks."

The officers swarmed inside.

Five men looked up in surprise from seats positioned around a long picnic table set with utensils and foil-vats.

"Get on the ground. Do it now. Do it *now.*" Gun barrels aimed at their foreheads, barring any thought of resistance.

Two men in oil-stained overalls stood up. They threw up their hands, knees shaking. Officer Brant kicked one in the chest. He crumpled with an "Ay comacho!" The other dropped to his knees. Two more kicks spread-eagled him.

"You cain't be serious," one of the jean-clad Anglos mumbled.

"You fuckin rednecks hit the deck." Two cops grabbed the first and handcuffed him roughly from behind. Before his face hit the floor, they had jumped the second.

The second Anglo groaned as he collapsed under the weight of three cops. "I know my ri—" Officer Brant kicked him in the ribs.

"Bill. That's hardly needed—"

Brant glared at Marla but backed off. "Where's Mr.

Green Vest?" he shouted at the Anglo on the floor.

Green Vest fell forward through a back door where he had attempted to slip away. Two more cops appeared behind him and cuffed him as well.

The police went silent.

"Hold everything, gentlemen," Marla said, her eye wandering over the picnic table.

"Don't mean nothin," Brant snorted. "Search this shit. There must be something hidden in all this."

One of the cops brightened. "Well, if there isn't, I call dibs on these tacos right here." He laughed.

"And put me down for the peach tea," another cop called.

More officers chuckled as they inspected the table laden with the makings of crisp tacos, soft enchiladas, peach tea, and long-neck cervezas. Five half-eaten plates sat where the suspects' meal had been interrupted.

Dragging the five suspects painfully to their feet, each handcuffed from behind, the officers stood them around the table.

"Now, if I have our lab analyze all this shit, they won't find anything illegal, will they?"

"Hey-ell no, Officer Sir." One cowboy risked a smile. "Maybe a little bullshit, but that's all the shit you ever gone find in these parts anyhow. Everybody knows that Okwalla is Bullshit Town, USA. Kind of Ground Zero." The others laughed until the cops' glares silenced them.

The two Mexican laborers grinned also. "We got lots of tacos. You want some? All you had to do was ask." A ripple of laughter spread through the five suspects.

Several cops frowned.

"Shut up." Brant yelled.

The auto workers kept grinning. "If we geeve you

some tacos and enchiladas, will you let us feenish our sieesta?"

The two cowboys snorted and grinned.

"I said *shut up.*" Brant stepped closer, ignoring the disapproving stares of Marla and several other officers. "Or I'll shut your mouth for you." He tore off his sunglasses and pointed them at the prisoners, lecturing, "Your lawyers will tell you, you shouldn't say a word."

"*Lawyers*? Heyll, we don't need no stinkin lawyers. We ain't done a damn thing wrong." The first cowboy glanced at the second. "Except maybe use too much chili." They laughed again.

"Let's inspect the truck." Marla's quiet voice calmed Brant and he paused.

"No need for that," Brant said.

"He must have some reason for being in Okwalla."

"I said there's no need." Brant looked toward the suspects. "Our information was wrong. That's all there is to it."

Marla risked a diplomatic smile. "Can't hurt, though. It will make the paperwork worth it." She motioned to two deputies, who exited the front door before Brant could intervene. Twenty minutes later a thorough search of the 18-wheeler turned up no drugs, as did a search of the warehouse, and the Escalade.

Brant took Marla aside. "Satisfied?" He sniffed. "I told you this morning we didn't have enough to go on. And turns out I was right. You're new to Okwalla, little gal. I've been cruisin these streets since you were wettin your diapers. Believe me, I know when somebody's doin' somethin...and when they're not."

"Take them downtown," she called to the others. Then in a lower voice, "Even though I'm sure we'll find nothing. Either they're all innocent...or someone tipped them off."

Brant snorted. “Tipped. In Okwalla? Not in my lifetime. Nobody would *dare.*” The other officers returned sheepish glances as Brant stared them down.

Reluctantly, the officers packed the suspects in the back seats of several police cars while one stretched yellow tape across the warehouse’s front and back doors and more started up both suspect vehicles to drive them to the police impoundment lot. In another few moments, the alley was empty except for casual bystanders who had gathered to watch the drama. The action over, they dispersed.

***

“Ralph. Is there anything else you need?” Lori adjusted her waitress uniform and inspected her ample bustline in the hallway mirror. She had gotten used to the stares, though she still did not understand why Tom, the owner of the Bronco Grill and her employer, always insisted that his waitress’s uniforms be so revealing. She shrugged. *Money is money.*

“Zilch. Nothing. Bye already.” Ralphie crossed and recrossed his wheelchair behind the closed door to his room. “Don’t be late.”

“Okay, I’m gone.”

“Who asked you to stay anyway? Go to work, Lori.”

One last listen at Ralph’s door and Lori headed out to work. Somehow every time she left her brother alone she felt a twinge of guilt. But money was short. Someone had to make it. She smiled, more in relief than pleasure. Her wedding was just around the corner, and the torrent of late and unpaid bills that left her and Ralph wondering how long the lights would remain on would at last halt.

The front door banged shut as Lori left.

The rubber wheels on the carpet behind the hallway door slowed, then stopped. Silence ensued, as if someone had paused to listen, to ensure that no one else remained in the house.

Creaking slowly open, the door framed *Brando* in a wheelchair, James Dean hungry to kill The Man, de Niro in mohawk waiting to ambush a President. The arrows on the chair glimmered in soft light as Ralph carefully inched forward, minding not to scrape the imitation wood paneling on the walls of the hallway. A fanny pack jammed with several screw-top water bottles hung around his neck, next to two thick gloves made for mountain climbing.

A coat-stand equipped with hooks at waist-level stood by the front door. He snatched a white cap slash-printed *Bad Rap* and carefully ensconced it on his head, ignoring his neck-length black hair that still bore traces of henna. He adjusted his dark glasses hooked on a neck string. *Fuck the world that fucked me. It's time to fuck back.*

He swung the front door wide, backed his chair out the door onto the porch, and pulled the door shut. He locked it. No point in leaving Lori inconvenienced. She would worry once she realized, but nothing could interfere with what his heart desired. *The heart wants what it wants. And that's what it will have, whatever the cost.*

Down the L ramp and onto the concrete walk, he paused his chair in front of the tan Voyager van with white trim. *His* van. In *his* name. Not his parents'. Not Lori's. He had known precious few such victories. For a moment, sitting in the morning sun, he reflected how swiftly his school friends had forgotten him after his hospitalization. How soon he had become nameless and friendless once the other children had seen his wheelchair. How hopeless any notion of employment had proven once he had grown. The insults. The: "But you have no experience," rejections by smug persons unaware that they were gifted with two healthy legs while his life was forever on hold, forever held up by an endless series of one-inch Mount Everests everywhere he tried to go. "At least *try* to find work," Lori would whine while holding another medical bill, which alone was larger than his entire social security check. *If she can't understand, what hope is there that anyone else will?* And soon, not even her to complain to. Because she would be marrying *him*.

At last—there was a way out.

He clicked the new key-fob. The van side door slid quietly backward to reveal a darkened interior. Like his life: quiet, dark, and—as always—alone. His private hell, but at least now his *portable* private hell.

Progress.

He clicked again. With a loud clang, the metal ramp jerked into action, extruding from the van to a sound of loud beeps, as clanky as a space shuttle heading for its launch pad. Several neighbors paused from their yardwork in alarm. *Don't help him Trish, you know those people like to do everything for themselves,* he had once overheard. He had remained stuck in the sun for half an hour that time until some kid mercifully gave him a push out of the gutter. He'd be damned if he would ever ask for it.

The ramp crunched onto the concrete. Circling his chair, Ralph backed onto the ramp and clicked again. The intolerable missile launch sequence resumed and the neighbors glared.

Once inside, he swiveled his chair to the left, then propelled himself forward so his chair was adjacent to the driver's seat. With some difficulty he lifted himself out of the wheelchair and into the seat. But he felt good. The soft comfort of the new material surprised him. Unlike the chair, the seat had not had time to conform to his body. He clicked the seat belt—with a twinge of sarcasm. *A bit late for that.*

He wriggled his toes and stretched his lower legs. Life was there—always had been. But atrophied, weakened, the nerves too impaired to respond to the decade of efforts by therapists to regain control and enable him to walk again. One hand gripped the handbrake that had been installed at chest level just for him; the other touched the hand-accelerator next to the brake. He glanced down the street. The neighbors had all either fled inside or resumed their gardening. It would not do for him to be interrupted. He was not supposed to drive by himself yet. But who knew, except Lori?

The engine purred to life.

A feeling of ecstasy took hold, mingled with a chill of the possible consequences should he have an accident. There would be no more van. No more Lori. Maybe even time in a jail cell. A jail within a jail. But that was always a possibility given his flirtation with Rose's miracle substances. If they arrested him, he was sure to be clamped in irons...stuck in isolation. A drugged-out cripple in a wheelchair alone in a cell in the dark—Public Enemy Number One. He snorted. *That's how society deals with its throwaways. It labels them a public menace, then buries them alive.*

The van jerked into gear.

Hesitantly, his hand slowly pressed the accelerator and the van rolled forward. The road was empty of traffic, for which Ralph was grateful. With his other hand he tried the brake and the van halted. Squeeze one, then the other. One, then the other. He jerked all the way to the end of the street, then turned aside to take a back route.

Although he had never driven alone in his life, he knew the lay of Okwalla like the floor map of his own house. Left—then right—pause for the traffic to vanish—then slowly ahead and again turn. In a few minutes, he was out of Okwalla's only suburb and tooling down the southern turnpike, as nonchalant as you please. *Freedom. Like a spaceship to Mars.*

The southern pike turned into the West Loop and there were no more potholes, and his driving smoothed out. On the left-hand side by a cutoff, a worn filling station crept by, a figure in dirty white overalls standing hands on hips—good ol' Len Squires—glaring death at every car that failed to stop and tank up. Minutes later, a new motel glided past on the right side, its eternal *Vacancy* sign inviting him to spend money he did not have, like those credit card invites that assured him: "You are pre-approved" when he knew damn well he would never be approved: pre-, post-, or otherwise.

He crossed an ancient rust-red railroad track. At long last the side road he sought appeared. On the dirt track he crunched to a sudden halt and extracted the equally ancient road map he had pilfered from the local library about Okwalla's past, after exhaustive searches of online websites had yielded nothing. He peered again as the sun crossed midday. He looked back at the map, scrutinized it... Yes, there it was—the tiny dot with the equally tiny blurb: *M.P.* So small...as if the mapmaker had hoped it would be overlooked. There was only one thing that could mean in this backwater of civilization, a landmark forgotten—or deliberately ignored—by the modern world.

Peering out the window, he nodded.

The van crept carefully onto the side road. Fields of potholes returned. Shaking and swaying like a Portuguese caravel heading for an undiscovered world, the van inched its way deeper into the unknown, the opportunities for returning or bailing out on its purpose shriveling and dying with each mile that elapsed.

The sun passed from midday to afternoon and still the van had not come to the end of the pitted dirt road, whether due to the condition of the path or the inexperience and errors of its driver, Ralph often stopping to lower a window and peer outside with increasing apprehension as the level of the gas in the tank steadily dropped and the air cooler wheezed louder from combating the growing heat and dust. But the van never turned away. Each time, after a brief inspection out his open window, it resumed inching forward to negotiate the next pit and hole.

Afternoon had grown into latenoon as the van mounted a last rocky ridge and finally pulled onto the surface of a massive block of brown stone baking in the sun. Pulling forward to within six feet of the edge, the van halted alongside an antique pickup truck with four disintegrated tires around four rusted rims that had been abandoned for so long that it had left rust tracks on the rock's surface.

In front rose an eight-foot-high wooden fence with a large gap close to the truck where the fence had collapsed; someone had once strung barbed wire in its place. But the wire itself had rusted and sagged, leaving nothing to impede intruders. Two boards contacted the ground where someone had once used them to press down the barbs. Removing his new sunglasses, Ralph peered. He could barely make out the faded words: *Mystery. Pueblo.*

Ralph shook with excitement. *So goddam far—so goddam good.*

He glanced between the truck and the fence and sighted a collection of debris strewn up to the fence line. A pair of what looked like reptile boots, whitened by the sun. Torn remnants of a jacket and shirt, with dirty rain-soaked jeans, lay alongside several more items of clothing. Resting beside a faded Western hat, now mottled and covered with dust. Over the boots looked like what he first took to be a wig, then saw it was hair. *Scalped?* A twinge of fear chilled him, until he saw the discarded knife and realized it was someone's braided queue that had been tossed carelessly aside. Years ago. *No more Injuns in these parts.* He sighed in relief.

The sun was low and dropping fast. Which was good because the heated slab of rock was more lethal than Death Valley and wider than the Grand Canyon. Not even a mountain bike version of his wheelchair could manage its many small ridges and crevasses, though he believed that the far side might present something different. Planning—that was the key. He continued to run the van's cool air, watching the slant of the sun's rays incline and the air currents that rippled over the heated slab gradually lessen, then cease. He recalled Sam's words for the thousandth time: midnight. That's what he needed.

Midnight it would be.

He sighed, his excitement growing by degrees. No more day. No more spying, snide neighbors impatient for him to die or move away. No more alms dropped into a shallow tin cup by passersby with pitying expressions. No more...you-know-who, sucking what little life remained out of him. For a decade his life had been a shadowy existence with endless midnight struggles, heroic victories in savage battles unwitnessed and unsuspected by the privileged outer world. What would they know? He was a superhero. He had vanquished monsters, conquered deadly vistas unguessed by the universe. Now he would leave it all behind.

A new world beckoned.

Sinking below the anterior ridge, the sun

darkened, blackened, and reemerged in some nether region awakening to unguessed possibilities. The currents had finally ceased rippling. Ralph lifted his head, shook himself awake. The last rays of dusk arched overhead to plunge the farther regions into mystery. There was no need to waste more time.

Ralph clicked the button to open the side door amid a raucous clanging and beeping. For the last time. Riding the angry metal ramp down, his chair seemed to expel itself onto the face of the dark brown rock. He checked his fanny pack. Unscrewing one bottle of water, he swigged twice, then reclosed it. A crush-resistant flashlight proved in good order. He donned his mountain climbing gloves.

One last step...if that was the word.

A last glance around and it was time to discard what he would no longer need. His hat dropped, landing next to the snake-skin boots. His sunglasses went on top of the weathered discarded clothing. He tested the bottoms of the new blue sneakers clad on his feet—suede, of course. Never used, but a good fit. A last glimpse at the stars twinkling in the sky. He glared at them defiantly. Soon they won't have Ralph Drumond to kick around anymore. *Who gives a goddam fuck?*

He launched.

Sliding from the wheelchair, he spun it back toward the van, and threw the keys after it, leaving the van's side-door wide open.

CHAPTER 12

The antique Oldsmobile's blue hood vibrated as it exited Southmore Street, turning in the direction of the equally antique Young Men's Christian Association boarding house—the part-time adventure of an elderly couple with a local monopoly on the name, and the federally-assisted bank account that came with it. They arrived from their church at the same moment that Sam found an available space, jiggered his car until he found the exact center between the painted lines, and entered the ageing building, careful to avoid stepping on cracks in the sidewalk.

At the same time, across the street, a new Lexus pulled under a copse of trees, the bright sun rendering the car virtually invisible in the shade. In the driver's seat, a golden-haired man in Western jacket fingered a matching tan hat.

"Straight from Lori's house to here." Rose stabbed a narrow glance at his companion. "Did I tell you? Or did I tell you?" His laser-like stare redirected to the edifice across the street.

Steve matched his glare, squint for squint. "Damn if you didn't."

"Take a good look. We need to know his car anywhere." Rose rubbed his nose. "Can you believe the nerve of this guy? Comin back to Okwalla where he's not wanted no-way no-how, and shovin his nose in where it don't belong—right into the pussy of my fiancé. Goddam prettiest girl in this podunk dump of a town that I'm stuck in, and the only damn thing worth fuckin in this burg." He spun back to Steve. "Which I ain't even got to do yet, in case you're thinkin what I think you're thinkin."

Steve risked a nondescript turning of innocent palms up, knowing better than to voice an opinion where Lori was concerned.

"Don't even think it, faggot." Rose slapped his hands on the steering wheel. "That's a situation that I'm damn well gonna cure and pretty damn soon too. And if I find out that Mr. Buttinski overturned my apple cart before I cross the finish line..." He peered toward the parking lot. "Let's just say you won't want to be anywhere near two little love birds if *that* were to happen. Not after I damn near broke my bank account with all those pussy payments just to get on Lori's good side."

"Pussy payments." Steve chuckled. "That's good, Rose."

For a moment Rose turned a shade of red. Then relaxed and grinned. "Yeah, ha ha. That *was* good, wasn't it." They both laughed.

Rose pursed his lips. "Blue. Oldsmobile. Ancient hunk of tin. You gettin this, Steve-O?"

"Yeah." He scribbled on a piece of yellowed paper. "And what about *my* car, Rose? When do I get it back?"

"Hang onto your goddam horses, bro. That business I mentioned was finished just a couple hours ago. Your car will be waitin for you tomorrow in the parking area behind the Rose Realty office. It's safe and secure 'til then; you got nothin to worry about. But meet me at five o'clock at Daddy Dear's office. We gotta put the spin on it."

Steve rubbed his chin with one hand.

"Relax, Steve-O. I'll drop you off with your *chilita*." Rose grinned. "You gotta play. You know...too much wood breaks the chipper."

He laughed. "Yeah, wowza. And what about *your* chilita?"

Rose snorted. "Which one? The chili-*hita*, or the chili-*hota*?"

Steve sniggered. "What do we care? A hungry pussy is a hungry pussy."

"And don't forget my new chili-*chinga*, who you haven't even seen yet."

"AfroMexiWhite will do just right. Here's to ho's, bro. White, black, brown, or purple."

"I'll smoke to that."

Rose leveled a reproving stare at Steve. "You better not be samplin our shit again, Steve-O. I told you, that'll screw us up."

Steve tore open a cigarette pack.

"Not in my new Lexus, dammit. Wait 'til we get to Main Street. Let's go. It's time I collected on some debts."

The engine leaped to life. Rose put on dark glasses and popped the Lexus into gear, and in seconds it sped into the distance.

Minutes later, having dropped off Steve, Rose braked on Southmore in front of a faded yellow wooden two-story residence, stopping directly on top of matching tire marks deposited earlier that day, and directly under an ancient oak whose roots steadily widened cracks in curb and concrete. Rose glanced up and down the street for anything unusual. One hand patted his wallet in his right rear pocket. The other hand patted his other wallet in his left rear, the one that had *correct* names on the photo IDs and driver's license. *Nothing like freedom of choice*, he reflected.

The sun was setting and he still had not received word on the results of the vehicle searches. The spin was in, his contact had it covered, but still he was conscious that possibilities remained for things to go awry, no matter how remote those chances may be, and he now found it necessary to spill a certain pile of beans to his father, the Judge, just to make sure. Paranoid? Maybe so. Still, his nose for the unlikely had preserved him so far. Keep your own nose clean—that was the most important Lesson he had learned from *Daddy Dear*. Let others get their hands dirty in case the shit ever hits the fan—and it helps to own the fan. And whatever you do, no matter how bad the situation seems, don't *ever* tell the truth—not even God can help you if you fuck up so badly that you make *that* mistake. That was Lesson Number Two from *Daddy Dear*'s lifetime on the bench.

Rose knocked on the door.

A passing cloud exposed the sun, and he put his wide-brimmed ranch hat back on his golden curls.

Moments passed. The door opened.

"Wanna buy some gold?" Rose smiled his best smile and removed his hat. "Get your scissors and I'll give you some for free." He fingered his hair.

Lori forced a smile. "I'm not twelve years old anymore, Rose."

"If I had known you better when you were twelve, I would have given you some back then."

He pecked a kiss. She received it on one cheek.

Entering, they paused in the front room.

Giving her a look askance, he asked, "You okay, Lori?"

There was still a trace of red around her eyes from the day before. She rubbed it away. "I'm fine, Rose. Just a little upset about Ralph, is all."

"How many times do I need to tell you? I'm gonna take good care of Little Ralphie. Just you see."

"Please don't call him Little Ralphie. You know he hates that. He's twenty-one years old, for goodness sake."

Rose dropped his hat and jacket on the couch. *His* couch. He threw up both hands in don't-shoot fashion and grinned his best. "Ancient history. Won't happen again."

"Tea or coffee?"

"I need a jolt, babe. Pour them in together."

"When did you start doing that?"

"This week."

"What for?"

He peered at the floor, suddenly disconsolate. "Do I really need to tell you?"

She let a deep breath drag out. "No. I wondered when you would find out. I should have mentioned it the day Sam came back."

He stood and put his hands on her elbows. "Don't worry, Lori dear. He's part of your past. Part of this town's past. You have every right to renew your acquaintance with Sam Trencher. Just..."

She looked up at his face. "Just?"

"Just don't forget who loves you *today*. Now."

Smiling, she shook her head. A tear appeared. "I haven't. And I won't." She turned and hurried to the kitchen. Banging pots and kettles, she soon emerged with two small mugs and placed them on the coffee table in front of Rose.

"Here. You can mix them yourself, or drink them straight, as you like."

Rose sat and poured some cold tea into the hot coffee. He sipped. It was good.

"So, are we still on? No problems with the date?"

"Uh-huh. July 3rd it is." Lori radiated gratitude—or relief. "Thanks for paying for the chapel hall. And the gown. And everything else that a bride's father is supposed to pay for but can't. If I even knew where my father was."

A reproving glance was returned. “We’ve discussed all this before, Lori. I commanded you not to give it a second thought. The money means nothin to me. It’s nothin...nothin, that is, compared to one of the most beautiful women I could find in this dump of a town...I mean, the most beautiful woman anyone can find in this town, and the entire state. And I’ve been all over this state and had plenty of time to look.”

A puzzled expression settled on Lori.

He sensed his error. “How’s the couch holdin up?”

Lori nodded, non-committal.

“And the car?”

The smile returned. “Perfect.”

“And the wardrobe?”

She beamed.

He paused. “And the...bedroom suite?”

A hard look returned. “Let’s not go into *that* again, Rose. Please don’t. You know my feelings on all that. My Christian beliefs.”

“Just askin, babe. I didn’t mean a thing.” Rose frowned, then bit his lip. *Don’t screw this up, not at this stage. You’ll screw things in good time...with or without a wedding.* He forced the smile again. “Not to worry, Lori. You know my feelings just as well. Whatever my bride-to-be wants, she gets.” For a brief moment, a jumble of emotions twisted inside him. He reflected on how his own parents’ divorce and his mother’s angry absence had left him equally angry and with an empty void waiting to be filled by just the right woman. One hand reached out and closed again on her elbow. He stepped closer.

Lori’s eyes grew narrow. “Oh, the tea is still boiling.” She rushed off.

His frown returned.

Glancing in the direction of the hallway, Lori called out. “What’s that, Ralph? Oh, I’m sorry. You’d like some, too? I should have offered." Hammering ice cubes into a tall glass, she poured brown tea over them and stalked off to Ralph's room. She returned empty-handed and resumed her place on the couch beside Rose.

She sighed. "July 3rd it is. I confirmed it yesterday with Mr. Patel."

He smiled halfway. "That's good, Lori. I'm glad. A small ceremony, just like we agreed. In and out. My Dad really likes you. He'll record the marriage certificate himself that very day."

She nodded, more tears appearing.

They both stood. He took her hand and fondled it. "Aren't you happy, Lori?"

No response—just tears. Then she nodded.

"Do you believe when I say I will take care of you?"

Another pause. She nodded again.

"Believe it, babe."

He got up and walked to the door. Hesitating, he turned. "Oh, and Lori. By the way...I don't want to see Sam Trencher anywhere near you. Or me. Or at the wedding. In fact, the sooner he leaves Okwalla, the better for everyone...and *especially* for him."

The door closed shut behind Rose and his steps sounded down the front stair. Moments later the engine of his Lexus growled, and Rose lanced down the street and out of sight.

Back in the house, instead of abating, the tears flowed stronger. For a full minute Lori Drumond sat sobbing on *her* couch in *her* clothes, looking at *her* furniture. She stood. Walking slowly into the hallway, she drifted its length, noting its emptiness and arrived at Ralph's door. The door swung open to reveal an empty room and a full glass of iced tea resting on a table.

CHAPTER 13

"There are two kinds of people in this world, Brant. People who have no kids. And people who *wish* they had none." Though he seemed to address Officer Brant, Judge Alexander stood staring daggers at his tall son Rose, his usually dignified eyes about to pop and explode. The judge's hands clenched then unclenched. With a sudden move, the Judge banged his fists on the shiny expensive wood paneling that lined the wall of his office.

Officer Brant stepped back to avoid the hammering. Almost as an afterthought, he clasped the ornate doorknob and pulled the thick door the remaining half-inch. It shut with a soft thud. Brant flipped the heavy bolt lock into place to prevent any accidental intrusions into Judge Alexander's private chambers when he was in one of his moods.

The Judge turned and looked again at his son. Rose stood sheepishly, hands in pockets, half-hidden beneath his Western jacket's double leather frills. The Judge pointed a finger. "Are you telling me that after all I told you, after all my warnings over the years, that you launched an illegal *drug* business right here in Okwalla? Are you *insane?*"

The way his father gesticulated in the air with his fists reminded Rose of old newsreels of Hitler speeches. He struggled to keep from smiling.

Steve-O whitened. Following Brant's lead, he retreated a step. The middle of a family feud among the

Alexanders was the last place he wanted to be.

The judge continued his rant. “Insurance fraud is one thing. Sharp business practices are another. But those are just white-collar. In the end, they’re just *business. Good* business.” He stepped closer to Rose and shook his hands in the air. “But drugs? That’s nuts. That means the DEA all over this town...all over *my* town. Life sentences, property forfeitures, cash seizures. A lifetime of effort, *my* effort, down the drain.” The Judge’s face turned several shades of red.

Finally, he calmed. He collapsed in the sagging hidebound armchair behind his desk and stared at his visitors with a mixture of anger, resignation, and the kind of fatigue that sneaks in the back door with the passing of too many birthdays.

At length he looked up, like a boxer down for nine. “Okay. What’s the story, Rose? And I mean the *full* story.”

Rose and Brant exchanged brief glances.

Rose spoke. “We brought it in from Reynosa in a commercial truck. It wasn’t going to stay in Okwalla...only long enough to unload it in a warehouse and send it on to Denver. But before we had a chance to unload...it was busted.” Rose spoke directly, calmly.

Brant interrupted. “Your Honor, I heard about the bust just before it went down. I managed to get out a phone call in time and made sure that I was on the team. Everyone involved got the message...so nothing happened. Over my objections, that bitch Officer Marla searched the truck. Luckily, she didn’t find the stuff.”

“That’s right, Dad. Officer Brant saved our ass...er, saved the day, I mean.”

Dropping a tired gaze on Brant, the judge nodded. “Thank you, Brant. I can’t express my appreciation enough for what you’ve done for me.” He looked back at Rose. “Some situations, however, don’t improve with age." He glared. Tapped a finger on his desk. "So, what the hell do you expect *me* to do about it?"

Rose smiled broadly. "Get the truck released. The back-room released Steve's Escalade already, but the truck is still in the impound lot. They said City Hall has an interest. I'm very concerned, Dad, that if Officer Marla goes back and searches it again, she'll find the stuff, and..." Worry transformed his face. "And Steve and I...and maybe Officer Brant too...will be in trouble."

Alexander snorted. "*Trouble?* Boy, have you got that right. In this day and age, you don't want even a wrong name on a goddam prescription bottle. To fix things like that, you need to go a lot higher than a municipal judge holding court in Jerkwater, USA."

A subtle exchange of glances again, this time between Rose and Steve.

"So, can you get the truck released?"

The judge steepled his fingers in the superficial manner that a lawyer's instructional course had once advised him to do to intimidate people, a manner which had now become habit. He thought. Nodded. "Jackie owes me a favor...in a way. Between the mayor and me I think we can get your truck back on the street by 5 p.m." He chiseled his glare. "And you better get it the *fuck* out of Okwalla by *midnight.*" He emphasized his order with a shout.

Rose broke into a grin.

A sigh of relief came from Brant, who stared at Steve. Steve's hands rubbed one upon the other, then were thrust into his back pockets. The revelation that his own car had also been searched did not fill him with confidence.

"What about this Officer Marla, Brant? This isn't the first time she's crossed us."

Brant frowned. "No, sir. She's been jumpin in

where she's not welcome ever since she came here. Always askin questions. It seems she never misses a chance to second-guess me in front of the department."

"That's personal. This is business."

"But with her, business *is* personal, sir. When it comes to departmental matters, she..." Brant glanced at Rose and Steve, "well, she just doesn't *play ball.*"

Lips rippling, the judge rubbed one cheek. "You mean little matters like the Dead District... She sounds like a goddam problem. Okwalla is *our* town...*my* town. I don't like anything or anyone who gets in the way of the Grand Plan." He looked up at Brant with that look that always seemed to be looking down on one. "Still, we don't want to take any chances. The law is still the law. She's a jealous mistress but you can't divorce her any more than you can your own wife...when there's children involved." His eyes stabbed at Rose again, who directed a hard look at his palms.

Rose spoke up. "And there's the little problem with...Sam Trencher."

Puzzlement crept over the judge.

Eyes narrowing as if about to release a concern that had gnawed at him for some time, Rose put his hands on his hips. "The little firebug. You remember..."

Judge Alexander flicked his fingers in way of extracting an old memory, while Steve looked at his shoes, trying to look smaller than he was. "That old man," the Judge said, "whose house burned way back. The Army..."

"I put the kid in the Army after we caught him with drugs," Brant said. "But now he's back."

"And he's seein my girl," Rose interjected.

"You mean that sweet little darlin who you promised to marry?"

"Yeah. Lori. The little bastard won't leave her alone. Last time I saw her, he even left her crying." Rose stared bug-eyed. "Just like he did that time with *Josey.*"

Now the Judge narrowed his eyes. "After Josey got married and left town, I thought I had nothing left. I've been hoping that sweet little Lori will one day take my daughter's place...and settle you down. Now you say somebody's makin *her* cry?"

"Maybe more, Daddy dear. Maybe more."

The judge blinked.

Rose stepped forward. "We want your permission to—" Rose and Brant locked glances again, "*discourage* him. Strongly."

"Officers like Marla are one thing, that's a clear No. But some punk kid interfering in my family affairs? That's something completely different." The hard look returned. "It would be just too bad if this Sam Trencher had a problem with the law while he stayed here in Okwalla." He glanced at Brant. "A *serious* problem. Wouldn't it, Officer Brant?"

A steely look took hold of Brant while Steve's eyebrows arched. Rose's smile grew broader, reaching ear to ear. "Yes, sir, Your Honor. It would be just too too bad for one young punk named Sam."

At a nod from the judge, Brant snapped open the deadbolt to the chamber and swung the large door wide, and Rose and Steve happily strode out.

After they had gone, the judge shut the door and turned toward Brant.

"Time to put on your fireman's hat. Is your report ready?"

Brant nodded, expressionless. From a briefcase, he extracted a card-bound batch of white papers, with *Fire Incident Report* stenciled across the top. He recited aloud.

"Ferguson's warehouse had bad wiring. It's a common problem. No way was there arson involved."

The judge nodded. Placing the report on the Judge's desk, Brant exited, shutting the door behind him.

With a broad smile, Judge Alexander carefully read the report. He signed it. Putting it aside, he turned over a stapled stack of papers and read the lettering at the top: *Last Will and Testament*. He signed it too. Sliding the will inside his desk, he stood, opened the thick door, and carefully avoiding the company of his favorite policeman where the public might see them together, walked to lunch alone.

***

Ralph's thick shirt and mountain gloves served their purpose, protecting his skin from projections in the stone. Crawling forward on hands and forearms, he soon reached the end of the slab. Away stretched the forested valley to the far side of the next ridge, and for a moment Ralph chilled, unable to make out anything that he expected, that he needed to find. His eyes lit on a teepee-shaped dome, viewed from above, located just below the edge of the brown slab of stone. A quick stab from his crush-proof flashlight jammed into the V of his shirt proved this was correct and further revealed a circular opening in the top of the teepee, with regularly shaped pockets descending within.

Reversing his body, he slowly negotiated the slab until he rested on the very top of the teepee. He gazed into the dark interior. The Round House. When he was younger, it was just a word. A challenge to his bravery before girls and an emptiness waiting to be filled by whatever his child's imagination could conjure. Now he was an adult, and the words took on menacing significance. Now his imagination had no limits, his fear no bounds. Did he dare enter?

He dared not.

By his side someone had left a rope. One stained

and dusty end had been tied around a rocky protuberance while the other descended into the bowels of the teepee, offering a means of ingress that would surely be more certain than a mad clinging to the quickly darkening walls.

Ralph tested it.

It held.

Without another pause, he swung himself over the edge and lowered himself, the light eerily cutting a downward spiral as the rope untwisted, its bright round scope illuminating the expanding interior one spiral at a time.

He could see the floor, more items strewn testifying to prior visits by...similar pilgrims? Somehow Ralph doubted that any one of them could be remotely similar to him. That was his curse. He was always unique. And this was why he was resolved to go forward. But for the rope he was grateful—and more, upon spying a series of deep handholds dug into the sides of the pueblo which the flashlight illuminated. Who knew what the future might hold for one such as he, what his future needs might be?

From somewhere a low moan drifted and he paused in his descent, his rough gloves clinging to the rope like velcro, his muscular shoulders rippling, flashlight tracing its ghostly spiral. Sweat beaded on his forehead. This was a lot even for Brando. He coughed.

With a snap, the rope broke.

He seemed to tumble forever, but in fact instantly touched the live stone floor of the teepee, the impact raising a flurry of dust and a cloud of tangled wings disturbed by the sound. For a full minute he grimaced as a tsunami of pain washed over him from his childlike legs, while a torrent of bats, pouring from some unseen source, whirred about his head to erupt violently out the aperture into the black night above.

The torrent and the tsunami passed. Cautiously he extended both hands and delicately touched his legs and feet to ascertain whether anything had broken. To his relief he found he could still wiggle his toes and concluded that everything was intact. He blew a breath. Thank god the fall had not harmed his arms or his hands.

Mounting on one elbow, he used his free hand to aim the light. He paused. On either side of a darker aperture in a side wall of the pueblo, with a layer of broken brick showing that a portion of the wall had collapsed at some distant time, crude stick-figures had been roughly drawn on the walls. Men in animal hides, some with bows that unleashed stick arrows at meandering deer and buffalo. A few with exaggeratedly large eyes seemed to stand alone, staring upward in the midst of more sticks, vertical lines extending from their heads. A pyramid of stones stood near them.

What could it mean?

Another wave of pain from his emaciated legs distracted him. After it passed, his eyes finally turned to the aperture leading to the next cave. He clenched his jaw; he had business to tend to.

Congratulating himself for his foresight in wrapping himself in thick clothing appropriate for blunting sharp rocks, he inserted the flashlight in the tight V of his shirt and crawled forward, moving quickly over the detritus of brickwork,.

He arrived at a second cave.

A sleeve ripped and he paused again. Withdrawing the flashlight, he flashed it over the walls. The figures, before merely the work of children's crayons, here took on the detail of a consummate artist. The animal hide was clearly buffalo. The stick figures became pueblo Indians, with feathers and blue-dyed cloth caftans. More disturbing, the cartoons standing on sticks were now clearly Indians standing in piles of bones, surrounded by mysterious creatures with huge eyes that stared and aimed skyward, mouths open as if reciting some esoteric formula over the burning of a sacrifice. Peering more closely, he perceived that, while the sacrifices had hair that stood straight up as if from the effects of the flames, the anatomy topping the creatures' heads was hair-like, but *not* hair, rather something similar, though it too seemed to be mostly erect, or perhaps wriggled like an upended mop with gravity in reverse.

His pain and gritty determination distracting him again, Ralph drained his first bottle of water and popped the cap back on. Reaching forward, the other sleeve ripped. The flashlight tipped out. The constant crawling was mangling his shirt so the V would no longer contain it. Placing the flashlight into a cargo pants pocket, he resumed his painful crawling.

The next dark aperture beckoned.

Twenty feet on, the way seemed suddenly to ease. As if carved and smoothed to welcome visitors to the Mystery Pueblo, the path here opened wider and down, descending farther into the depths. Ralph breathed deep. Not so much from the exertion, which was difficult enough, but from fear. If he had had any notion of surviving his adventure, he knew that such was no longer possible. Without food and many days of rest, his strength could never recover sufficiently to return to civilization unaided, even if he could somehow replace the broken rope. He flicked the flashlight over more figures engaged in mysterious rituals.

At length, just as his strength seemed at last to ebb, and plunge him into despair, with his last bottle of water almost drained, cuts and scrapes on his exposed arms left a growing trail of blood on the rocky path behind, mixed with bat guano. The way halted between two high stalagmites and he peered over a deep crevasse, the result apparently of some ancient quake. A luminescent glow emanated from its depths, washing the roof of live stalactites with its flickering rays, bright minerals twinkling in the high ceiling in imitation of the real stars above.

He rubbed his eyes. Stung from sweat and blood, he used the last drops of water to wash his eyes clean so he could view the final wonder—or doom—whichever the fates had ordained.

The low moaning returned. From somewhere it cycled louder, then softer, then louder again, more of a muffled hum, now that he was closer to the source.

Sitting up, he let his skeleton legs droop over the edge of the crevasse as he rested, and he rubbed them again. What was the hour in the greater world outside? How long had he crawled? Who could say whether the passage of time in this world of eternal shadow was the same as outside in the realm of a healthy yellow sun?

He found himself mumbling what he had heard from Sam, from the mouth of the only soul in the Universe who had ever accomplished what he craved: *rescue* from the private hell that Providence had plunged him into. If he were to be buried alive, let it be here. *This* was his world. The phrase repeated itself in his mind: *Before Charlie kissed the Midnight Sun, I could hardly walk. Now, I have dancing shoes...*"

The hum strengthened. In time with his mumbling, the lights from the crevasse seemed to dart forth like sprites to play eagerly across the jagged roof, translucent wings fluttering across the rocky cavern to settle on Ralph's pale awe-struck visage, the ceiling now alive with sparkles. The sparkles outshining his flashlight, he flicked it off.

He swallowed.

The Sun emerged. Spinning slowly in imitation of the Earth, purple and violet hues giving rise to eruptions from its surface like sunspots, the ejections of ions spraying out to bathe the cavern in their essence. At length the black globe entirely cleared the cusp where the fractured floor would meet and revolved with measured calm. The stone of the floor crackled white as The Glow crept forward from its base. It crawled across the stone to embrace him in its fold.

Opening his mouth wider, Ralph gripped the handholds and lowered himself to the rocky floor just below the crackling sphere.

"I'm here. I want this. Give me what I came for." He was shouting, not so much at the Sun, but in the maw of an uncaring Providence.

With a final effort, his tattooed arms rippled in their last ounce of strength and inched him bloodily across the raw granite to the edge of the deeper source of the sphere. At the edge, he halted. White leprous patches appeared on his arms. The surface of the globe revolved inches from his face; its hum grew to a deafening whine. He pressed his lips against it...

CHAPTER 14

The judge walked past his office on Main Street without glancing at the pale stencils on the glass that read *Rose E. Alexander, Sr., P.C.* Rarely used, it served primarily as headquarters for his reelection campaigns—and for insurance in case he ever lost. He smiled at the double entendre implied by *insurance.* He kept walking to the smart little Chinese bistro with the tasty take-out that had recently opened on the next block.

Inside the law office, the blank white rear door resounded a knock. A hand swung the metal door to reveal a man in plaid shirt and freshly scrubbed but still soiled green vest. On his head rested a white cap, *Duval St.* sewn on the front in black letters.

"Zavalo." Rose welcomed him. "Glad you could make it. Park your ass over here."

Steve held the door while green vest entered, then shot the iron bolt so no one else could enter his father's Main Street law office without a key.

"Sorry about the detour, amigo." Rose's jacket fringes dangled while he directed Zavalo to the luxurious leather furniture that filled his father's office, ignoring the thick layer of dust.

Steve slid open opposite panels on a cabinet to expose a cornucopia of liquor. "Whatcha want? Whatever you fancy, we got."

Zavalo pointed an oil-stained finger at a Cuervo and soon was sipping it on ice. He sat on the edge of an armchair. Rose and Steve watched closely, reading each other's moods as much as their visitor's.

"That was indeed a little...inconvenient." Zavalo spoke with a slight trace of Mexican accent, his English almost perfect. Rose noted Zavalo's smooth-shaven pale skin, remembered his Anglo settler ancestry in the mountains of Durango, making him as much at home in the U.S. as in Mexico.

"How was Florida?"

"Miami responded, as you said they would. They are just as interested in your laundering idea as my partners in Reynosa. They can send the items through Key West, using a cruise line."

Rose nodded. "Good. Good."

"I noticed an Escalade parked in back." Zavalo looked inquiringly at Steve.

Steve opened his mouth, was silenced by a quick glance from Rose.

Rose blinked. "Here's the dope, Zavalo. *First*, thanks for delivering the product from Reynosa—"

"My partners..." Zavalo interrupted and Rose halted in mid-sentence, "want to know the status of the facilities you promised them, Señor Alexander. And when you will have the next batch ready?"

Rose nodded. "The facility is fine, Zavalo. A little rough launching it, but now it's blowin and goin. Now that you made your delivery, the next batch is in the pipeline and will be ready in two weeks. That was *Second*." He sucked a breath. "*Third*, as soon as you dropped off your merchandise at the Motel, I arranged a little circus at the Okwalla police department. Sorry we didn't have time to fill you in, amigo, but we wanted you to have—uh, *plausible deniability* I think is the phrase—when the police picked you up."

A frown settled on Zavalo.

"You see, we've had a little problem converting the

entire police department in Okwalla over to our way of thinking, so we had to come up with a way to separate the good guys from the bad."

Zavalo continued his calm stare.

"Therefore it was I who called the police." Rose glanced once at Steve. "Just before I sent you there to meet my guys...I turned in my own warehouse."

Steve's eyebrows crawled up as he turned a surprised gaze at Rose, then glanced nervously back at Zavalo.

Rose continued. "I knew that since you had already dropped off your shipment, the police would find nothing in your truck, so you were in no danger, my friend. Now that they've searched your truck, the entire police department knows that Vaya Gonzalez trucks are clean. You're above suspicion now and will have no more problems when you return to Okwalla. In fact, your truck is being vacuumed and cleaned right now, courtesy of the police department, and will be released by five p.m. I even sent two guys in Steve's Escalade pretending to be me and Steve, just to help smoke out the true blues. In fact, I had a heck of a time making sure your truck *was* searched. That's how good my protection is." Rose glanced at Steve, whose eyes alternated confusion and admiration. "It worked. We've been takin names...and we're almost ready to start kickin ass—with the assistance of Okwalla's finest."

Zavalo began to smile. He sucked another drink. "So Okwalla will become like Reynosa. No more hiding like little children."

"*Almost*, amigo." Rose leaned forward in his chair. "But there's still the matter of kickin ass." He paused, glanced at Steve. "We have a little favor to ask."

Zavalo arched his brows and leaned back to listen.

"Look out the window. You see a place across the

street called Bronco Grill?"

Zavalo peered through the wide glass windows of the Alexander law office to the Grill across four lanes of road.

"In a half hour a young punk will park his car in front of the Grill and saunter into the place like he owns it." Rose's voice grew taut. "This guy has been in town only a few days and has already gotten too close to our operation. He's been asking questions...lots of questions. In the wrong places."

Zavalo looked back at Rose.

"We've arranged, with the full cooperation of the top people in Okwalla, to give this punk a one-way ticket to Hell. No stamps; no refunds. He's a loner with no family and no allies. He won't be missed, and no questions will be asked." He crooked his neck. "All we need is someone to put some heroin behind his seat, and a pistol on the floorboard."

"And then?"

"Okwalla's best will do the rest." Rose smiled at Steve. "No more young punk asking questions. And now that we took names at the warehouse, no more *true blues* either...if you get my drift. One hundred percent *conversion*."

Impressed, Zavalo slowly nodded. "Reynosa right here in your very own...fast-growing metropolis." He smirked.

Rose did not react. "Small, boring, and below radar...just the way we like it."

"Why me, my friend? I know good help is hard to find, but don't you have any trustworthy rancheros here in Okwalla?" His glance wandered to Steve.

Steve turned pale.

Shaking his head, Rose leaned forward again. "No can do. My people will be recognized. They live here. You're a stranger. No one will recognize you if you approach a car in daylight. Besides, from what we've heard about your...accomplishments in Reynosa, you're the man for the job."

A half-smile settled on Zavalo's face. "They weren't as many as you heard..."

Rose and Steve listened attentively.

"They were *more.*" Zavalo grinned and gulped his drink. "It is actually not so hard to convert semi-automatic assault guns to fully automatic, if you try. Give me your gun. This little job is playtime for children."

"You'll need these." Rose stood and reached behind a desk. "Slacks, blue blazer, blue cap. You'll dress like Okwalla's parking attendant. You even look like him. I got an official ticket pad for you. Everyone will think it's just our traffic cop *Al* writing another ticket. There's never enough parking on Main Street at lunch hour."

Zavalo was nodding. The prospect of achieving complete immunity from local law enforcement was worth a moment of risk. His partners in Reynosa would be pleased, and a little fun a welcome relief.

Rose glanced across the street again. The sun was climbing. He opened a box and pulled out a brown wrapped parcel and a small black plastic cylindrical container with a tan topper.

"A hot Smith & Wesson .38 straight from police impoundment, and one ounce of heroin. Times a-wastin. The sooner this pistol appears on the floorboard of a certain beat-up blue Oldsmobile, and the sooner this container is dropped in the back seat, the better."

Zavalo stared across the street. "I don't see no Oldsmobile—"

"He'll be here before the lunch crowd arrives. Soon. When he goes inside, use this jimmy to pop the lock. Put the dope behind the seat, lay the gun on the floor, shut the car door, then walk back here to us. I'll let you in. You'll change clothes again, go out the back door, and take Steve's Escalade. The keys are in it. We'll meet you at HQ after the cops take the punk down."

Zavalo nodded again.

"As soon as the crowd sees that the cops found a pistol, he'll come out of the Grill. That's when the SWAT team will arrive with an APB that this punk is armed and dangerous...and the shooting will begin. Not too much, but just enough."

Zavalo stood. Discarding his work clothes, he put on the new outfit. He took up the pad and flipped the pages, pencil poised.

Rose and Steve whistled at the illusion.

Withdrawing the pistol from its wrapper, Zavalo spun the chamber. He play-aimed at Steve, who turned whiter. Returning the gun to its wrapper, Zavalo stepped to the door. Steve's heart resumed beating.

The three stood and stared, Zavalo's pad poised as if nothing were more urgent than an imminent excursion to a theater.

The sun climbed farther.

Steve rubbed his eyes, his confidence ebbing inverse with the growing heat that distorted the air over the pavement visible through the law office's front window. In truth he had become more eager to get Zavalo out the door than he was to finish off Trencher.

"Huh. How do you like that?"

"What, Steve-O?"

"Little Ralphie's wheelchair is back. By your front door. I can see those little arrows on the metal arm."

A blue gleam flashed.

"I see something."

At the end of the block a sequin-blue car hood turned the corner to enter Main Street, sparkling in the almost-noon sunlight, not a cloud to block the growing harshness of the suns' rays. The parking spaces angled on the far side of the street were filling with cars in anticipation of a crowd queueing for lunch at the Bronco. For now, the few spaces in front of the Alexander law office remained empty, shaded by two large oaks.

Slowing to a crawl, as if hyper careful of a collision, the blue car blocked traffic, cars backing up behind it. Sharp honks resounded.

"Is it—"

"Yeah…an Oldsmobile. With a blue hood."

Zavalo adjusted his pants-belt and cap. Fingering the paper-wrapped gun and container of heroin, he produced sunglasses and put them on. A hand wandered inside the blazer to adjust a hidden object.

"He's pulling into a space," Steve said.

"But is it him?" Rose blurted.

Across the street, the Oldsmobile backed up, pulled forward, paused. Backed up again. More honks sounded from blocked traffic.

"What the hell's he doin?"

"I told you, faggot. The creep's a fuckin looney. Can you imagine that looney tryin to stick it to my girl?"

The car pulled forward, precisely between the white lines, and finally lurched to a stop. The engine quieted. Inside, a figure squirmed as if seeking the exact center of invisible lines inside the vehicle while parked in the exact center of the visible lines outside. After what seemed an interminable stretch of time, the door squeaked open.

Rose, Steve, and Zavalo squinted, their hands shielding their eyes.

"It's him. I see his tan zipper jacket."

Zavalo put his hand on the office doorknob.

Slam. The muffled noise drifted across four lanes

of traffic as the car door shut.

Zavolo paused.

"What's he doin? What the hell is he doin now?" Steve stared, mouth still open.

Sam had paused. Standing on one painted white line he stood bathed in sunlight, his face raised upward to stare into the great yellow orb, no hint of discomfort from its rays. Gently he raised his arms and began to turn, revolving in place.

"Now what? What the hell's he up to? He came for lunch. Why the fuck doesn't he go inside and get it?"

Sam's arms fluttered as if enveloped in a cloud of flying gossamer objects that no one could see but him. Abruptly, his arms lowered and he plunged his hands into his pockets where they shifted to explore the contents. His hands switched to the back pockets, then to his jacket pockets, then again to his front pants pockets.

"What the hell does he need a jacket for anyway, Rose? It's fuckin hot as hell outside."

Rose shrugged. "Who the hell knows? He's a fucked-up looney, Steve-O. What did I tell you?"

Keeping to one white line, Sam turned his back to the Alexander law office and walked to the Grill's front sidewalk. At the front door of the Grill, he paused yet again, turning to stare at the spot on the sidewalk beside the Grill's door where Ralph's wheelchair had always sat, now missing. One hand on the Grill's swinging door, Sam slowly turned and gazed across the street to gaze at the Alexander P.C. law office where his eyes settled on Ralph's wheelchair resting under an oak tree. Sam sniffed the air; his gaze dropped. Without a word, he placed both hands on the Grill's door handle and entered, his eyes inspecting the ground while he walked in as if the entry were strewn with mines.

Rose and Steve let out a breath.

"Now."

Zavalo swung open the glass door to the law office and stepped out. The blocked cars had found parking, or had gone. Traffic was still light and Zavalo had no issue jaywalking over all four lanes until he came up beside Sam's Oldsmobile.

Several parking spaces remained unfilled—the traffic picked up again. One car pulled in. Then another.

Extracting the jimmy from his blazer, Zavalo calmly slid it in the door window of Sam's Oldsmobile via its top edge. He paused. He smiled back across the street at Rose and Steve. The car door popped open by its handle—Sam had not locked it. With a quick toss, Zavalo dropped the film container behind the seat, and in another smooth movement, deposited the brown wrapped gun on the floorboard and slid it under the driver's seat.

So far, so good.

"Hi, Al." An elderly couple strolled by and waved.

Behind the sunglasses, Zavalo smiled and tipped his hat. Quietly, he shut Sam's door. Turning on a heel, he circumnavigated the tail end of a newly parked Taurus and stepped into the street.

"Hey! Well, ain't that just like damned City Hall. They give me a helper and don't say a damn word to me about it."

Zavalo stopped.

An officer in blue cap, blazer, and sunglasses stood ten feet away, facing Zavalo, ticket pad in hand. "What's your name, brother? When did they start you in this burg?"

Zavalo withdrew an object from inside his blazer.

"Yessir." Inside the law office, Rose spoke into his cell phone. "I'd like to report a guy inside Bronco Grill. He's crazy. He's got a gun in his car and I'm afraid he's going to shoot someone. No, you don't need my name, I'm just a citizen doing a public serv—"

"*What the hell?!*" Steve yelled.

Rose looked up in time to see one twin in blue blazer and cap aim a pistol at a second twin in blue blazer and cap, and the barrel flash. A muffled pop penetrated the windows. The second twin collapsed between a Taurus and an adjacent parked car. Dropping his gun on the pavement, Zavalo strode across the four lanes to the law office as nonchalantly as if he had just bought an ice cream.

Steve retreated into the office, his face turned to talcum.

Rose snatched up the green vest, jeans, and plaid shirt. Cracking the front door, he swung it wide as Zavalo sauntered in. Rose said nothing; his hands shook as he handed the clothes to the gangster.

"What the *hell?*" Steve yelled. "You shot Al. You shot the parking cop."

Rose leveled a glare at his comrade.

For once, the glare failed. "What the hell are we gonna do now?" Steve shouted. "You shot a fucking cop...in broad daylight."

Zavalo took off the uniform and quickly but calmly redressed in his street clothes, while the sound of sirens grew. When he was done, he looked up and smiled. "Now your *metropolis* is *exactly* like Reynosa."

Rose rubbed his fingers and thumbs together, his brain racing to catch up.

Zavalo shrugged. "Don't worry, *infantes*. It is almost Fourth of July. No one cares about a little firecracker. Anyway, gringos, I will have more questions from my partners about your operation when we meet later at your *HQ*." Zavalo grinned and headed for the back door. "You did not forget the Escalade's key?" He shook his head, still smiling. At the office back door he paused, hand on the knob. He looked back. "My friends. It is time for you boys to grow up. No more play time for children. If you want to be men...you must learn to pull the trigger." He laughed and took a deep satisfied breath. "I like it here. I feel more at home than ever."

A hand appeared from outside. Gripping the metal door, the hand flung it wide, throwing a flood of high noon into the office.

"Nnnnngh!"

Zavalo stared up. Six inches from his face glared the eyes of a large man—or the form of one. For a moment Zavalo peered blankly, uncomprehending. A mottled oval framed the man's eyes, pitted with purple and violet streaks that seemed to infect a diseased landscape of flesh, while beneath whistled a mouth round like an open sphincter with lockjaw.

Zavalo's face tightened. He grimaced. His retinas registered reflections of strangely thickened hair that rippled like wriggling strings and crackled, emitting sequins of light.

Stiffly, Zavalo backed a step. He staggered. Righted himself.

The thing burrowed from the scorching sunlight, sparks spitting from head and neck. Two arms knotted with tattooed muscles spread wide, and it strode with cocksure intent on rock-hard calves that ended in dirtied blue suede shoes.

"Burns! *BURNS!*"

A hand seized Zavalo's neck. For a moment he struggled—the other hand joined its mate, and the gangster's feet left the floor as he was lifted easily into the air.

Instinctively, Zavalo's hands clutched those of his assailant, only to flare purple. His eyes jerked toward Rose and Steve. "Heeelp meee," he hissed.

The pair were nailed in place, jaws open.

A louder hiss sounded and Zavalo's neck and head began to mottle brown, followed by purple, violet, pink. Yellow flame and gray smoke erupted, ripping tears in his darkening skin. A strangled yell escaped his throat. His hair stood on end throwing off sparks in time with the intruder's.

The thing dropped Zavalo and stepped back. Leaning to slam the door shut behind him, the intruder breathed deep in relief as if savoring an orgasm. Zavalo jerked from side to side and beat his neck and face as Steve and Rose jumped back. The flames accelerated.

"Aaaaaaaaaah!"

Zzzzzavalo exploded into flame from head and shoulders down. Staggering over couches and desks, he threw himself round the room in a frenzy until collapsing in the middle of the office, spraying embers and burnt flesh in a gruesome mess on the floor at his hosts' feet. A gray haze flooded the ceiling, hiding the white gypsum tile.

Still nailed in place, Steve and Rose finally jerked free.

"Now *that's* a rush." The mottled and burned flesh split in two and curled into a grimacing smile. The intruder took another deep breath. "Who could have guessed?" it rasped. A bloodshot eye peeked out of the still writhing mop of string that surmounted his head. He spoke with difficulty, a dog-like growl escaping. "You really gotta put this on your menu, Rose... You got nothin on this stuff... All you got is shit on a shingle compared to what I got in *MY GOD-DAMN FUCKING VEINS!*" Tautly muscled biceps erupted as he flexed both massive arms like a weightlifter.

Rose peered at the caricature of his former acquaintance. "Ra-Ralphie?"

"Yeah, *mon capitan*. Little Ralphie. Come back to

see his old friend. To give him a kiss...the same as Little Ralphie got not more'n a few hours ago. Give you a touch of the wild blue heaven...the deep dark yonder." The mottling seemed to pale as Ralph spoke; the smoke abated, and the weird writhing of his hair calmed into straight vertical upthrusts, sparks glittering above. "Whadaya know? Gettin kind of cold in here now. Now that I shot my bolt...gave a light to a scarecrow... fingered the freak show of death."

Steve and Rose exchanged glances, faces corpse-white.

"What ha-happened, Ralphie?"

"Oh, now that's a damned long story. A long sad tale full of sound and fury that's way too long to tell to Tweedledee and Tweedledum." Ralph reached down and rubbed his legs. The bulging muscles stood out like a drum, tight and massive. He leaned forward on one leg to stretch a calf in one and quadricep in the other; they emitted a ripped sound like cloth tearing and Ralph grinned. "Is that the sound of music? Or the music of the spheres?" He looked wildly above him and chuckled. "Or could it be the music of Even Steven and Readie Eddie...soon to be guests in Little Ralphie's *Funland*...where no one goes away cold and hungry. And everyone gets their *just desserts*."

His hair began snaking again and the sparks rose from the depths like a shower of stars as the energy returned. His biceps and quads bulged as the skin turned a darker shade of brown, violet and purple streaking across their surface, leaving red valleys behind.

He panted. "Let's see how far you can run, *jackos*, when I've turned your legs to mush."

"Now-now, Ralphie, you know we can do something about this." Rose maneuvered behind the desk. "I've got lots of stuff that I know you like..." Rose dove and resurfaced clutching an old-fashioned hunting shotgun. Rose attempted to load two red cartridges in the barrel, but, hands shaking, dropped the cartridges to the floor.

Ralph grinned and advanced, arms outstretched, yellow licks erupting from his head. "Little Ralphie wants to play. He has ten years of catching up to do."

"You're not well, Ralphie," Steve stammered. "Look at you. You're sick. We can call Doc Henry and get him down—"

"Ha haaa ha ha!" A smoking arm swung at Steve, who dodged and bolted behind Rose. "If you think Doc Henry can do any good for your *crispy fried friend on the floor.*"

The other arm swung at Rose's leg—missed.

Rose scooped up the cartridges and crabbed to one side, trying to gain the street door, while Steve kept himself behind Rose, showing an unexpected agility in keeping Rose between him and Ralph.

Visible through the glass office windows, Sam calmly exited the Bronco Grill and approached his car.

A key turned in the door to the law office. The glass door opened. Inside, three heads turned. A suit walked in off the street, one ear cocked to the approaching sirens.

"Rose, I've got another bone to pick with you." Judge Alexander stopped short as the door clicked shut behind him. "And what the hell...happened...here?" The judge's voice trailed to a whisper. He peered at the tall figure spitting yellow and orange flames.

Dashing for the door, Steve pushed the judge aside, thrusting him farther into the room. Rose leaped close behind, and using both hands, shoved his father directly at Ralph. Rose and Steve flung the door wide, and in their panic to escape, stumbled together at the threshold.

The oval landscape split into another grin. "Howdy, Judge. Welcome to Little Ralphie's Theme Park."

The gnarled hands closed on the Judge's shoulders. Lifted from the floor as easily as Zavalo, Judge Alexander exploded into a maelstrom of flame like a Fourth of July fizzler, his sparse hair springing up like steel wire, sparks and lisping torrents of purple and orange twisting about his shoulders and head. His hair twisted while purple and violet streaks jetted down his torso. His tie burst in a red glow and evaporated in smoke.

Ralph threw aside what was left of the judge. Not pausing to watch the judge's death throes, Ralph strode out the door, the touch of his hand scorching the handle. On the sidewalk in front of the office, Ralphie leaped after Rose and Steve.

Unable to outrun him, they turned. Rose again tried to thrust the stubborn cartridges into the shotgun, his gold finger rings rattling against the barrel while Steve took refuge behind Ralph's wheelchair and spun it to keep the chair between him and Ralph.

"Ha haa ha ha! Hey, Steve-O. *This Sterno's for you!*"

The shotgun clicked shut.

Ralph turned to look.

The shotgun aimed.

Burped.

The echo of the blast melted into the oak trees as the force of the pellets propelled Ralph backwards into the wheelchair, and the wheelchair rolled backwards into the street.

Inside his car, Sam guided his Oldsmobile out of the angled parking space and turned the wheel counter-clockwise. He had not seen.

A loud clang shook the car.

Inundated by deafening sirens, Sam emerged from his car to see Officer Brant, Marla, and several other police erupt from their vehicles and aim their pistols at him from behind opened police car doors, several with black SWAT vests over their blue uniforms.

A megaphone appeared. "Get on the fuckin ground, slimebag. We got your ass now."

Turning behind him to look, Sam's eyebrows lifted in surprise as he glimpsed Ralph's wheelchair crumpled in the middle of Main Street, a body—which could only be Ralph—sprawled on the asphalt, plainly dead, and looking as if viciously run over a dozen times.

Calmly, Sam opened his trunk.

Ignoring the surprised stares of the police, he withdrew from the trunk a collection of brooms and mops. In a few moments, he had arranged the poles in two neat squares, one square around the body of Ralph; the other around himself. While the sirens one by one fell silent, Sam raised his arms and again revolved slowly in place, face uplifted to the sky.

Seconds later, Officer Brant had him face-down on the hot asphalt, handcuffed.

Entering Sam's car, Brant triumphantly paraded a brown-wrapped gun and a plastic tube of heroin before the other police, while Rose and Steve watched from the shade of oak trees, where Sam thought he had seen Ralphie's chair, strangely out of place and draped in red metal, and which he had tried to understand but failed, knowing that what he saw could not be real. Only now, lying prone in the street with his hands cuffed behind, did he notice Ralph's new tan and white van parked under the densely shaded oak trees, clearly real, and two more police dragging a body in blue uniform from behind a car that was parked next to his Oldsmobile, real as death.

"You know what, you goddam punk? You just got fucked in the ass."

His last view before everything went black was Lori standing in front of the Bronco Grill's still-swinging front door, shock and disappointment on her face. Wiping away tears, she ran inside as a downpour of rose petals rained about her.

CHAPTER 15

Counter-clockwise. You turned right, now to make things balance you must turn the steering wheel counter-clockwise. Sam rocked side to side as the police cruiser accelerated down the Main Street of Okwalla, avoiding sniping traffic and parked vehicles. Sam's eyes were closed, and his tongue could feel the imprint of the asphalt on his cheek, able to ID every gritty pebble. He caught his breath and gently blew out his cheeks to assess the damage. He was okay. Relieved that he tasted no blood.

Cautiously he peeked. Maybe he could glimpse his face in the cruiser's front seat mirror.

Blurs.

Gradually his eyes adjusted.

"The little prick has decided to join us." Brant appeared in the cruiser's internal mirror looking back at him. "How do you like that, Officer Marla? This prick sells dope to his own uncle, burns him out, then comes back six years later to do the same damn thing to poor Ralph Drumond. And as if that's not enough, he fuckin runs him over a few times to make sure he can't testify. Can you believe the balls on this guy?" Brant stamped the brake to avoid colliding with a truck, its bed filled with chickens.

Marla angled her head, then straightened it. "We don't know all that yet, Brant." She turned to glance at Sam. "But I gotta admit it doesn't look good for him right now. Once he recovers, we'll see what he has to say."

Sam noted the short clipped black locks on the back of Marla's head. Military style. Or possibly a sign of indeterminate gender. Her hair style suggested blocks, and a black line appeared forming right angles around her head like some mathematician's halo.

Brant snorted. "How much you wanna bet he gets a New York Jew lawyer and clams up. Good luck gettin a word outta him then."

"He's entitled." She shook her head and the squares vanished. "But it sure won't be Judge Alexander."

An ambulance passed the cruiser, having loaded up several bodies under police supervision.

"Maybe he did run over Ralph and shot Al," she continued. "But I haven't seen a car yet that can run over two people inside an office with the doors closed."

Brant stole a brief glance at his partner. "Yeah. That's weird, ain't it?"

Rubbing a palm on one leg of his pants, Brant shifted the mirror away from Sam in the back seat to himself. He glimpsed sweat glistening on his temples and switched the mirror back. He cranked the air conditioning higher.

"Son of a bitch."

Marla looked at Brant who was staring at his hand.

"The little prick is so filthy he left a stain on my palm." He turned his palm up to show a dark patch. He rubbed it again and grunted. "Fuckin age spot? I ain't that goddam old. I got more propane in the tank than a dozen Minit Marts." He stole a sly glance at Marla's uniform-clad breasts, ample despite the layer of blue cloth.

Marla blinked and absentmindedly shifted to face away from Brant as if a long acquaintance with subtle remarks had taught her where they were likely to lead if allowed to escalate.

"I think Dr. Correa is in order in this case," she said. "There's really something wrong with this guy."

The shortness of her hair emphasized the fullness of her figure, but Sam could see only squares and black lines. He wondered, as always when the visions came, what it portended about her.

The car jerked to a stop as traffic backed up.

"Dammitohell." Brant honked. When the chicken truck failed to move, he flicked on the cruiser's siren. In a few moments, the truck edged over, and he sped past. The police station appeared, and he pulled into the down ramp under the station.

Stopping in his assigned space, Brant and Marla stepped out and opened the back doors.

Sam closed his eyes, moaned.

"The bastard had better not have puked in my back seat. I'll fuckin break his head open."

No puke.

Relieved, Brant dragged Sam out. His eyes opened again as the other cruisers parked and expelled more police.

Pushing him against the side of the cruiser, Brant removed his glasses and pointed them, resuming his favorite lecturing pose. For a moment he breathed deeply. The Okwalla heat seemed hotter than usual.

"You wanna tell us why you shot Officer Al? And why you beat Judge Alexander to death in his own office and set his body on fire? Where did you get the heroin, you goddam little punk? The same place you got the goddam shit you gave your own uncle before burning him to a crisp six years ago? What kind of a creep are you?"

Marla stepped closer. "Brant. You know you can't interrogate him without reading him his rights. We gotta book him first."

Brant opened his mouth to speak, then suddenly released his hands from Sam and stared at his palms. The age spot had appeared on the palm of his other hand. He loosened his collar with one finger and looked around, sweat beginning to stream down his neck.

"I need some fuckin AC. What is it, fuckin 120 out here?"

He motioned for a handcuffed Sam to start walking but remained a foot or so away without touching him again. They walked up concrete stairs and passed through two heavy metal doors buzzed open by some invisible console. An open office with several desks appeared behind a waist-high barrier surmounted by a white formica mantle. Lining the opposite end of the main room loomed the vertical steel bars of a small holding cell, and a corridor where more cells resided. While Marla laid out fingerprint forms and an ink pad on the mantle, Brant gingerly unlocked Sam's handcuffs.

Brant strode off, leaving Marla with Sam.

Marla stepped near.

"Excuse me," Sam said, "but you don't want to touch me."

She halted her approach, puzzled.

"I-I have what you might call a disease. If you touch me, you might get it. Like..." he glanced at Brant who stood across the room, washing his hands repeatedly in cold water. "Him." As she watched, Brant dried his hands and stalked to a cold vent where he removed his tie and unbuttoned several shirt buttons of his uniform. His eyes shut as he exposed his face to the cold blast with obvious relief.

Sam shook his head. "It won't help. He's infected."

"So *you* say." But she stepped back.

"Please, it's only contagious if I'm touched. Then..." He shook his head. "I had better do the fingerprints myself. I've done this before. But it's best if absolutely no one touches me...for their own safety."

Quickly Sam stained his fingers, his own temperature rising, the cold ink providing a modicum of relief. He rolled each finger and thumb on both hands in the appropriate places on the cardboard form and quickly wiped off what ink he could on paper towels. He used a spray bottle of alcohol to clean the rest, again welcoming the temporary relief from the evaporation.

"Take off your shoes and belt."

Without a word, Sam complied.

"Empty your pockets."

Sam looked up. "That's also a bad idea."

"You said you know the routine, Mr. Trencher. Now empty your pockets." She tapped the desk.

He shook his head. "That's a *really* bad idea." Spare change jingled as he felt out the same exact amount in each pocket.

"I'll have to put you back in handcuffs if you refuse to comply, Mr. Trencher." The black lines erupted around her head and began to spin a black web composed entirely of right angles.

"Okay, okay. Here." A tinkling of change appeared on the white countertop. He plopped down his wallets, then pulled his pockets inside out.

"I need to check them myself."

Sam stepped back. "I understand, ma'am, that you're devoted to rules and the law. You have lawyer," he glanced at the steadily darkening angular web, "written all over you. There is no need to expose anyone else to my infection, though. Please take a moment to think. Just tell me what you need and I'll do it without anyone having to touch me. Otherwise..." He glanced at Brant leaning over the AC unit.

She hesitated. For a moment she seemed to

consider his comments but finally shook her head. "Brant's right. We'll need a specialist to evaluate you."

Sam shrugged. *Nothing new about that either.*

"Walk that way." She pointed. Several other police paused to stare.

Knowing better than to argue procedure with a policewoman who had the soul of a lawyer, he walked past the holding cell, down a hallway, and into a white-painted room entirely bare of pictures. The thick metal door with a single small square window locked shut behind him.

He sat in one of only two chairs at a table, thankful that they were metal frames that afforded him another small opportunity to cool down.

A camera in one corner of the room briefly moved.

He tapped his fingers on the table. This won't do. Subtly, he slid one hand into his shirt where he unfolded a hem out of sight of the camera to expose a sequence of paper clips sewn roughly into the lining. Eyeing the silent cam, he extracted a half dozen paper clips and placed them in his pockets: two in each front, replacing the coins; one each in back, replacing his wallets. His temperature instantly dropped two degrees.

A half-hour later, a face appeared in the window. A stranger.

A buzzer sounded and the metal door opened.

The stranger entered. Smiling broadly, he swung the other seat around and sat in it backwards, extending a glad hand eager to make contact. A delicate pointed beard was just beginning to gray beneath wire frame glasses and receding frizzled dark hair.

"Hi. I am Dr. Correa." He trilled the R's like a native of Madrid.

Sam inferred an excessive ethnic pride and joined it with the total lack of accent to yield *forensic psychologist with affirmative action resume.* From long habit, Sam unconsciously glanced around as if seeking an escape route. “Nice to meet you, doctor.” His hands remained under the table.

After a pause, Correa’s offered handshake was withdrawn. The *insurance-agent* smile remained. “Well, let’s see now. From what the officers tell me, you’ve had quite an adventure today. You want to tell me what’s been happening?”

Sam fingered the paper clips in his pockets and relaxed a trifle. “Not much.”

Correa twitched his head to one side. “That’s a hell of an understatement. Four people died in a space of five minutes. The worst crime wave this town has ever seen. And it seems you were at the center of it.”

“Nothing to do with me.”

“Surely there is something you can add to help clear up what happened. The police out there will be very disappointed if I leave this room and can’t tell them anything at all.” He peered at Sam. “You don’t *want* to disappoint them, do you?”

Sam pursed his lips. “Cold water.”

“What’s that?”

“Cold water. Glass full of ice.”

“You want water?”

“Yes, please. For me. And for Officer Brant.”

The broad smile returned, indulgent. “For Officer Brant.” Dr. Correa’s eyes opened wide in genuine surprise.

“He’ll need it. Soon.”

The smile grew skeptical. “I think Officer Brant is capable of getting himself his own drink of water. Don’t you think so?”

“Not today. Not in this case.”

“We can certainly accommodate you, though.” Correa stood and approached the metal door. He buzzed a buzzer. The intercom came on. “I would like a very large glass of ice-cold water, please. Pronto.” He trilled the R pridefully.

In moments, a clerk brought the water and the door clicked shut again.

He placed the glass on the table and Sam reached for it with both hands. Correa thrust his own hand in front of the glass, again extended in a hearty handshake. Paling, Sam snatched his hands back and thrust them back under the table.

“Now how do you like that?” The smile turned vague. Correa cocked his head again.

“You really don’t want to do that, Mr. Correa. It’s really a bad idea to touch me. For your own sake.”

The doctor flipped the chair around and leaned back, arms folded. “Now why would you think that? Care to explain?”

Sam remained deadpan. “Waste of time. You wouldn’t understand.”

“Mr. Trencher, I have a Ph.D. in Clinical Psychology from a leading educational institution, with many medical courses under my belt.”

Sam finally detected a hint of an accent, long suppressed, but which surfaced in moments of stress.

Correa’s smile turned superficial, condescending. “Do you think that I am not capable of understanding? Do I look like an imbecile to you? Do I have *imbecile* stamped on my face?”

“No. But you have yellow flames in your hair.”

The smile broadened again. “How’s that?”

Silence.

“But I have no hair, Sam. Or only half of it left I should say.”

“It will all be gone soon. And you’ll have no more worries.”

The smile vanished. Dr. Correa unfolded his arms

and tapped his chin. Pointed. "Why, Sam, do you keep your hands in your pockets?"

"Balance."

Leaning forward, Correa nodded. "Now we are getting somewhere. What do you mean by *balance*? You don't seem in any danger of falling over to me." Correa shook his head. "And if you were to fall over, wouldn't it be safer to keep your hands out of your pockets so you could catch yourself?" He smiled triumphantly.

Sam felt his temperature rise a degree. The water on the surface of the ice glass was condensing in a pool on the table. He adjusted his chair, which halted the increase in temperature.

"There. What was that for?"

"For—"

In a swift movement, Sam grabbed the glass. Before Correa could intervene, Sam downed most of the water in a few gulps. He closed his eyes with relief and breathed deeply, savoring the coolness as it surged down his throat.

Correa frowned and half stood, but before he could remove the glass, Sam had crunched the ice and swallowed it so only the empty glass remained. His temperature dropped. He stopped sweating. As Correa watched in puzzlement, Sam drenched his hands in the water that had pooled on the table, and wiped the liquid on his forearms, as if attempting to bathe in it. Raising his wet hands above his head, he dried them in the draft of cold air emanating from the AC vent. The evaporation dropped his entire temperature another two degrees. Sam breathed in relief.

Correa's eyebrows uplifted in astonishment.

Calmly, Sam unbuttoned his shirt, and after smoothing the hems to hide them, laid it out on the table between the two of them so that it lay in the exact center of the room, leaving himself bare-chested. "Mr. Correa, could you do me another favor, please?"

A blank look. "*Dr*. Correa."

"Dr. Correa. Your chair. Can you adjust it so that it matches the position of my chair exactly? Just a trifle to the left. They should mirror each other."

Correa's jaw dropped farther. He adjusted the chair then said, "Now we're really getting somewhere. You are not so mysterious after all, Mr. Trencher. In fact, I think I have you completely figured out."

Correa looked at the ceiling. "Let's imagine for a moment. I wonder how a person might react if certain people who had become part of his life, and which people had, let's say, become inconvenient to him, like maybe complaining about his drug usage, or giving him a parking ticket, or passing judgment on him, or otherwise were forcing him to...go *out of balance*?" Finger wandered to cheek. "And let's say that such a person had great difficulty distinguishing reality from fantasy, such that he really could not tell the difference anymore. I wonder what such a person would do if those people...those clumsy ignorant *stoopid* inconvenient people," the accent surfaced again, "were preventing him from preserving his *balance*."

He looked down at Sam.

"Do you think that such a person might do certain things, do whatever it turned out was necessary, no matter who it hurt, to restore his *balance*?" He smiled at Sam knowingly. "Let's say a family member told a young man: "No more drugs." If that family member were gone, life would be so much easier for the young man. No more uncle...balance restored. Let's say a certain immigrant who just took his oath of citizenship refused to provide the young man with heroin from *Mehico*."

Sam noted the ethnic pride again.

"No more good citizen immigrant...balance restored. And let's say a certain traffic cop gave the young man a ticket when he could not afford to pay it. No more traffic cop...balance restored. And let's say a certain crippled young man in a wheelchair got in the way of this young man's attempts to date an old girlfriend who lives here in Okwalla. No more crippled little brother...everything in balance once more." He peered almost sideways at Sam. "What do you think of my supposition so far?"

Sam stared back flatly. "I think you should get another glass of ice water. Soon."

"You just drank one."

"Not for me. For—"

"Officer Brant, I know, we already went over that." Correa leaned forward again. "Now about brooms and mops—"

"There's only one way to stop it," Sam interrupted, speaking calmly. "You need to stay in alignment, in order, in balance. I'm not educated, I don't have any Ph.D. from anywhere. I don't know theory. All I know is if you touch The Glow it will take you, absorb you... I don't know how to say it...*infect* you. I can only tell you: don't kiss the Midnight Sun. And don't touch anyone who has. If you do, it won't stop. Fast or slow, wherever you go, The Glow will come. It doesn't care who you are. Doesn't care who it kills. Use brooms, mops, coins, whatever. All you can do is put it on hold, delay it, by staying in balance. Until..."

Correa's mouth dropped open again.

At length, he closed it. "You know what I think, my young friend? I think you're a young man who has decided to be lazy. You bummed around from job to job, stealing, embezzling, doing anything you could to take whatever you wanted without bothering to knuckle down and actually work for a living like everyone else. You jumped ship from the Army. You quit everything you ever attempted. You got so used to being lazy and letting everyone else support you, and the prospect of working for a living was so bad in your lazy redneck eyes that you decided to invent this little scheme. It's a perfect cover for you, isn't it? A masterful self-deception. But I think there is nothing at all wrong with you. Nothing that can't be fixed by some *tough love*." He smiled again. "What do you think of my little hypothesis now?"

Sam leaned forward. "Don't touch Officer Brant. And don't let anyone else touch him. Or me."

Sam stood, the chair jerking back an inch. A high-pitched whine began, which registered before Sam's gaze as the color turquoise. He gazed above and behind Correa, who involuntarily glanced behind himself in response. A flurry of turquoise paper had appeared over his head, circling down to envelop Dr. Correa in its spirals and create a layer of paper on the floor. Sam peered closely to ascertain the source of the paper but realized that Correa saw nothing. There was no paper.

But it continued to dive and soar. The papers turned white and solidified and took on hardness. The whiteness invaded his nostrils as an acrid smell, and he sniffed and sneezed to clear it. As Sam watched, the papers elongated and began to resemble white metal pipes, and he could not understand why they did not crush Correa's skull as they dropped from the ceiling in torrents. The pipes on the floor morphed into logs, and Sam wondered what kind of stove used white logs to burn then noticed that the logs had grown fulsome termini at either end, round and smooth and twin-jointed. With a start he realized that what he saw was bones accumulating around Dr. Correa, spilling around the table to encompass his chair.

Sam sighed. "Go home, Dr. Correa. Before it's too

late."

Slowly, Correa stood. The smug smile returned. He looked as if he were about to proffer the glad hand again, but thought better of it, and stood straight with his arms at his side. "Well, that's about it, Mr. Trencher. They'll be coming in soon to read you your rights and take you to your cell." He bowed briefly. "Thank you and goodbye."

The buzzer buzzed.

As the steel door slammed behind him, locking Sam alone inside the white room, Correa approached Officer Marla flanked by two Okwalla policemen. He slowly shook his head.

"What's the matter with him?"

"Impairment of the intercerebral corpus callosum. He sees sounds. Hears colors. Right-hemisphere, left-hemisphere confusion. If you place a pen between his hands, I'll bet he would not know whether he is right-handed or left-handed. His grasp of reality is more than tenuous...it's non-existent."

"Does he know right from wrong?"

"As much as anyone. His problem is perception... classic schizophrenia. Probably triggered by many years of illicit drug use on top of an inherited family predisposition. His preoccupation with a rigid pattern of behavior is most unusual, though. I would say it's classic obsessive-compulsive, but to a degree that even the textbooks have not seen. He seems quite unable to break free...and doesn't want to. Some professor could make tenure just studying his case."

"But is he criminally responsible?"

He shrugged. "That's for the courts to decide. He's just as capable of making plans and executing them as you or me. But God help anyone who interferes with his behavioral patterns. Somehow, he knows how to get rid of people who interfere. He warned me repeatedly, and he especially seems to have it in for Officer Brant. Passive-aggressive and the worst case of self-delusion I've ever seen. It's all due to his inability to distinguish reality, coupled with criminal tendencies, after all, you did arrest him, and that proves his criminality as far as I'm concerned." He stepped back. "I'll submit my report tomorrow. In the meantime, you should probably put him in his own cell. Touching him seems to trigger his passive-aggression. You don't want an incident between him and another inmate. At least not 'til you figure out how he is managing to murder everyone who gets in his way."

Dr. Correa exited and climbed the stairs down to the parking garage. *Who do I give my report to again? All these redneck gringos look alike to me.*

Inside the room, Sam slid the paper clips into his pockets and put his shirt back on just as the metal door buzzed open, sliding both arms into the sleeves at the same time. Buttoning the buttons on his way to his jail cell, Sam's eyebrows raised. *They never read me my rights.* He shrugged. *You can't lose what you never had.*

***

"Two more days. We'll tie the knot in a very small ceremony, stay the night here at my father's place, then off to Miami."

Lori ceased crying in her hands and looked up. "Do you really think we should go through with it right now? I'm not sure I can get married only two days after Ralph's funeral."

"Yes, babe. Everything has been planned for weeks. Too late to change anything." Rose took Lori by the hand and caressed it. "Look around. This was my father's house. Now that he's gone, it will soon belong to me. I can finally sell that four-bedroom dump that

that old...um, that my father stuck me with and move up to this classy six-bedroom estate." He grinned as his eyes passed over the high carved rafters and luxurious pool visible through the back French-windowed doors. A vast acreage rolled into hills behind, no neighbors visible for miles. "I'll sell my old dump for a million or so and we can take a plane overseas. Our own private plane."

She cleared more tears. "But Rose, your father just died. How can you be thinking about money before you even have his funeral?"

"Money's important, babe." He stopped smiling. "You know funerals gotta take a back seat to business. That's why the wedding is just for you and me and a few family and the judge...that is, whoever will substitute for my father. I just can't afford anything big."

Lori looked puzzled. "Overseas? I thought we were going to Miami."

"Uh, yeah, is that what I said? I meant Miami."

A sigh escaped her. "I just can't understand. I can't believe it. Why would Sam do it? He's never been like that. The police said he ran over Ralph...not once, but several times." She buried her face in her hands again. "I saw him back up. But only once. And suddenly Ralph was by his car. There wasn't time for anything else." She sniffed. "But his body...oh, Ralph's body." Again her face collapsed into her hands and she cried. "It's almost as if he had a terrible accident then someone pushed him into the traffic. I just don't understand it."

Rose turned hard. "There's no point in trying to figure his shit out. You heard what they said. He's crazy. Crazy as a loon. I have it straight from the department that a psychiatrist warned them to keep him locked up in solitary before he kills someone else." Rose whistled. "Four people in fifteen minutes. You gotta hand it to the little punk. He knows something we don't know about how to do people in. I'd sure like to learn how the hell he... Well, let's not dwell on that." He put a comforting hand on Lori's head. "You're better off without him. And much better off with me."

She glanced up briefly, then buried her face in her hands again, still sobbing.

"And don't forget Ralph's accident insurance. As soon as our wedding is over, give me the death certificate, and I'll send it in. I've already been talking to Doc Henry. He owes me a favor. There won't be any problems with the examiner's opinion. It was all Sam's fault." He gazed at the ceiling and suppressed a smile.

She shook her head. "I don't know if I can do it."

"Sure you can, babe. Little Ralphie always wanted an insurance settlement. If not for you, or for me, then file the claim for him...for his memory. This is what he would have wanted." Rose stared at the ceiling again. He lowered his voice. "You did put me down as one of his beneficiaries like I asked, right?"

She nodded.

He breathed easy. "Strange case, that Sam. They found not only my father's body in his law office, but the body of one of his clients. Seems he had it in for Mexicans too." Standing straight, Rose thrust his hands in his pockets and allowed a smile to form. "Too bad he also shot the parking attendant. The police are really pissed. Just too too bad for one young punk named Trencher."

"You must be sad about your father, though, aren't you Rose?" Lori stood and wiped away the rest of the tears.

"Oh-oh yes." A sad look took hold. "In fact, I keep tearing up about it." He rubbed his eye. "We were...very close, you know. Since Josey moved away and my mother died." He sniffed. "He was...all I had." He looked back to Lori with his lip out. "Until I found you, that is."

She moved a bit closer.

"Your happiness is all that's important to me now." Rose's eye wandered to Lori's full figure, which the new wardrobes he had showered her with failed to cover. With some effort, he restrained himself and embraced her only around her shoulders. His eyes settled on a clock on the wall. *Countdown to the finish line.* Mentally he loosened his gun in his holster...nothing would be allowed to upset his apple cart now...whatever the future may hold.

Nodding, she accepted his embrace and put her arms around Rose. "You've done so much for me, Rose. I don't know why you've been so good to me and Ralph. You have a good heart. I've dreamed of my marriage for years. After we marry, I'm really looking forward to going away with you."

Rose smiled and petted her head. "That's my babe." As they embraced, he inspected the ceiling.

CHAPTER 16

Sam Trencher gazed through the off-white painted steel bars of his jail cell and counted the seconds between the extinguishing of each light as the police prepared the jail for another night. The second, the third, the fourth flicked off, and shadows filled the corridor, and the cacophony that echoed from the other cells finally quieted. The voices from the other cells did not bother him. The voices they awoke in his mind did.

Sam reflected on his fate. What does the average person know of what it means to be an outsider...a *true* outsider? Not someone merely inconvenienced, or paid a bit less, or passed over for a meaningless promotion. But someone whose luck ran out the moment he was born, someone who had struggled against Niagara his entire futile life, and every moment that he almost gained the shore was met by a pole to his chest thrust by some outraged Fate determined to keep him in his place, followed by a rush back down the Falls.

He sighed. The stars were not right. He could not see them, his cell having no window or skylight, but he knew it—felt it. Corvus the Crow, the Pleiades, was in control. He had just missed being born under the dog star Sirius. If he could survive long enough, keep his temperature from rising, maybe the dog star would return and bring things back into alignment.

How mortal am I?

He rubbed sweat from his neck. Yes, he could die. Would he grow old like others? He glanced at his foot and wondered. Who knew? A year...a century? How long did he actually have to live after his most extraordinary communication. And communication it was. Of that he had no doubt. But with what? For what purpose? What secret had the pueblo Indians of prehistoric Okwalla possessed that induced them to build the Round House, decorate it with various images documenting their discovery—then wall it up again to block future access? What secret did old Injun Willie keep in his half-civilized breast, the only person who had ever been inside, which always made him clam up when anyone asked him about it.

"There's nothing to see there, you had best forget it," was all he would ever tell the town's youth when they asked, vying with each to prove their boyish courage. Then he would fix a fearful glare on them, and deep in drink, whisper, "It's the *Round House*. Don't go there after dark."

Coughs and grumbles echoed from the cell next door, spoiling Sam's reverie. True to their word, the police had put him in a cell alone, to his relief, and he could not see the other cells or their inhabitants, and—even better—they could not see him.

His fingers clutched the paper clips he had restored to each pocket. He thanked whatever gods may be that the police in Okwalla had overlooked this—or perhaps they had finally decided to take his comments about contagion seriously and now wished to avoid contact. But the metal clips were not enough. The sweat was increasing. He needed water, and soon.

Squeaking open the broken cold-water spigot, he tried to drink.

At first nothing.

A dirty trickle leaked out. Quickly he remedied the imbalance by squeaking it counter-clockwise, which shut off the trickle. Glancing once more down the empty corridor, he turned and peed into the toilet. Then he flushed it once, twice, a third time. Finally, he dipped his hands in the water, as clean as it would ever be, and spread it over his forearms, neck and face. He exhaled a sigh of relief.

It was not enough.

Removing his shirt, he placed it carefully on the floor in the exact center of the cell over the drain. Then removed his pants—now minus his belt—and underwear and placed them, carefully folded, directly in the center of the shirt. For good measure he parted his hair down the middle. Dipping his hands back into the toilet, he splashed its life-giving fluid over his entire body from head to toe and stepped onto the folded clothes.

Relief.

Standing still, the evaporation rapidly cooled until he felt he was again approaching normal. He peeked through one eye. Rather hoped no one would pop in for a visit at this precise moment. What could he say? He knew no one would understand—even the psych docs were totally at sea when it came to comprehending what he was dealing with.

Even Lori...

He sighed again, now with sadness.

Even Lori. It had been difficult enough to get her to understand, to get her past his standing her up at seventeen, and to reestablish their relationship. Now even she was gone, defecting to the Other Side. How could he get her back with her marriage to Rose coming up?

Sam shook his head. She loved *him*—not Rose. Of that he was certain. She had said as much, and he was certain that that at least was real. Eventually she would realize her error, learn Rose's nature, what he was up to. But how long would that take? How many years could Sam survive? Could he survive even this one night?

Yellow flames.

Eyes closed, he could see them. From somewhere they erupted. In Okwalla—or close by. They were being extinguished, then burning like an ember, and erupting again. From somewhere he thought he could detect a low hum cycling, just like what he had once heard so long ago when he had first visited...*The Place.* He wondered what he and Charlie and Lori had awakened that day, what phenomenon they had triggered, what wheels had commenced to turn. Could others have followed him into the Round House? Was it possible that someone else had kissed the Midnight Sun? What might be the consequences if such a person had no knowledge—or no desire—to learn how to remain in balance?

Somewhere burned...yellow flames.

He needed sleep. Now that he had cooled a few degrees, he lay upon the clothing so that his head and feet rested directly on the concrete floor. In the light of a soft glow emanating from down the corridor, he glanced one last time around the cell to ensure that every item was arranged in right angles, or matched in even pairs, or colors appeased with sounds. In this last regard he found himself humming a cadence that he supposed might offset the too-white paint of his cell.

Soon he was at peace, soaring over a crowd of friendly faces as they welcomed him one by one as if he were a long-lost comrade.

A metallic reverberation flicked his eyelids. From somewhere the echo briefly traveled through the corridor and rested gently on his ears.

Silence returned.

Apparently, the sound was not enough to have awakened the other inmates of Okwalla's jail cells, and

Sam lay nude on his back, arms still outspread to either side, exactly matching, like the contre-temps of a cross, eyes open in the darkness, waiting the next iota of information.

A footstep drifted.

Another.

And another.

Each time pausing as if its owner were hesitating, searching for something, only to resume.

Out of the corner of his eye, a hint of light slowly grew. Sam stared at the ceiling, not wishing to move.

A ham-like hand curled the corner and grasped the farthest steel bar on the front of his cell.

The soft light grew, accompanied by a hissing. A large burly figure still wearing the scorched remnants of a blue uniform stepped into view, purple and violet streaks having ripped his face and torso as if beaten with bats, steam escaping ~~from~~ his shoulders. The figure grimaced—the only expression it could muster.

"Grip with both hands. That will help."

The other hand joined the first and for a moment the figure stood clinging to the two cold steel bars, exhaling with relief from the degree or so of coolness that they afforded.

With an effort it ejaculated a tangled attempt to communicate as if from the bottom of a well, already drowning in its depths.

"How...*the hell?*" Brant sucked an agonized breath. "What the *hell*...did you do to me?"

Sam blinked. "Nothing. Nothing at all."

Brant shook the steel bars and exploded with a guttural burst. "You knew. *You knew.*"

Slowly Sam sat up. Calmly dressed.

"What kind of goddam voodoo curse did you put on me, you lousy punk kid?"

Approaching the bars, Sam looked on the tragic

development with pity. “No curse. But I warned you not to touch me. *Begged* you not to touch me.” He shook his head. “Now you have it, too.”

Brant shook the bars again. “Have *what*, you goddam little punk? What the fuck do I have?” The steam increased and Brant twitched in pain.

“Cold water. That will help.”

The bruised face with its red-shot eyes turned left and right, then Brant produced keys and inserted one in the lock. Brant brandished his police revolver and stepped back so as not to endure another accidental touch with Sam.

Sam walked out.

“That way.” Brant motioned him left with his pistol.

They walked up the corridor amid the silent stares and open mouths of the other inmates, all of whom were now awake, shocked silent witnesses. Passing into the main office, Brant opened the smaller holding cell that opened onto the main area, and after Sam entered, Brant relocked it. Laying down his gun, Brant rushed to the corner water fountain and drenched himself, steam blasting from his corrugated skin. Rushing to the department’s kitchenette, he extracted all the ice he could find and plunged his face into its midst until it melted, which lasted only seconds. He breathed, somewhat relieved.

In surprise, Sam suddenly noticed the body of one of Okwalla’s policemen collapsed over a desk. Blood dripped from the back of his head. Sam looked back to Brant, who ignored it.

“What’s the secret? How do you stop it?” Brant gripped and ungripped his hands, already feeling the temperature rise relentlessly. “What can I do to reverse this thing?”

From behind the bars in his new cell, Sam shook

his head. “Reverse The Glow? You can’t. All you can do is control it. Maybe. And only with great care.”

Steam hissed from Brant’s neck again. He threw a plaintive glance at Sam. “Please, Sam. What can I *do*?”

Sam pursed his lips. He had never wanted this. Had done his best to prevent it. “Do you still have pockets?”

Burly hands thrust into two side pockets. One found a bottom; the other thrust through to encounter empty air.

“Can you change your pants?”

Brant glanced desperately around the office. His eyes lit on the body of the other policeman. Moving swiftly, he tossed the body on the floor, undid the belt and yanked off the pants and exchanged his for the new pair. Within seconds, yellow flares erupted and the pants tore.

“Alright. Try this.” He glanced at spare holsters encasing pistols in a locked glass case across the room, but hesitated to mention guns. “Take two metal handcuffs and attach each one to your belt, one on each side.”

Brant quickly did so. Groaned as more steam hissed.

“Add two radios.”

They followed and seemed to help. But only for a moment.

“Remove your shirt.”

In one movement, Brant tore the remains of his scorched shirt away.

“Throw more cold water on yourself and stand in front of the air vent. The evaporation will help.”

Hurrying to comply, Brant did as he said. A minute later, however, more purple streaks appeared on his flesh. His cheeks swelled, threatening to block his sight. “What else?” came the desperate plea.

Sam glanced around the department main office. “It’s this place. It’s not in balance. One desk here—another over there. Crooked pictures...”

Before he could finish speaking, Brant began to rush about the room pushing furniture like toys, every few moments pausing to look at Sam for a smile or a frown. “Will that work?” “Is this the right way?” The body of the policeman Brant dragged into the corridor of cells where the inmates watched in stunned silence.

Rushing to the walls, Brant straightened every picture in the room and removed the only odd one that had no match elsewhere, flinging it into the hallway that led to the cops’ private offices where the glass and frame shattered from one end of the hall to the other.

He paused to catch his breath and his hair began to wriggle. “I don’t get it. What else can I do? What can *anyone* do?”

“Officer Brant. Have you ever heard of spontaneous human combustion?”

A wild-eyed glance was returned. “Spontan... human. That’s...that’s ridiculous.”

“You don’t think it really happens?”

“But it can’t. It’s nonsense.”

“How do you think those people the other day died?”

“You...you touched them.”

“Is that an explanation?”

“Can’t be no...goddam spocktaneous...”

“What do you think happens when people ignite for no apparent reason? Such cases are fully documented. Could my touch by itself really do such a thing? Do you have a better explanation for what happened to those people? For what is happening now? To *you*?”

Terror seized Brant. “What else...tell me what else I need to do to stop this.” Brant brandished his pistol again. "Or I'll end it all. I'll finish you, you fuckin monster, I'll—"

The buzzer to the front door buzzed.

Stabbing quick glances about the wrecked office that he had thoroughly ransacked and up the corridor where lay the body of the other officer, Brant warily approached the door. He pressed the button on the console, releasing the lock, then stepped to the wall.

It opened, the first light of dawn seeping in.

A female voice sounded. "Derek, where are you? The night shift can't raise you on the—" Marla stopped short. Behind her a gun barrel contacted her head.

A husky voice cracked. "Move over there, you *bitch*." The barrel pushed her forward. "Don't think. Just do it. Move."

Marla swiftly raised her hands and hurried toward Sam's cell. Brant unlocked it and made as if to push her inside as Sam retreated to avoid contact.

"Don't touch her, Brant. Don't touch anyone. Or the same will happen to them as what's happening to you."

Brant squinted in reflex. Glanced through a grotesquely swollen face at his half-burned hands as if contemplating some new-found power. He grunted and smiled. "Some age-spots, huh, Marla? I wonder if Dr. Schol's has an over-the-counter medicine for this?" She stepped into the cell, and Brant slammed the bars shut and relocked the lock.

His straw-thick hair wriggled like worms. Steam hissed from his neck, ripping holes in his skin, and flashes erupted from the ends of the worms to cascade over his head like a miniature Fourth of July. Hands on knees, he bent until the eruption passed. He stood again.

"Funny thing," he croaked. "All this time I thought you were just some run of the mill punk who needed a good kick in the pants. Now look at you. My life...in your goddam little punk hands."

"Not my idea, Brant. Not what I ever wanted."

Marla stared in shock. Slowly closed her mouth.

Sam signaled to Marla with his eyes to glance at the hallway, where the feet of the dead policeman were just visible, his pants gone.

She peered and paled.

"Well, ain't that the bull's balls. Don't that just put the fuzz on the cunt. That goddam Judge Alexander squeezes me under his thumb for twenty goddam years, making me file false reports about those warehouses that his son Rose was burning down, just so he can get kickbacks from the fire insurance. And that little jerk Rose squeezes me to look the other way so he can keep selling heroin and crack to people like your Uncle Roy and Little Ralphie Drumond. Twenty years of being squeezed. Only to find out that spontaneous human combustion is running loose and has put me on the *fast-track to hell.*" He laughed uproariously as purple licks took on tinges of yellow.

"Just a punk kid after all." The swollen eyes stabbed at Sam and Marla. "Yeah, I planted that dope by your window so's we'd have a way to get you out of town. I guess the thing to say now is...I'm sorry." He struggled to catch his breath. "And Rose and Steve and the judge...they planted the gun and the dope in your car yesterday. And their drug-running friend Zavalo from the Reynosa cartel shot Al just for getting in his way." He blew his cheeks out. "I just did as I was told...so I wouldn't lose my job."

Marla's eyes grew big, her ears taking it in.

"And now it's your turn."

Sam looked puzzled.

"I stripped for you. Now it's your turn to strip for me. How do I stop the *fire in my body?*" He lurched toward the cell.

Marla and Sam stepped away from the bars.

"Touching things helps."

"Touch things...touch things." Brant grabbed the steel bars and pressed his body against them, sighing for just a moment in the temporary relief they gave. Flames burst from his chest and he lurched back. Rushing about the room, he scooped up more handcuffs and radios and hooked them to his belt, but yellow flames replaced the purple, and dark streaks descended in spirals down his torso where they ripped tears in his pants. Brant ripped away the remains of his uniform to reveal black and purple streaks that wound about him from top to bottom. The belt disintegrated, crashing his collection of objects to the floor.

Rushing to the bars he slammed against them. His hands thrust through, tried to seize Sam and Marla in their grip, in his haste forgetting the existence of keys.

They hugged the back wall of the cell, out of reach.

"Nnnngh!"

He paused. Turning, he rushed to the water dispenser and again tried to bathe himself in its life-saving purity only to raise such a cloud of heated steam that he was pushed back to the center of the room. Desperately, he stood in the center with arms raised and began to twirl.

"Balance," he hissed to himself, "balance."

The buzzer rang again.

Like stone, Brant halted. Stealing to the console, he buzzed open the door a second time.

Sam jumped to the bars. He shouted at Marla. "No. Don't let him do it. You can't let him do this."

Marla joined. "Brant, don't. We'll find another way."

Swinging wide, the steel door slowed, then paused.

"Here's your report, my friends, I finished early and thought I would drop it off on my way out of town…" Dr. Correa stopped, still as death.

"Run! Don't stay. Get out!" Sam and Marla shouted together.

The doctor peered skeptically, taking in Sam and Marla in one glance. "How did you get in there, Mr. Trencher, my young friend?" His gaze switched to Marla. "Has he a gun on you?" Correa stepped behind a desk. "This won't work, Mr. Trencher. Let Officer Marla go."

Marla shouted. "It's not Sam, Dr. Correa. Look behind you. Get away. Quick!"

Still confused, Correa stepped closer to the cell, his eyes looking for evidence of the gun that Sam must be holding on Marla. "You think you can escape from a jail by holding this woman hostage? It will never work. Think, young man. You don't have a firm grip on reality."

A quiet snap sounded behind Correa.

He stopped.

Slowly he turned.

For a second, he wondered why he had not heard the hissing that bombarded his ears and now transformed into a roar. Correa's eyes grew round, white on black. Before him cascaded a torrent of yellow and violet flames that ended in electric explosions like firecrackers in the air over a mass of yellow wriggling worms, Brant's massive body bulging with boils that burst into more flames.

A guttural squeal cracked. *"I need a hug, Doc."*

Yellow arms embraced his shoulders and the swiftly blackening face propelled directly into his own, Brant's body merging with Correa's in a single roaring tornado, Marla and Sam soon unable to distinguish the two as they spun round the room like two twisters merging.

For minutes, the two struggled in a single phantasmagoric image from Dante's lowest hell, rolling and kicking until the mass finally stopping twitching—then exploded. Only an empty cavity seared into the concrete of the office floor remained as witness to the violence of the eruption. Smoke covered the ceiling like a Dakota winter.

Marla staggered back and collapsed to lean against the wall at the back of the cell. Her hand wandered to her forehead. She finally glanced up at Sam, who continued standing, hands fingering the paper clips in his pockets.

"It's like shell-shock. The kind veterans get." Sam turned and looked at her. "It will take time to understand...longer to accept."

"Then it wasn't you—"

"Like I said. I'm just a bad-luck kid trying not to lose the only person in his life who he ever loved. Nothing more." He turned back toward the room. "His pants are there."

She followed his gaze.

"The keys are in his pants." He pointed.

Understanding, she nodded and stood. "Officer Derek's belt." Removing her own policewoman's belt, she tossed the buckle toward the dead policeman's belt and soon had it pulled within reach. Tying them together, she managed to retrieve what remained of Brant's pants. After several tries, she extracted the keys.

The lock popped open.

Turning, Sam looked at Marla. "I can't stay," he said. "I can't let you keep me here." The black rectangular lines—for a change—were entirely absent. But rose petals continued to rain down as they had for the past few days everywhere he went. The rain was growing more intense.

Her attention was on the floor and the body in the corridor.

"You'll find that Brant's gun has that policeman's blood on its barrel. Brant killed him so he could get to me."

"I believe you now. Like you said...just some punk kid." Looking at what was left of Brant, she took a step back. "A punk kid who should never, *ever* be touched."

He smiled. Pressing the console button to open the outer door, Sam walked out.

CHAPTER 17

"Move it and jump in, faggot. You can straighten your tie later while Tom lays out lemon legs and chickenade. Go figure. Eggs and pancakes he can do...but not a lunch buffet?"

Steve grinned. "Yeah. Lemon legs and chickenade. That's good, Ed...I mean Rose."

For once Rose did not level a reproving stare at Steve, and as Steve settled into the passenger seat of Rose's Lexus, smoothing his rented tuxedo, Rose screeched the tires and barreled toward the West Loop. Rose's free hand adjusted the tie on his own rented tux.

"I can't believe all the shit that this shit-town has gone through in the past few days. With my father's funeral yesterday, I had to scramble to whip up a new judge for Operation Pantyhose."

"You don't want to hold off a few days?"

The glare appeared. "Fuck no. And I've got my reasons, in case too much wood in the chipper is any of your business."

Steve laughed.

"And too much green in the flower box where it ain't doin no one no damn good. *My* green." Rose banged a pothole. "And my inheritance from Dear Old Dad ain't any of your business either."

He sped up, steering with one hand and reading text messages with the other. "Be happy that Jackie Lantern stepped in," Rose added. "He picked up Lori and they're there now."

"What's your hurry? Afraid they'll start without you?"

Rose flashed serious, then flippant smirk. "I just don't want to miss Pancake Tom's crappy food, or be late returning this damned tuxedo, or most important, miss our appointment with..." He glanced at Steve, who returned the glance knowingly. "Those people aren't known for their patience."

Steve stared. "Do you...do you miss your father, Rose?"

The engine momentarily slowed. Rose looked at Steve. He bit his lip. "Would you miss someone who ran your mother off, never answered your phone calls, called you a fuck-up to your face for years in front of everyone he knew, and was a total hypocrite in everything he did? And finally tried to reach out from the grave to control the rest of your life?"

"Maybe not." Steve sighed, gazed out the window. "But that was a strong push you gave him."

"Not strong enough to suit me. Never strong enough to suit me. But I had to attend his goddam funeral...for reasons. And I would have pushed him sooner or later, anyway, when the right time came. It just happened to be sooner as things turned out. And for the better."

Steve snickered. "I wonder what lemon legs and chickenade would really taste like?"

"Probably just like chilichinga pie." Rose sniggered.

They both guffawed as the Lexus pulled into the parking lot of the Haven Motel. The car swung into the second-closest space next to the portico-covered front entrance.

Steve looked about in surprise. "Where's all the cars?"

"Like I said, Steve-O, that ain't in my budget. I've

made enough payments to land this pussy...I got other plans, and I ain't handin over no more blank checks just to keep Goody Two-Shoes in a good mood. All I want is to cross the finish line. *Tonight*. Then I'm gonna get a certain insurance application in the mail and turn a new page, and it don't matter a rat's ass who cries about it."

Rose popped the door and stood. Glancing cautiously about, he leaned back inside. "Check it out."

He motioned at Zavalo's 18-wheeler that had reappeared in the far corner of the motel's parking lot, fresh from impoundment release.

"Don't forget the gear, Steve-O. I want it handy."

One hand felt on the floor of the back seat under a black tarp to encounter several assemblages of steel and smooth hard plastic. "Locked and loaded," Steve said.

Rose nodded. Together they walked through the entrance. Behind the welcoming counter, a raised hand from Patel's Mexicana concierge waved them to the right.

Lori, in a flowing white dress, stood at the entrance, staring into a cozy side-room with double doors thrown open to reveal a carpet composed of colorful swirling curves and ocher walls hung with tapestries of thickly forested hunting scenes. Her attention seemed to be on two bowling-ball-round maids who were busy sweeping and cleaning at the bottom of a thick curtain that split the room in two, shrinking its small size even smaller.

Instantly, Rose's face transformed into a wan smile. Both hands extended to embrace his soon-to-be bride.

Lori turned.

Rose stopped short and embraced her. "Tears? Why, babe? Isn't this what you've been waiting for?"

Others inside the room stared at them.

She sniffed. “I’m crying for your father, Rose. He was always so kind to me.”

Rose forced his smile to remain a bit longer as Lori continued talking.

“He told me many times how much he wanted me to marry you, that he thought it would be good for both of us. And now...he’s gone.”

Looking up, Rose took her hands in his and patted them. “Yes. My dear father. Fate took him from us too soon.” While he spoke, Rose gazed at the ceiling with a hard look.

“And also for Sam,” she said.

Rose dropped the hard look upon her.

“I still can’t believe he was responsible for what happened, Rose. I know him. I know he can’t have done what they say he did.”

“Believe it.” Rose almost yelled that, then regained control. “But you haven’t heard the latest from the police department.”

“I heard about Officer Brant, that he killed two people yesterday.”

“Don’t be surprised to learn that it was really Sam responsible for that too, and for killing Brant.” His eyebrows rose. “They say he has some kind of...ninja killing technique.”

Her eyes grew limpid as she stared up into his. More tears flowed. She buried her face in Rose’s chest. With a look of relief and triumph, he accepted her embrace and closed his arms about her. A wink aimed at Steve.

“Well, how da ya like the spread?” A figure approached almost apologetically, ranch hat in hand, mustache entirely hiding both lips to tickle his chin. “Texican style just like little Lori ordered.” The owner of Bronco Grill smiled at her, though only the nether ends were visible beneath the longhorn muff. “She’s smart fer sure.”

A half-smile responded from Rose. “It’ll do, Tom. My thanks to the Bronco Grill. It will do just fine.”

The walrus chin angled inquisitively.

Taking the hint, Rose stepped away from Lori so he and Tom could talk in private. Tom whispered: “I can expect your check soon then, Mr. Alexander, sir? Things have been a bit tough lately...more expenses than I expected.” A subtle glance stole in the direction of the lectern.

Rose hesitated a moment in thought, then: “Tonight, Tom. Before we leave.”

Tom grinned and backed away as if departing the presence of royalty, to be replaced by several pairs of long-lost cousins who, Rose supposed, must have broken speed records to attend, since the few invitations he had sent had only just gone out, delayed until the last possible moment by the disasters of recent days.

Rose rejoined Lori. He reflected again on how Okwalla had been thrown into chaos from the moment that punk Trencher had rolled into town. After all—Rose remained silent as he shook hands and pretended to smile at total strangers—the word he had gotten was that after Brant had massacred several people and then killed himself, Sam, whom he felt was somehow behind it all, had walked merrily away and was now as loose as he pleased, wrecking Rose’s entire elaborate frame-up. Even now he could not be certain of events, since Brant had been his eyes and ears in the department.

He patted a bulge under his arm in reassurance.

Across the room beside a lectern on a short dais stood an older man in a suit, Mayor Jack. Jack signaled Pete Patel.

Lori and Rose watched as Patel hurried in

response. Without acknowledging them, Patel crossed to a tiny console where he turned a knob and traditional wedding music began to blare through chintzy speakers. More knobs turned the lights lower, the lights with bulbs that still worked. A dark woman in flimsy Indian garments trotted behind him everywhere, though doing so little that she seemed only a shadow. The maids exited with Patel's wife by way of a small door behind the lectern, only to reappear briefly through the main double doors to retrieve their forgotten brooms, then exit again.

Patel attempted to take up a position behind the buffet, but Tom pushed him away and motioned him toward the dais where he stood uncomfortably among the guests wondering what to do with his hands and wondering if the Chinese bistro would still be open after the wedding was done.

With Steve in tow, Rose and Lori approached the dais.

Rose said, "Glad you could step into my father's shoes, Mayor Jack, Your Honor, sir."

The mayor shook Rose's hand with vigor. "The least I could do. My condolences for your father, Rose." A sad expression hung about the Mayor. "I'm glad to pitch in. With the judge gone there's really no one else in Okwalla qualified to perform a wedding. Without Sue Ann, I don't know how I could have managed." He smiled at his new assistant who stood next to him and a little behind, holding an instruction book. "Don't know at all." Mayor Jack looked back to Rose. "Have the two of you met?"

Rose and Sue Ann looked level at each other without expression. "No. But word gets around," Rose said. Their hands connected and briefly shook.

"Nice to meet you," Lori said, also touching hands with Sue Ann. A glint seemed to cross Sue Ann's eye.

Through a side window, the sun dipped below the horizon, making the gloom behind the curtain that enveloped half the party-room darken to blackness. Behind the buffet, Tom Borger inspected his own tuxedo as if concerned that contamination may prevent the return of his rental deposit.

"Let us thank our Lord for allowing us to meet on this happy occasion..." At a signal from Rose, the Mayor picked up the pace and rattled through the rest of the preliminaries. He rushed to the meat of the matter.

A paternal glance fell on Rose. "Do you, Rose Edwin Alexander, Jr., take this woman for your dearly beloved wife, to honor and cherish 'til the end of your days?"

Steve, grinning more than usual, stepped back, hands on his rump and elbows out.

Rose frowned. Glancing at Lori, he blurted, "Damn right I do. What do you need, spurs? Get on with it, Jack."

Jack cleared his throat. "Do you, Lori Trepolis Drumond, take this man for your dearly beloved husband, to honor and obey 'til the end of your days?"

She was staring at the floor. With a quick glance around the room as if seeking a last lost opportunity, she looked briefly at Rose. All doors were shut. "I do," she whispered.

"The ring, please."

Everyone stood silent, no one moving.

Rose frowned at best-man Steve who stood as if frozen.

"Oh yeah." Steve grinned sheepishly and hurriedly explored a pant pocket. He soon produced an unadorned ring, which had all the appearance of gold but none of its weight.

Rose hastily screwed it onto Lori's left middle

finger. “That’s done.” Taking her by one hand, he gave her a peck on the lips.

“Let the good times begin,” the Mayor yelled, his loud youthful voice seeming to contradict his shock of white hair. At a signal from Patel, his plump wife cranked up the music, and the colored lights accelerated. Two couples began to twitch in imitation of an attack by nerve gas. Others rushed the buffet table and kept Tom busy.

Lori and Rose stepped away from the lectern to watch Patel’s wife wheel a stunted eight-inch white wedding cake toward the buffet, Mrs. Patel still smearing icing on the edges with a plastic knife. Lori quietly removed the ring and screwed it on her third left finger.

She turned to Rose. “Do you...you want to dance some?”

With a slow deliberate sweep around the room, his eyes lit on hers and his arms encircled her and squeezed her tightly against him. He was not smiling. “You know what I want. And it ain’t dancing.” He leaned over to whisper in her ear, a hand firmly planted on her rear. “You’ve denied me for weeks. I’ve done everything you wanted. I won’t be denied again.”

She leaned back and looked away. “Is that all you want?”

“What else is there?”

“The honeymoon.”

He shrugged. “I want what I paid for...now. This place has lots of rooms. Any room will do.”

Grabbing her firmly by an arm, Rose took a step in the direction of the exit, when his eyes caught a figure standing in the double entrance doors of the party room.

Rose halted, alert.

Short and swarthy, the newcomer had recently

exchanged his tank top and shorts for Levi's and Polo with leather jacket. An ostentatious buckle with crossed miniature pistoleros contradicted the expensive Rolex that hung on his too-small wrist. The jacket's left breast bulged as if covering a sizable object.

He entered and paused several feet from Rose.

"Señor. You must think I am only some *borracho pendejo*. I don't need no more vacation. It's time someone pays me my money." He spoke just loud enough to gain the attention of several revelers, and Patel's wife, ever eager to serve and thinking the party must be over, and it was time to turn to business, turned down the music and increased the lights as if the night's celebration was done. Distracted, Rose found himself a trifle surprised and definitely annoyed at her unexpected efficiency. He glanced at Steve, who quietly exited the door behind the lectern, then in the corner of his eye thought he glimpsed a movement behind the curtains and suspected that the intruder was not alone, that more pistoleros had infiltrated as backup for the intruder.

"Not a problem, my friend, but as you can see I am very busy tonight—"

"You know, you must have *cojones de plomo*, my freend. Do you think Hector is like these, how you say...fat stupid maids?"

"Not at all—"

"Do you think you are talking only to some wetback? Mi amigo Zavalo goes to meet Saint Jesús Malverde, then our truck, she disappear, and when it come back I *still* don have my money."

"No problemo, my friend. There's never a problem with paying."

The intruder walked farther into the room and paused one meter from Rose. His hand crept behind the jacket's lapel and the bulge loomed larger. "You still think this little brown man will leave without his money? I think you are wrong, Meester."

His gaze passed over Rose toward the back of the party room, and his eyes grew larger, and in the white around his pupils Rose could see the reflection of Steve as he re-entered the room. Approaching the lectern, Steve quietly placed a large black box across its top and extracted an AR-15 rifle, locked and loaded.

Rose straightened and took a step forward. He emphasized his point by letting the visitor see his own hand wander to the interior of his left arm where it contacted the butt of a revolver. Seeing the move, Lori and the guests jerked back.

The visitor squinted. "You must pay me, my freend. I have a long drive back to Mexico, and I do not want to stay here any longer."

With the motion of a single finger, Rose signaled Steve, and he strolled forward. Cautiously, Steve handed the rifle to Rose who held the barrel almost level, then Steve stepped to within two feet of Hector. He handed Hector the wrapped package and stepped back. Flashing the rifle, Rose smiled and waved. "Enjoy your trip, amigo."

A single shake of the box sufficed to verify its contents, and Hector broke into a broad happy smile. He stepped backward toward the entrance, still keeping his hand on the bulge in his pocket.

At the door, he turned and exited.

An explosion of chatter erupted among the guests.

"Who the *hell* was that?"

"The nerve of that guy."

"I think we just got robbed," Pancake Tom said to Patel. "Call the goldarn cops, Pete. We'll stop his ass fer sure."

"No," Rose yelled. "I don't want any cops here on my wedding night. It's nothing at all to worry about."

He turned back to Lori where she stood pale and open-mouthed, staring not at the exit but at Rose. Leaning the rifle against the back of the lectern, Rose returned and loomed over Lori, seeming to speak directly to her. "Let's just thank the Lord that no one was hurt, and that we can all now return to our—"

Two shots rang out.

As the lights flared, Hector silently backed through the entrance, stepping slowly, clumsily, a heavy pistol weaving in his right hand. The box was gone.

He swayed. Without uttering a sound, he fell backwards and thudded on the carpet where a gush of red clouded the colorful decorations on the rug.

A man in casual street clothes with an overlaid black vest rushed into the room and aimed a Smith & Wesson police issue gun. The vest read: FBI.

"Get the fuck down. *Get on your fuckin faces now.*"

From behind the lectern, another intruder appeared with another black FBI vest.

"Do it now. Don't think about it. Do it now. Get on your fuckin faces."

As one, almost everyone in the room hugged the floor, rushing to obey.

"Put your hands behind your heads."

The second Agent looked up at Rose and Steve and thrust a barrel in their faces. "You too. Get on the fuckin floor."

They moved slowly, but obeyed.

A familiar face appeared. Wearing another FBI vest over standard issue Okwalla police uniform, Officer Marla entered, carrying Hector's package in one hand. Laying it on the floor, she walked toward Rose and Steve as they lay face-down on the carpet. Holstering her heavy pistol, she brandished two handcuffs, and with a kick to spread his legs twisted Rose's arm behind him, then the other, and cuffed him. Before Steve could react, she snapped more metal cuffs on his wrists, while the other two agents handcuffed the Mayor, Tom, and Sue Ann.

Patel sat on the floor—he jumped up, then found that his knees shook so badly that he had to sit again, his hands striving but failing to calm his squirming legs.

Marla motioned to one of the agents. "Let Patel up. In fact, they can all stand."

In relief, everyone struggled to their feet, except Patel who attempted to stand but whose knees shook so violently that he again sat on the carpet to prevent fainting.

Rose's mouth opened.

"Shut up," one of the agents yelled before he could make a sound.

Rose closed it again, alternately squinting and glaring. His cuffed hands squeezed repeatedly as if strangling a series of necks.

Marla turned to Patel. "Gary, put the cuffs on Patel also."

Pete Patel froze as Agent Gary approached. With a gulp, Patel fainted.

Lori caught Pete and braced him up until he woke again. "Don't hurt him," she yelled, tears streaming. "What are you doing here? Don't hurt anyone. Why does anyone have to get hurt?" Sue Ann, Jack, and Tom directed puzzled looks at her sudden outburst. "Remember? This is supposed to be my *wedding*."

Marla glanced at Rose and Steve who, though breathing quickly, sullenly returned her stare. Her glance moved to Patel and she nodded.

"Mr. Patel."

"Yessss...yess, ma'am?"

"I'm Agent Marla Lefkowitz of the Federal Bureau of Investigation. Several months ago I was given an assignment to investigate illicit drug transactions in the town of Okwalla done by certain individuals whom we believed to be Judge Alexander and his son Rose."

Patel's eyes grew big.

Rose's glare narrowed.

"Since then the FBI has documented your involvement with Mr. Rose Alexander and his accomplices in an interstate drug operation that puts *you*, Mr. Patel, in the middle of the whole thing."

"No!" He gasped and moaned, hands on his cheeks. "Oooh."

"Would you like to see some pictures of a certain transaction that took place here in your motel just last week?" She reached for a small manila folder deposited in a back pocket. "I'm arresting you for paying a cash bribe of $10,000 to Judge Alexander, and for running a drug lab for his son Rose."

"No. That money was not mine." Some starch reappeared in Patel's knees. "That was Rose's money. It's counterfeit anyway. Rose paid me fake money, so when the judge told me to pay Mayor Jack I gave fake money to him." Patel took a deep breath then resumed talking non-stop. "And I have videos on flash drives showing the judge bribed Mayor Jack to help him with insurance fraud. I took the videos to protect myself from what the judge was making me do. It wasn't my fault." Not yet cuffed, Pete pointed at Rose and Steve. "*They* threatened to kill me if I didn't let them use my motel as their drug headquarters. I never kept any of the money, I gave all of it to the judge and the mayor."

Now Jackie Lantern's knees began to shake. He thought quickly then blurted. "Not me. I knew the money was fake. I was just playing along so I could turn it in the police the first chance I got."

Rose turned a contemptuous glance at Steve, who looked equally disgusted listening to Patel and Jack. Steve spit into the carpet.

"Don't handcuff me, please, Miss Officer Marla," Patel shouted through a gush of tears. "Okay, I will show you. I'll show you everything." He managed to steady himself and rushed to the edge of the rug, now stained with blood. Rolling Hector's body to one side, he peeled back the rug to expose a differently colored patch in the floor. Pulling on a hook, he lifted a board showing a series of white-wrapped plastic containers beneath. Glares of hate from Alexander & Co failed to deter his rush to ingratiate himself with Marla and the FBI.

"This is it. This is the heroin that Hector and the Reynosa gang delivered. Their meth lab is in my kitchen." He leveled a desperate look at his wife. "Oh, I cannot live without my Chinese takeout specials. And my hard-working wife, she cannot run the motel without me. Can you tell me when I can run my motel again, please, Miss Agent Marla?" In the back of the room beside the stunned long-lost cousins, Mrs. Patel stood with both hands covering her mouth.

Marla shook her head. "What motel? Haven't you heard of drug property seizures?"

Patel caught his breath—promptly collapsed again into Lori's arms.

Marla turned to the remaining guests, who had not been handcuffed, and were now standing by the curtain in confusion. "You all can go home. The action is over. There won't be any more entertainment tonight."

With hardly a word, all the guests filed out, a few happily snapping cell phone pictures of the most memorable wedding they had ever attended. Only Lori remained frozen in place as if catatonic, forgotten in the commotion as Agent Gary proceeded to handcuff Patel, but paused a moment while the motel owner stood and cried with his hands over his face.

"What about *me*?" Sue Ann stood calm and quiet, still handcuffed. Beside her, Mayor Jackie Lantern and Pancake Tom rounded out the guest list who were still under suspicion for the crime of hailing from the crime capital Okwalla.

Marla shrugged. "Let her and Mr. Borger go. I have nothing on them. But I'm sorry, mayor, you and I need to have a talk about arson and insurance fraud. You'll have to stay handcuffed."

Agent Gary took out a key and unlocked the cuffs behind Tom. Tom rubbed his wrists in relief but, in truth, was breathing more freely due to having heard Marla state that she had nothing on him, more than due to his physical liberation.

Moving to Sue Ann, Gary snapped the cuffs off. Sue Ann stumbled and swayed. Catching her with one hand, Gary helped her up then walked back to Marla's side.

Marla snapped several pictures of the heroin for evidence. "Agent Wang, let's get this stuff loaded up." Wang and Gary holstered their guns and leaned to extract the white bags of heroin, which were surprisingly heavy, and Gary soon paused to remove his vest, the exertion making him sweat.

"I'm outta here." Tom paused to look at Marla. "That is, if that there's okay with you, Miss Marla. I mean, I do have a restaurant to tend to."

Marla nodded.

Quickly flicking off all the controls on the buffet, Tom rushed out the exit.

"One goddam fucking moment," a man's enraged voice roared.

The three agents caught their breath. Lori and the

Patels switched their gaze from the bags of heroin back to the lectern where Rose stood gripping the AR-15, the barrel aimed at a trio of de-vested FBI agents.

Their hearts climbed into their throats.

Sue Ann clicked open Steve's handcuffs and stood beside them both, smiling and swinging the handcuff key she had slipped off Agent Gary.

Turning to Rose, Sue Ann planted a kiss on his cheek. She pouted, "Aren't you through playing with that little whore, Rose dear? I know you had to marry her to inherit your father's millions, but now you've done it. We don't have to delay a minute longer. We can fly to Rio tonight. It's time for you to keep your promise to marry me. I have our tickets, honey. I'm ready to go."

Rose slipped one arm around Sue Ann and pulled her close.

Walking slowly, almost baby steps, Lori approached Rose.

No one breathed.

She halted one foot distant—more distant than a thousand miles. "Sam was *right*."

Rose dropped his arm from Sue Ann. He looked hurt. Even now the mention of his rival pained him, even as he made an irrevocable choice to steal her happiness and throw her overboard for someone else.

"You *are* a drug dealer. You *are* a criminal. Just like Sam said."

He smirked, looked away, then looked back. "You can say that...after what your little pal Sam did?"

Marla spoke up. "Lori, I was with Sam at the police department yesterday, and we had a nice talk. I don't think he murdered Brant, or Ralph, or anyone else in Okwalla, or anywhere for that matter."

Rose frowned again.

"In fact, the police lab says it was Rose's shotgun that killed your brother."

Catching her breath, Lori stared harder at Rose. "Long ago," she blurted, "in the Round House, that *was* you who chased me. It *was* you who beat up Sam...and beat up poor Charlie." She shook her head, crying. "You...*you* killed Ralph."

Rose shifted his weight and glanced nervously around. He pursed his lips and spat on the floor. "Of course. You didn't really believe my little lies, did you?" He laughed. "Come on. No one can be that stupid. All I wanted was a roll in the hay. If my father had not forced me to marry you by putting this charade into his will, I would already be gone. Can you imagine the nerve of that guy? He was hoping *you* would improve *me?* A dumbass waitress from dumpwater Okwalla?"

She stepped forward. Slapped him.

He squinted as the flat mark reddened on his face. Putting his foot on the front of her wedding dress, Rose shoved her. She stumbled but stood.

"Okay, bitch. You want to know what happened to that pissant Little Ralphie? Steve and me wasted him. Just like we ran his pissant little bike off the road when he was a punkass little kid, when we ran him into McReynolds' pickup truck. Yeah! It was us! And now his pathetic drug-addict pissant little life is over and done with, and I ain't about to spend another moment more than I have to with his prissy older sister who don't even know which side of the bed she's supposed to get fucked on."

"It's Sam." She looked at the floor. "It's Sam that I love."

Still no one breathed.

Even Mrs. Patel watched, hands still covering mouth.

Steve looked at Rose.

"It's them or us, faggot," Steve said.

Rose handed his pistol to Steve and frowned.

"There ain't no arguin with the ever-fuckin truth."

One long second passed—longer than an epoch.

Snapping their pistols out of their holsters, Marla and Gary fired several quick shots as Rose unleashed a barrage of rapid gunfire from the assault rifle, spraying bullets across the room, blood bursting from chests and limbs.

Steve stumbled, his pistol spitting flame, Agent Wang falling backward, bloody, collapsing, Marla on her face, white package exploding, throwing puffs of white into the air mixed with puffs of red.

Agent Gary stared at the ceiling. He slowly exhaled, wondered silently if the faux barrel vault should be called baroque or rococo. He had always wanted to be an architect. His eyes closed.

Rose lay beside the lectern, smoke streaming from his weapon. At the first moment, he had thrown himself sideways, finger tight on trigger, and a quick glance revealed he had not been hit. He glanced at three unmoving bodies across the room. Agent Wang lay across Marla's legs. Marla was face-down, her arms splayed.

"Fuckin-A." Steve picked himself up and inspected a red crease that had nicked his arm. He spat.

"How about you, Sue Ann?" Rose helped her up from behind the lectern where she had dived. She shook like wheels on a rickety grocery cart. Without a word she bolted out the door.

"Sue Ann," Rose called.

No answer.

Patel moved subtly toward the back door.

His eyes narrowing, Rose barked, "Not you, Mr. India. You and me...we've got a bone to pick."

"Ooooh," Patel screamed and ran faster than a vacationer skipping his overnight bill. A spray of bullets hammered the wall about him as he disappeared through the exit, one resulting in a red geyser.

"After him, Steve-O. That squealer's not gettin away with this."

Rose and Steve ran through the back door in pursuit, guns peppering, while the party room emptied of its remaining survivors.

Except one.

Standing quietly, Lori stared at a growing spot of red in her upper chest. *Gee, I wonder what the honeymoon will be like?*

The curtain parted.

From the back of the room, Sam appeared and rushed to her. Her eyes closing, she fell into Sam's arms, his sad face looking down upon her the last thing she saw.

CHAPTER 18

Cradling her in his arms, the Castaway staggered out of the Haven's main entrance, no one else in sight. The parking lot was now empty of vehicles, except Lori's yellow Taurus, Sam's steel-blue Oldsmobile, a dormant 18-wheeler, and two black sedans with U.S. government plates that flanked a black Lexus.

"Do you," he wheezed to the universe, "Samuel Louis Trencher...take this woman for your dearly beloved wife, to honor and cherish 'til the end of your days?" He stumbled, paused to rest, letting Lori's legs contact the ground. "I do," Sam replied to himself, breathing hard.

Moments more and he lifted her again and labored toward his Oldsmobile.

"Do you...Lori Trepolis Drumond...take this man for your dearly beloved husband, to honor and obey...you don't have to worry about that part, darling...forever and ever?"

He reached the car.

Digging into his pocket for a key, he encountered only coins, then remembered. Since he had no duplicate key to balance it, he never removed the key from his car, so it was always left unlocked.

Holding her up with one arm, he laid the passenger seat back and gently draped Lori on it. He glanced once at the steady stream of red that had stained half her white wedding dress, and now dripped on the floorboard. He clicked the seat belt.

"Can you hear me, dear? Are you still with me?"

No answer.

Glancing at her arms, Sam spied a dark splotch. He caught his breath and hurried to the driver's side.

Right of the Haven's portico, two figures approached the front entrance from the darkness of the back lot, weaving gun barrels that glinted with starlight, their eyes tracking spots of Patel's blood.

"We'll find him," Steve muttered.

"He's got to be here somewhere. He can't go far with a bullet in his back."

Steve grabbed Rose's arm. "Lookit."

Across the front lot, Sam shut the passenger door on a figure in a white dress, then hurried to the other side of his Oldsmobile. Entering, he gunned the engine.

"Isn't that Sam?"

"With someone dressed in white."

The tires squealed and moments later a shrinking blue trapezoid sped over the darkened West Loop.

They stared at the highway. Rose's eyes narrowed. His key beeped his Lexus.

"Get in, Steve-O. We'll finish Motel Pete later. He'll be easy to find after he bleeds to death. No one runs off with *my* goddam wife...sure the hell not a goddam little punk named Sammie Trencher."

On the West Loop, Sam pulled the seat belt over Lori, for once ignoring the failure of the interior of his car to balance. Another glance revealed a second dark splotch on her arm. "Forever and ever...*forever and ever.*"

Accelerating down the Loop, the Oldsmobile soon left the motel far behind and passed several broken-down developments that had failed to develop. Taking a curving exit, Sam departed the Loop and entered a side road that barreled northwest.

A clear expanse of sky enveloped them, the sharp

drop-off of city lights left the dark canopy awash with glittering stars, as eternal and unchanging as when time began.

Potholes loomed in the headlights. A rust-red railroad track hammered the bottom of the auto, and the car landed on the other side with a thump.

"I'm here, Lori...your husband. I won't leave you again. I promise." He glanced at Lori's still form beside him, which had not reacted to the bump.

The radio erupted in a shower of static.

Grabbing his chest, Sam jammed the brakes.

The static melded into music—Sam breathed in relief—jammed the pedal again. The railroad had merely kicked his radio on, and his CD had auto-jerked into play. The car lurched onward in the night, racing through the blackness, the constellations above urging him on as music filled the void:

You don't remember me
But I remember you
Twas not so long ago
You broke my heart in two
Tears on my pillow
Pain in my heart
Caused by you...

An unlit turnoff loomed and Sam slowed. His temperature rising, he cranked both windows down all the way using both arms while his knees steered, and he felt relief from the night air evaporating the film of sweat on his neck. He gunned the motor again, oblivious of the papers that blew about the interior and escaped the windows.

The potholes multiplied, forced him to slow. With a start he saw a trace of smoke and glimpsed a white fog rising from beneath Lori's dress. He smashed the pedal and lurched over another half-mile of rocky path.

“I do! I do!” he cried.

Reaching behind him with one hand, he yanked a gallon jug of water, popped off the top with his teeth, and sprinkled its contents over Lori.

A hiss of steam clouded the cab, immediately escaping out the open windows.

“I take her...I take her...”

He let the water pour and drench her, and the steam subsided.

“Good. That’s *good.*” He jerked the wheel to avoid a looming crater.

His brights angled down, then up, crazy angles stabbing the thick night of what was, until not so long ago, empty wilderness, a rural countryside devoid of humanity except a few exiled Indians distrustful of outsiders, become outsiders themselves. Sam was returning, himself no different.

Reaching over Lori, he grasped her seat belt and clicked it in place.

More steam erupted.

He shook his head in frustration and unclicked it and unclicked his own seat belt to match. Slowing to swerve another large pit, he dug into his pockets and extracted coins. He unclenched Lori’s right hand and stuffed a quarter, dime, and penny into its palm, and her hand seemed to reclose, though he could not tell if the movement was conscious—or if there was any movement at all. He stuffed her left hand with the same denominations, and Sam refocused on the nightmare drive that would have challenged a Nascar pro.

For a moment, he glimpsed an endless landscape of craters and wondered how his moon lander would refill its gas tank. Then a shower of turquoise buffalo hides started raining down from a cloudless sky strewn with a myriad of incomprehensible constellations, their interplay hinting at zodiacs unguessed by mere earthlings, and the buffalo hides were followed by white bones rattling and bouncing about his car.

The gray whiffs from Lori had paused, but new sources were appearing from Sam's body, little flickers slicing holes in his shoulders. Between pinpricks, he wondered: might the curse affect other forms of life? Was there such a thing as spontaneous buffalo combustion? Clearly, old man Willie had known about The Glow. Why else did he warn his grandson Charlie to stay away from the Round House? And everyone else that he knew when he was hitting the bottle? But he had vanished. And now there was no way for Sam to find out the truth—except to launch himself forward, hurl himself and everything he held dear into the maw, demand of it one last miracle.

The car sped through a storm of white bones, rose petals, green lines that zigzagged about him like a jungle, yellow wheels that spun alongside like rebellious suns that refused to rest when they should. The grass itself seemed to come alive in his headlights with wriggling tentacles that spat sparks to pop overhead like electric bubbles.

A decrepit wooden fence burst out of the darkness. Its middle stretch was collapsed in a welter of rotten boards and rusted barbed wire. The Oldsmobile bounced to a halt.

Sam jumped out. Glimpsed an ancient rusted pickup truck. A soiled pile of clothes. From somewhere a deep cycling hummed. Despite an absence of more than ten years, he instantly knew its source.

Rushing to the other side, he swung open Lori's door.

She made no move.

He batted his eyes, put his hands to his head and squeezed.

"What next?...What next?...*How?*"

In confusion he ran across the brown slab of stone to stare down into blackness. The blackness of the pit. He remembered.

Rushing back to the car, he ransacked the back seat until his hand found what he sought. The flashlight's beam penetrated the darkness, forcing a temporary compromise on humanity's oldest enemy.

Back to the edge, he shined its weak orb onto the surface of the Round House. Distant memories raced back. The entrance was small—even minuscule. Not at all the gigantic edifice that haunted his dreams. Still, he knew the power of what lay inside.

Racing back to Lori, he pulled her out and lay her over one shoulder. Never strong or athletic, the feat was difficult and painful. He lurched to the edge and managed to gently lower her limp form over so that her feet rested on the surface of the round mouth of the pueblo. With one hand, he held her up by her arm while he lowered himself with the other. At last he joined her, letting their legs dangle over the lip of the aperture. He gently lay her back against the raw stone. Breathed deeply. He redirected the flashlight deep below.

His hands pressed on either side of his head again. "How, how?" He could climb down using the handholds inside the pueblo. But with *Lori*?

He lowered his hands and touched on a rough strand of rope. He brightened. *Just maybe...*

If he could wrap its length around her shoulders, he could lever her down slowly by wrapping the other end around some temporary winch. He reached for a white protuberance—his hand closed on air, the object taking flight to whirl around the entrance with the other illusions.

At least the rope was no illusion. He pulled up ten feet of it from the depths, and undeterred by its age and fragility, and a recent tear at its far end, he quickly tied it around Lori's shoulders.

The pale light of the flashlight flickered as the batteries weakened and fresh ejections of steam hissed from her torso. Desperately, Sam snatched the free end of the rope—only to discover that not enough remained to wrap around anything.

"I take this woman..." He gripped the rope, and without hesitation, began lowering her into darkness by hand. "For...my lawfully wedded wife." His voice strained. His feet braced against the circle of stone blocks as he lowered her three feet, six feet, eight feet into blackness, the rope now beginning to slip and accentuating the heat that already made the cold night air seem like a Turkish steambath.

"Forever and ever..."

Crack.

Sam propelled backward and slammed the back of his head on the cliff-face. Scrabbling the rope up, he stared at the fresh tear. Lori was gone.

Grabbing the flashlight, he put it in his teeth and half-climbed-half-dropped the length of the interior face of stones until he alighted at the bottom. Lori lay where she had fallen, eyes still shut.

He lifted her again, and with the light again gripped in his mouth, waddled backward through the aperture into the cave of detailed drawings, dragging her by a full nelson. At length he pulled her higher up and placed both his arms around her waist just below her breasts. Slipped on blood. But staggered on again.

He hummed. "You don't remember me... But I remember you..."

Wheeled suns whirled past, throwing spinning shadows about him.

"Twas not so long ago... You broke my heart in two..."

Green tendrils spread from the cavern's rocky

sides to envelop Lori as if to welcome her to their garden of paradise.

The stony path wound to either side and downward, ever downward.

"Tears on my pillow..." Violet and purple streaks appeared on her face and neck. "Pain in my heart..." Sam paused to inspect the coins and discovered they had fallen from her hands. "Caused by *you*..." Madly he compared stray pebbles, and when he found two that more or less matched, he thrust them back into Lori's cold grip. Stuffed two more into his own scraped and dirty pockets, then wiped the back of one hand over his sweaty unshaven face. Frantically he wiped the other hand to exactly match the movement of the first. The pinpricks in his own neck and face, he reflected, must look the same as hers.

The hum had grown to an overarching buzz as if an enormous tesla coil lurked just below his feet. He paused. He lay Lori upon the rocky path to catch his heaving breath.

"You...oo-o-oo."

Propping Lori against a rocky outcrop, Sam put his arms around her and kissed her on the lips. Released her as wisps of smoke hissed from her shoulders and neck. Yellow flames began to flicker behind her.

"Don't worry, my dear. My dear dear wife. Everything will all be perfect soon. You will be just like me. You won't mind. I promise. I'll show how to live like this, how to keep everything in balance. We'll be happy together, you'll see."

Encircling her again with his arms, he resumed staggering backwards until the walls of the cavern expanded around him and came alive with flickered light, purple, turquoise, violet, all lighting the high ceiling and cratered walls with waves of rippling neon.

The electric hum rang in his ears.

He paused at the lip of a rocky ledge, two mounds flanking him, staring down at a floor of rough stone unmodified by human touch. As if awakened by his presence—or supplication—the Midnight Sun had risen. Half the black sphere had emerged from the crevasse that led to unplumbed depths below. Despite his pain as the former pinpricks grew to patches in his skin and glowed like embers, the notion hung in his mind that those depths could have no end, dropping down and down to regions not limited by the earth, indeed to unguessable reaches, unsuspected dimensions, far from the comprehensions of mortals.

The sphere revolved more quickly, screwing—or unscrewing—ever higher. Squeaks like unoiled machinery squealed in his ears. On its putrid surface more embers appeared, spreading their violet and purple and yellow-tinged patches like some primeval fungus. How many years had The Glow lurked in those unmeasured depths? How long had the Will behind it nurtured its malevolence? He hated it—that he knew. But for now he needed it more than anything he had ever needed. Like an addict who thirsted for one last all-consuming high in the face of exultant promises to forever swear it off in the future.

A distant memory returned of him standing in exactly this spot as he had once sought to rescue a childhood friend, which had triggered the concatenation of events that brought him back after so many years to the very same spot.

Destiny.

Lifting Lori's red-stained body limply over one shoulder, steam escaping from her ever-darkening skin to mingle with tiny yellow flares now erupting from his scalp, Sam slid down the six feet of precipice.

His heart throbbed. Which was louder? The

maddening hum? Or his hammering chest?

He stepped closer. Those many years ago the contagion had only affected him indirectly, when Charlie had kissed the Midnight Sun and then touched him. Now he contemplated thrusting the heartbeat of his life directly onto its surface. But he had suffered only from a clubfoot; she was...he could not say it—could not think it.

He had one thought: *Am I in time*?

Inches from the glowing rotating surface he stood, his beloved propped upright beside him. At this closeness the surface seemed translucent, the outer layers transmitting inner glimpses, inner realities, from deeper layers.

Through the lower translucence a patchwork of faces seemed to take shape, triangular, ovaloid, round mouths open like eternally frozen sphincters, surmounted by glazed black pupils surrounded by sharply white irises. He stared transfixed. Crowning each ovoid expression licked yellow flames that took on the appearance of wriggling yellow worms—a meadow of wriggling yellow grass that merged with red at its edges, smoky wisps seeping through the whole.

A hand gripped the back of his shirt. He was suddenly yanked backwards so that he and Lori collapsed on the rocky ground.

A black tuxedo loomed above, sprouted a glinting six-inch switchblade knife.

"Tell me it ain't so, Steve-O. Tell me that life can't be this good to us."

A second tuxedo stepped close. "Seein is believin, bro."

Steve kicked Sam in the side—he urked a groan. Transferring his flashlight to his left hand, Steve's right hand flicked open his own blade.

"Well, well, ain't this been a long time comin."

Rose smiled at Steve. "But you know what they say, the best things in life are worth waiting for."

Sam noted in surprise that both their ties were still straight. And no blood on either one.

Rose's dress shoe slammed into Sam's other side.

"Goddam, this puke-ass punk has got some balls. Can you believe this shit? What did that fuckin little Mexican Hector say: *cojones de plomo?* That's little Sammy."

He touched the point of his knife to Sam's neck.

"Did you shoot my new wife Lori? Huh, faggot?" Rose took a deep breath. "*She ain't yours*," Rose shouted in his face. "Don't you understand that, punk? Alive...dead...or in between. And she ain't through with me 'til I *say* she's through with me." To emphasize, while Steve aimed his knife at Sam, Rose dropped to one knee beside Lori and leaned over, lowering his face close to hers.

"No, Rose," Steve sputtered. "God, look at her. You don't want to—"

"I don't give a damn, Steve-O. I'll kiss my wife when and where I want to."

One hand slid behind her head, and he lifted her and made ready to plant a kiss... He yelped and jerked his hand back.

It smoldered.

"Sonofabitch. She's fuckin burnin."

"Yeah. Just like Ralph and Zavalo and...and your father." Steve's neck prickled. "Are you sure she's...you know...look at her face, her body. Fuck, she's got those purple-black streaks all over her just like the others. And you know what happened to them."

Rose straightened and stepped back.

"What if you...I mean, what if once you touch one of those people...one of those *things*...you become just like em, sorta like infected?"

Staring at his hands, Rose wiped them on his suit.

"Goddam faggot," he exclaimed, stepping closer, "if I'm done, then so are you." Rose wiped them again on Steve.

"Dammit, Rose." Steve now straightened. "Faggot," he called back.

"Faggot to hell, Even Steven." Rose laughed.

Steve could not resist joining his laugh. "Yeah. Faggot to hell, Readie Eddie."

They both refocused on Sam, who sat up and backed away several feet.

"No more screwin around. Let's make this toad look ten times worse than my soon-to-be ex-wife, then we'll throw him into that fuckin purple globe that he likes so much."

"What the hell do you think it is, Rose?" Steve had to shout over the growing hum; and he cast a worried glance at the sphere.

"Who gives a fuck? All I wanna know is does it eat Sammy Trenchers."

Rose leaned toward Sam, knife extended, ready to begin. "How 'bout now, little Sammy So-So? You ready to say *uncle*?" He smirked and looked back. Steve stood erect, facing the source of The Glow, hands limp by his side, silent.

"Come on, Steve. Shake out of it."

As in a trance, Steve slowly turned and looked behind them.

As Rose looked back at Sam, Steve spoke. "I think we should leave him alone," he whispered flatly. His gaze was fixed on the ridge above them.

"Now why such shit, Steve-O?" Following his gaze, Rose turned.

He froze.

At the top of the short precipice which they had descended in pursuit of Sam and Lori, stood a young boy. His sideways combed black hair drifted partially over his freckled forehead, and his hair looked freshly cut, and contrary to the soiled and torn clothes worn by the others, the inevitable wear of having penetrated dark and jagged crevasses, his long-sleeve shirt and jeans seemed as if worn no more than a day. Barely scuffed sneakers disturbed pebbles that rolled to rest at their feet.

A whiteness seized Rose's face. He stepped back, squinted.

Steve-O dropped his knife.

Quickly scrambling to one side, Sam sidled next to Lori and cradled her.

Without averting his eyes, the boy slid down the precipice as from long practice. He halted no more than a meter from Rose and Steve.

"*No...*"

"*Can't be...* It must be that Thing behind us." Rose found he had to yell louder to make himself heard over the growing cacophony in the cavern.

"I remember..." Steve hissed.

"Yeah. It's Charlie."

"You're little Charlie Fremont."

Rose glanced at Steve. "It can't be. That's impossible. That was freakin eleven years ago. That little half-breed Charlie would be at least twenty-four years old by now. Besides, his father moved away and Charlie never came out of..."

Steve looked at Rose with a sick look.

"Why, this must be just some kid who wandered in," Rose spat out.

His glance directed back to the top of the precipice, Steve spoke hoarsely again. "I think maybe you shouldn't make with the insults, Eddie."

An elderly man had appeared between the outcrops and stared down at them, a buffalo-hide pelt draped over his torso, loincloth and head-feathers completing his sparse outfit. Red and white smears decorated his broad flat face, reminding one of old daguerreotypes of a frowning Geronimo.

A strong voice sounded. "Now is the time, my grandson. The kachinas must be satisfied. I give you permission."

Charlie stepped forward, arms raised.

Before Rose and Steve could react, a hand connected the throat of each, and they were lifted free of the ground as if by a large and powerfully muscled man.

Steve kicked, one dress shoe coming loose. He hammered Charlie's arm with all his strength, to no effect, and he vainly struggled to breathe, while Rose swiveled his legs like a child in a grownup's vise-like grip.

"Unnnnngh!"

Suddenly grown to six feet, Charlie shook both men like a doberman shakes a rat, keys and knives, coins and wallets raining about their feet. Charlie grew taller still. And older. With Sam watching from the lee of a rock-wall, streaks of purple and violet swarmed Charlie's neck, spiraling up to cover his face and down to encompass his body, cloth ripping as the energy flowed through him, around him, sparking through torn skin and cloth as they flashed yellow and red at their ends. His mouth grew oval, then round as his face darkened. His hair stood on end and began to turn yellow.

A pale fungus traveled down the length of his arms and merged into Rose and Steve, its glowing edge creeping forward purplish-yellow like paper thrust into a fireplace.

Strangled grunts sounded.

Sam shielded Lori as The Glow flowed down the

suspended bodies of Rose and Steve, their clothes exploding in flame as it progressed. Like a red tsunami, the tide flowed up, over their necks, and rippled across their faces until their hair spun and twisted like yellow wriggling worms.

Behind them, the sphere had entirely cleared the crevice, and a dark flood reached the coping and emerged into the cavern. The mass separated, individualized. Smaller than Charlie's youthful self, each figure inched forward on dogleg chitinaceous limbs, worm-round mouth surrounded by enormous black pools of eyes, fields of straw like wet mops rippling overhead to give forth electric pops. Thumbless digits folded and unfolded in anticipation of grasping their means of sustenance as if hungry after a long sleep, while more black waves crawled out of the pit under the sphere and creeped toward the conflagration, white bones enfolded in their hands, as insects drawn to a stray flame.

The first figures reached Rose and Steve and, without haste, embraced them, pressing their roach-like bodies into the midst of the flames as if to merge with it, consume it, feed on it. White bones dropped around their feet to drive the flames higher.

Charlie, having grown older and taller, stared down at his victims. Still expressionless, his face had become that of an adult, hugely muscled hands still gripping their necks and holding them in midair, gazing mercilessly while Rose and Steve stared pop-eyed with horror at the nightmarish concourse of insects gathering about their legs. High-pitched buzzing from the dense growing pack mingled with their own stifled attempts to shriek.

"Charlie, my grandson, we cannot allow the kachinas to grow strong. They want to invite more of their kind to come from *out there*, but we must not allow it. This is the secret of our people, why they abandoned the pueblos long ago, so people will stay far away from their kind. Take the sacrifices with you back below so the kachinas will follow you and not come to the surface and hurt people again. Since they need fire to survive, and feed on flames and chaos, they will follow you back below. There, if God wills, we shall help them go back to sleep and resume their dreaming."

With a brief nod, barely visible through the mounting flames that twisted around him and his two victims, Charlie turned and slowly inched toward the sphere, taking care not to harm the swarm of high-energy creatures that surrounded his legs. Reaching the cusp of the crevice, he stepped within and descended slowly into its depths, the dense concourse of the dwellers in darkness crowding him every inch to follow him as one, back into the pit.

Once they had disappeared, Sam thought he could hear a final cry of despair from two throats before they were silenced.

Injun Willie faded into blackness.

Sam looked back to Lori. "The Glow. It's here. We can finally do it, my love." He cradled one hand under her neck and the other under her arm, ignoring the jets of smoke that ejected where he touched her. Splotches were appearing on his arms and legs just as hers. They expanded at a slow but steady pace.

"We'll be together after this."

He lifted her to her feet, still struggling.

"Forever and ever."

He partly dragged, partly carried her toward the black globe that seemed to swell in anticipation. Electric arcs shot toward the jagged ceiling.

"Come on, Lori, you can do it. One foot in front of the other, just slide your foot out, then the other."

Lurching under her weight, he closed half the

distance. The orb grew gigantically in his view, a maelstrom of swirling clashing currents playing out their tangled lives in its obscure depths. He thought he glimpsed constellations, entire galaxies imprisoned within, and—ever beneath—the swarms of black beetles thirsting for heat, outstretching their prehensile appendages, ready to grant immortality to whomever had the courage to touch, to embrace, to kiss their source of life, their Midnight Sun.

On the cusp of the crevice Sam stood, his eye drawn down, below and through The Glow. Blurred images swirled and swam, evanescent and translucent, purple and violet and yellow tingeing all he saw. For a moment the swirling paused. The images took on shape and form, and he thought he glimpsed corridors and chambers faced with green glass, orderly, premeditated, cycling machinery glowing in the deep, vast spaces opening up before him such that he knew could not exist underground.

He clamped his eyes shut. Standing silent, he let the subterranean reverberations of the rotating sphere move through him, within him, cycle as they had for who knew how many centuries.

Reopening his eyes, he stared into Lori's face. "Now, my love. The Glow is waiting."

Placing one hand under each arm, he pressed her slack head forward so that it merged with the outer edge of the sphere, entering its orbit to kiss the whipping winds of its tangled stratosphere.

"That's it. Your lips, my love. It must touch your lips."

Spreading from the interior of the black globe, a pale distorted fungus with yellow edges burned its way from the core to the surface and erupted over Lori, flowing over her face and neck and spreading to the rest of her body. Sam's hands tinged as well. As long as he could stand it he endured the contact, then finally pulled her back.

He dragged her back to the lee of the stony outcropping and sat her gently down.

Exhausted, unable to move, he stared.

Minutes passed.

Lori's eyelids twitched.

The smoky wisps were calming, and the splotches had paused in their progress across her body.

"Yes, my love. Lori, it's me. Fight, my dear...come back to your husband."

The eyes moved.

He held her hand and caressed it, ignoring the renewed heat that this caused the both of them.

"I take this woman as my wedded wife, to have and to cherish forever and ever." He laughed. "I do. I do."

Slowly the eyelids retracted. Lori stared straight ahead for several moments. Her arms stretched out and pressed against the stony floor, and with a deep breath, she rose to a crouch. Slowly, she stood.

Standing with her, Sam stepped into her gaze. "Welcome back, my love. I promise nothing will ever come between us again."

Her eyes settled on him. The blood-stained white wedding dress sagged and began to tear from the shredding it had suffered. Behind Sam, the black ball hummed and ground on, sending waves of energy that rippled her hair so that it stood up straight and spat sparks.

She glared.

Raising her arms, she placed her hands carefully on either side of Sam's face.

"Yes, my love," he said. "Do you see? The Glow has cured you, it repaired your heart, brought you back to me. It made you the same as I am. I hid behind the curtain at your wedding and repeated the entire ceremony. Rose is dead. We are married now, you and I. Now that we're the same, we can remain together forever."

Snarling, her hands gripped his throat and pressed to choke him.

"You did this to me," she growled. "You...you made me come back. I didn't want to come back." Fiercely, Lori shook Sam.

He pried her hands off. "No, Lori. I'll show you how to live, how to survive, how to stay in balance. I know how to survive once you've been touched by The Glow. Just listen to me."

With a scream, she wrenched free and scrambled away to spin and vanish in the turns and twists of the cave's many shadowed paths.

"Lori. No, you must stay with me. Only I can show you how to cope with it. You must listen. You must stay in balance. Or...or..." He chased after her, turned down one hall of stalactites, then another, but soon halted in confusion. His own heat was rising yet again, and the puffs of smoky steam were ripping into his back.

"Balance," he wheezed, "we must get back in balance."

Running back to where Rose and Steve had been taken, he rummaged through the items that Charlie had shaken out of them and quickly snatched up two quarters and two dimes. On the keychain he found two keys that almost exactly matched, and taking these items, he inserted them in his pockets in as matching a fashion as he could manage. The heat lowered.

In relief, he took up one of their flashlights and resumed the search. But soon gave up. His calls produced no response and he finally sat to rest.

After a time, he stood. Walking sadly back to the cave's entrance, he paused to view the things in buffalo hides that were gathered around the burning sacrifices etched on the walls and felt he could now add his own graffiti to the story. It was a warning, he now understood. As clear as the pueblo Indians had known how to state it. Shrugging, he passed through.

His torches revealed the side handholds in the teepee chamber and he clambered up, the flashlight stuffed into his belt. Halfway up he paused, puzzled by an accumulation of spider webs that he could have sworn had not been there during his earlier descent. Pulling them away, he reflected absentmindedly that they appeared more angular than concentric and vanished the moment he tore them.

At the top of the pueblo he stood. He surveyed the night-enclosed countryside that stretched before him. Dawn could not be far away and cold mists hung over all, the stars hidden, a blanket of black fog covering all.

Turning, he climbed the short distance to the brown granite stone where the vehicles were parked. He climbed carefully over the detritus and rubble and approached the vehicles. The flashlight stabbed into the dark mist.

His Oldsmobile remained where he had left it. Next to it stood the crumbling rusted pickup truck, which he now recognized as Injun Willie's. Closer was a black Lexus, the door still open, reflecting Rose's haste to catch up with him and Lori. He glanced inside and glimpsed a slew of weapons, enough to make a gun collector proud.

The round shaft of light wandered again.

Stopped.

A fourth car.

Peering into the damp field, he spied a second black sedan, sides glistening with rivulets of dew. Leaning, he blinked. The door to the fourth car was open like the other. He thought—could Rose and Steve have been followed by someone else just as they had followed him? Searching his memory, he was certain that only the pickup truck had been there when he had arrived with Lori.

He jumped.

The twin barrels of a shotgun glinted. Thrust in his direction, the barrels approached, shaking. The figure holding it swayed, took another step and staggered in an effort to remain standing.

A blue uniform stepped into his shaft of light. Peppered with red holes that streamed blood onto the pebbles.

"Where are...Rose and Steve?" Her black hair crusted with blood and dirt, Officer Marla squeezed the sweat out of her eyes and cocked one of the barrels. "I followed them here. I know they went with you, Sam. You went away together."

Sam caught his breath.

"No. Not so, Marla."

"Don't lie to me, Sam," she shouted. "I know now you were working together." She swayed again. Blinked away tears and more sweat. "You lied to me in the station. Now...I'm gonna have to ask you to turn around...put your hands behind you. And put these cuffs on. I'm gonna take you in. Even if no one touches you, I can't let you walk away."

Behind Marla, a subtle movement obtruded into the flashlight's beam. Blinking in turn, Sam glimpsed a flicker of yellow. The yellow grew, seeming to rise up from the ground, and he suddenly realized that it was emerging from the teepee and climbing onto the brownstone. The flame swirled and extended, purple and violet swarming in a twister, straight-up hair rippling like yellow worms or tentacles, arms and legs dark and blotched, red streaks ripping open to emit jets of gray smoke that merged with the mist, remnants of white stained-red clothing still clinging to parts of its scorched torso.

The pillar of flame walked slowly. Picked up speed.

"You don't understand, Marla. You think you know, but you don't. You've got to put the gun down. I can explain...but you must put the gun down."

"Not this time. You threw in with them, Sam, and now I'm taking all of you in, you and Rose and Steve."

She cocked the second trigger and brandished a pair of handcuffs with her free hand. "I'm telling you one last time. Turn around, Sam—"

"Eeeeeeeeeeeeaah!"

Marla spun.

Her eyes fixed on Sam and arms outthrust ready to throttle, Lori rushed past Marla, ignoring her. Nails like claws flashed in the midst of flames.

"Marla... No!"

The shotgun exploded. Once—twice. The second explosion caught Lori in midair and flung her across the slab of brownstone where her body flared like a torch, flames shooting into the misty sky.

With a guttural cry, Sam plunged into the black Lexus and emerged with Rose's assault rifle.

Turning back, Marla tried to reload, struggled to hammer another cartridge into the chamber.

Too late.

A spray of lead ripped her apart.

***

Below, in the near-blackness of the nether realm, a weathered hand reached for another brick and carefully placed it on the threshold leading from the chamber of stick-figures to the chamber of finer art-work, a detailed warning that had done its work too well. Another brick slid into place; more were placed on top. The passing of time of no concern, the broad flat face with feathers stuck in its hair and red and white paint smeared on its cheeks slowly continued placing bricks from the inside one by one until the entire threshold was once more blocked by a wall of bricks. From the darkness one last brick emerged and slid into place. No more light came in.

***

In the west, the sun verged the horizon, its prism of soft colors spreading their comfort over the land as it hurried like a lover to meet its destiny, its rays, cast to the winds like seedlings, warming a sparkly steel-blue hood. Vibrating with the hum of its steady motor, the blue Oldsmobile turned another loop of the winding road that climbed the wild hills. Sam smiled. His car seemed to know where to go. With the deepening of twilight, he found his destination at the peak of the highest hill, and parked.

He stepped out. Took in the vast concourse of glittering worlds above as each found its turn to shine. His smile was joined by a deep sigh of satisfaction. Turning, he reached into the passenger seat and carefully, lovingly, cradled a mangled body wrapped in a white sheet and carried it to a square block of concrete, the foundation of a development that had failed to develop. With a kiss and caress, he carried it to the exact center and gently laid the body down.

A portable lamp plugged into the car battery flicked on—its lambent glow relieving the growing darkness more than enlightening. In its light, he lifted the trunk lid and extracted several items. Two mops with equal numbers of strings. Four brooms exactly matching in length. A dozen cinder blocks of precisely the same make and condition.

Around the wrapped sheet, he placed the mops and brooms so they formed perfect squares, then added angles to reflect the relation of certain stars to others. The cinder blocks followed, some placed under the broom handles at strategic corners, others spanning them, all shifted, adjusted, and aimed with the precision of a surveyor. His feelings guided him. And the ever-present mercury that rose or fell in his mind.

After a pause to verify the presence of exact change in each pocket—every coin represented in the precise calibration—he unloaded containers of liquids. Two gallons of cobalt-blue glass cleaner. Four gallons of orange juice in clear plastic containers. Two liters of washing liquid, with both its plastic container and fluid contents transparent. Gallons of pink and purple Kool-Aid; bright red translucent floor cleaner; and clear gallons of water, which he had dyed with tinctures of various strategic colors to link with select constellations.

From under the white sheet, streams of gray smoke escaped.

Unhurried, Sam placed the containers in symmetrical locations around the sheet and at the corners of the concrete slab, sniffing the air to determine the precise location of each color. No fence or wire could protect better.

When all was done, he stood in the center of the second square, which joined the first at precise 45 degree angles, as directed by the secret messages from the star Sirius above, and extending his arms as in a cross, he began to turn, his face upturned to receive the messages better.

The portable lamp clicked.

Static crackled inside the car, and the CD slid into play.

If we could start anew
I wouldn't hesitate
I'd gladly take you back

And tempt the hands of fate
Tears on my pillow
Pain in my heart
Caused by you...

More static interrupted. The car radio crackled:

"And the Okwalla City Council reports that in an effort to increase revenue from tourism they have decided to reopen what once was Okwalla's chief landmark, the old Mystery Pueblo, once a popular destination but now long forgotten by most. The council's newest members, Mr. Tom Borger and Ms. Sue Ann Raft, have expressed confidence that guided tours of the Pueblo will put the town back on the map and help its citizens achieve a happy healthful life—"

Sam paused. Over the next ridge, he glimpsed a hint of a flicker of light where the Round House lay. He walked to the sheet and pulled back its corners to expose a darkly streaked face, glowing embers creeping forth from below.

The eyes flicked open. "Sam..."

"Hi, Lori. Welcome back."

Returning his face to the heavens, Sam closed his eyes and smiled.

Glenn Lazar Roberts is an international attorney and writer of sci-fi, horror, satire, and adventure fantasy novels. Glenn has taught college, professionally translated Arabic and Russian, and credits an eclectic group of famous writers for inspiring him to write, including Jack Vance, Robert E. Howard, Edgar Rice Burroughs, Mervyn Peake, H.P. Lovecraft, Ray Bradbury, Arthur C. Clarke, Isaac Asimov, and H.G. Wells, among many other Masters of the Art. "I love language. I am perpetually afloat on a sea of script." Roberts has edited the work of other aspiring writers and hosts a writing critique circle. When he's not writing he enjoys swimming. He lives in Houston with his wife and kids.

www.ingramcontent.com/pod-product-compliance
Lightning Source LLC
Chambersburg PA
CBHW071130260626
47162CB00003B/731

* 9 7 8 1 9 5 9 7 6 8 9 6 8 *